D0344167

THE TERMINATORS

When an important Soviet official disappears after his plane is hi-jacked on an international flight to Calcutta, British Intelligence, the C.I.A., and the Indian Government are deeply concerned and perplexed. British agent, James Wainwright, is sent to investigate but he also disappears and it is feared that he might have defected. The cynical, but dedicated and resourceful agent, Idwal Rees, is detailed to track him down, and the Russian too, if possible. After a rigorous and dangerous trek across the mountainous border region of India, Pakistan and Nepal, Rees and his faithful Pathan servant, Safaraz, rescue Wainwright who was being held captive. Later they are all involved when investigating sinister happenings at the refugee hospital run by Claire Culverton in an old fort near a remote mountain village. She and Rees had been in love but had parted a few years before, realizing that love and his career as a spy were incompatible. The situation is tense and further complicated when Rees at last locates the captive Russian, more dead than alive, and also learns that Wainwright and Claire are apparently in love. . . . The mountain wilderness of Northern India provides a grimly fascinating setting for this thrilling story.

Also by
BERKELY MATHER

★

THE ACHILLES AFFAIR
THE PASS BEYOND KASHMIR
THE ROAD AND THE STAR
THE GOLD OF MALABAR
THE SPRINGERS
THE BREAK IN THE LINE

THE TERMINATORS

*

BERKELY MATHER

THE
COMPANION BOOK CLUB
LONDON

This edition, published in 1973 by
The Hamlyn Publishing Group Ltd,
is issued by arrangement with
William Collins, Sons & Co. Ltd.

Made and printed in Great Britain
for the Companion Book Club
by Odhams (Watford) Ltd.

600871568
1.73/256

Prologue

HE CAME OUT OF THE LOBBY of the Hollywood Roosevelt Hotel and turned right and hailed a cab. 'Airport,' he said shortly, and added, 'Step on it, will you. I got to make the New York plane in half an hour.' The last wasn't really necessary, but a cabby driving fast was less likely to get into conversation with a passenger. Under strain he was apt to talk too much and there was an ever-present danger of his English accent coming up through the carefully cultivated American one. Even those two short sentences had required rehearsal. He would normally have said, 'Hurry, will you please. I've got to get the New York flight at half past three.' Yes, you had to be with it the whole time. Fork in your right hand when you were eating, and no 'thank you' at the news-stand. He was probably being over-cautious—but they'd certainly check on the passenger list afterwards, and one unclaimed Englishman on board would undoubtedly give *some* clever dick a lead.

The driver risked a forbidden U turn and sped back up Highland on to the freeway. A long run now, through North Hollywood and Sherman Oaks, then down the San Diego Freeway. They'd be hard put to it to make it in half an hour. He should have said forty-five minutes.

He yawned ostentatiously and sat back in the corner, closing his eyes. If the driver had been sufficiently interested to risk a glance into the rear-vision mirror he'd have seen a tall, well-built early middle-aged man, crew-cut hair, clean-shaven, pleasantly California-tanned, in a smart lightweight grey suit, wearing wrap-around sunglasses and with an expensive Japanese camera on a neckstrap. His luggage consisted of an equally expensive air-travel suitcase with a few—but not too many—labels on it—all American. He was, in fact, just about as anonymous as one could get in Los Angeles—and as indigenous. And if they did manage to trace every cabby who had dropped a fare at the airport today, this one would remember, if he remembered at all, an American going to New York—not an Englishman to Miami.

He paid off the cab outside Departures, adding an adequate but not over-generous tip, and went through the glass doors into the flat air-conditioning inside. They were calling his flight now, half an hour earlier than usual to allow for the recently imposed security routine. He went to the desk and handed over his ticket. A pretty girl stamped it and handed it back with a boarding card inside it, and reminded him to leave his luggage unlocked when he checked it in. Then she smiled mechanically and said, 'Have a good trip, Mr Hatchman,' and was dealing with the next passenger.

'Hatchman?' he wondered as he walked to the luggage desks. Who had chosen that name? And the home address in Charleston, S.C.? Who indeed had bought the ticket, which had come to him through the mail, in yet another name, at his hotel yesterday? Good job this was an internal flight and that there was no passport involved. They'd no doubt have coped with it very efficiently though, if there had been.

He saw Booth as he approached the security barrier. He wondered what *his* real name was. They would have been next to each other in the queue in front of the turnstile, but Booth wandered off to the news-stand at the last moment, and when he rejoined there were several people between them. Hatchman wondered who the other two men would be. He hadn't met them, but Booth would know them, of course. 'José' and 'Miguel' he had been told. There seemed to be several Latins travelling.

He was up to the turnstile now. On the other side was a black-curtained cubicle, and he could hear an intermittent Geigerlike buzzing rising and falling as passengers went into it singly.

His turn came and he entered. There were two uniformed men there, standing beside two bare metal poles, with a third looking into a dial in a console. One of them said, 'Just raise your arms to shoulder height please, and stand here.'

The buzz rose shrilly and he looked startled.

'That's all right,' one of them said reassuringly. 'The beam's hitting your camera. Mind if I have a look inside? Just a matter of routine.'

'Sure, go ahead,' he said. 'There's no film in it.' He handed it over and the other unbuttoned the leather case and expertly clicked it open, glanced inside, closed it and put it on a table clear of the beam. The other man mumbled an apology and asked him to empty his pockets of everything metal he was carrying. They yielded a lighter, a nailfile, a fountain pen with a gold cap and a few loose coins, and when he had removed his wristwatch and tie clip the buzzing dropped to a subdued murmur.

'Clean,' said the man at the dial. 'Less belt buckle.' Hatchman started to undo it, but one of them said it was all right, and he stepped out of the beam and reclaimed his possessions. A taped voice said softly, 'We are sorry for this inconvenience but we are sure that you will appreciate that it is for your own protection. Have a good trip and thank you for your co-operation.'

There was no waiting the other side and he went straight through the covered gangway into the aircraft. Three stewardesses were taking hats and raincoats from the few that had them and hanging them in the curtained closet between the first and tourist sections. One took his boarding card, injected into her smile the extra modicum of welcome its first class status rated, and showed him to a seat just clear of the entrance.

'Welcome aboard,' she said. 'You can change your seat later if you have any preference. There are only seven passengers in this section. Take your camera?'

'I'd rather carry it, if you don't mind,' he said, returning her smile. 'Thank you.'

'You're welcome,' she said, and went back to her duties. He took a copy of *Life* from the rack in front of him and leafed through it idly. Booth entered a few minutes later and passed him on his way through the curtain to the tourist end.

He was conscious of two men standing in the alcove between the bulkhead of the flight deck and the first class toilet. Just two men—young, neatly dressed—cleancut would have been the term, except that one of them had a slight acne round the chin. They weren't studying the passengers obtrusively, but he felt they weren't missing anything. Just a quick, impersonal but all-encompassing cop's scrutiny for each one. The new skymarshals, he decided. .38 Police Magnums in shoulder holsters, loaded with the new break-up bullet and reduced charges. Quite enough to kill, but not, it was hoped, powerful enough to puncture the skin of the aircraft in the event of an overcarry.

The loading went on for the better part of an hour. A muted babble was half-submerged by the treacly outpour of the Musak. The passengers, except for a handful of more than usually excited children, were for the most part subdued. There were one or two jokes in passing about riding shotgun in the Old West, Wells Fargo, and how's about that half-quart old Jim was carrying in a metal flask, which the stewardess was now holding for the trip—and then they were all aboard. About eighty in the tourist section, he reckoned, and the seven the stewardess had mentioned up front here.

The doors were closed and he heard the whine of a motor as the gangway was withdrawn. A man's voice said over the speakers, 'Welcome aboard, folks. This is your captain, James McFarrow speaking. We will be taking off in about ten minutes for Miami. Flying time about three hours forty-five minutes. The weather should be fine and clear throughout and we'll be flying at thirty-seven thousand feet. I shall be talking to you from time to time as we pass over places of interest. Thank you.' Then one of the stewardesses was demonstrating the emergency oxygen equipment, the 'No Smoking—Fasten Seat Belts' lights flicked on, and they were being pulled smoothly out backwards from the boarding dock.

He listened intently as the jets were cut in and run up. One of the newer ones, he decided. Pratt and Whitneys instead of Rolls. That was all right—he'd handled both in the past. Bit slower in reverse-thrust reaction, if he remembered rightly. One had to watch it on landing.

And then they were off. Palm trees bending in the wind—the beach and white surf below—the blue of the Pacific—and the port wing lifting as they swung to starboard—the beach again—Santa Monica below and Malibu to port, and the boundless checker-board of greater Los Angeles stretching to the foothills.

He sighed and relaxed for the first time in—how long? Five days? Balls. This had been building up since that morning a month ago when they first contacted him in London. Well, the die was cast now. Committed. Over the top with the best of luck. Crossed the Rubicon—and all other apposite clichés.

He wanted a drink, but Booth had warned him off that.

Not a snifter until it was all over, he had said. The stewardess, handing a miniature pinch-bottle Haig-and-Canada-Dry to his neighbour across the aisle did nothing to help when she smiled inquiringly at him. He nodded and mouthed, 'Same, please.' The hell with Booth. Who did he think he was? Some nonentity who had worked on a drawing-board in the Boeing plant according to his own story. Certainly not a flyer.

He waved the Canada-Dry aside when the girl came back, and took the scotch straight in one long gulp. It relaxed him still further. He could have done with another, but he knew his limitations. The girl went back to her pantry and came out with a Cona of coffee and cups on a tray. She went through to the flight deck and he had a glimpse of the solid, white-shirted backs of captain and co-pilot, with two others of the crew in front of the big instrument panel behind them. Cautious types. They were still hand-walloping her in a steep climb. They probably wouldn't go over to automatic until they were out of the turbulence you always got to a greater or lesser degree in this narrow shelf between sea and mountains. The girl put the tray down beside the chart table and came back, closing the door behind her.

He looked out of the window beside him. The blue smog haze was thinning now and fingers of desert were reaching down into the outer fringes of the urban sprawl. He looked at his watch. Two hours and twelve minutes to go. He had synchronized times with Booth by phone before leaving the hotel. He hoped to God that there was nothing wrong with the expensive Rolexes they had been provided with. Half a minute either way could wreck everything. The brief, euphoric moment of relaxation was passing, and he felt hot and prickly under his shirt.

He rose, stretched and yawned, then made for the toilet. The young men had separated. The one with acne was sitting on the stewardesses' seat that folded against the bulkhead and faced backwards down the central aisle. The curtain between the sections had been pulled aside and he could see the full length of the plane. The other one would be down at the back somewhere, looking forward. He stepped over the young man's feet with a smiling apology and went into the toilet, locking the door behind him. He studied his face in the mirror over the washbowl. He wondered if he ought now to take off his sunglasses. They were no longer necessary, but he felt safer with them on. It didn't really matter. Lots of people wore them habitually, outdoors and in. He took them off tentatively. Yes, he thought he was showing signs of strain around the eyes. He swilled his hands and face in cold water and used a mini-bottle of cologne from the locker, then he checked things again—the two-inch glass capsule in the tiny pocket inside the waistband of his trousers and the small piece of Elastoplast in his wallet. He wrapped the capsule in his handkerchief and put it carefully into his breast pocket. Christ, he'd have to be careful of that. Suppose he dropped it and had to scrabble for it under the seat at the last moment? Curtains. He took the handkerchief out two or three times experimentally. No, the risk of fumbling it was too great. He'd be better with it loose in his side pocket. But suppose he banged against something solid and it broke—? He swore at himself and turned his attention to the Elastoplast. The back of his camera case was where he had decided to carry that. He removed the cellophane wrapper from it and carefully stuck it on to the leather by its adhesive side. Handy—under his eyes—but unnoticeable.

Somebody was rattling the door of the john. He looked at his watch. He'd been here nearly ten minutes. Too long. He came out and mumbled apologetically to a fat lady who passed him in a fluff of indignation and slammed the door behind her. If that door had caught his side pocket——

He needed another drink badly, but he steeled himself against it. He would have loved to have taken a stroll the full length of the plane—people did when they got cramped. Yes, just a casual stroll, passing Booth without a sign of recognition—to show him that everything was under control—quite cool—not to worry. Show who? Booth or himself? He was getting jittery. Oh God, for a drink. Just one.

He stepped over the young man's feet again and sat down and took up his copy of *Life*—but the pictures and the print were just a blur. A draught from the adjustable air vent over his seat was catching him on top of his head. He reached up and turned it away. He hoped that Booth would have briefed the other two to do that also. He felt himself getting sleepy. It would have been heaven to let himself go for an hour or so, but he couldn't risk it. The thought of his sleeping through that vital five minutes chilled him back to wakefulness.

He was glad when the stewardess started to serve a late lunch, but when it came the sight of the clinically white slices of Tom Turkey and thousand-island-dressed salad and over-perfect, completely tasteless fruit, turned his stomach. He settled for a glass of champagne, but it was pink, sweet and semi-frozen, so he sent it back and asked for black coffee and a brandy. Booth, if he could see from wherever he was sitting, wouldn't have approved—but the hell with it, there was nothing he could do about it.

The in-flight movie came on then. He watched its flickering inanity for some time without turning up the sound on his phones, and when he could stand it no longer he closed his eyes—and presently his head dropped forward on his chest.

He woke in an overwhelming surge of panic, and

looked at his watch. He'd only been asleep for some fifteen minutes. He rose unsteadily and went to the toilet again and was sick.

He thought the young man looked at him somewhat curiously as he returned to his seat. He must have heard his agonized retching. But what the hell? People *were* sometimes sick on planes, weren't they? Actually he felt better, as if some of his stomach-torturing nerviness had gone down the pan with his bile. He had no difficulty in staying awake after that. He just sat on—and on—going over the steps of the drill. Hour and a half to go. One hour. Forty minutes. He had to fight down his overpowering desire to look at his watch too frequently. Twenty-five to go. Count in sixties, at the speed of the gong strokes when a boxer goes down. One minute—two—three—Holy Mother of God! Hurry—HURRY!

The captain's voice came up over the speakers: 'The large lighted town you can see on the left, ladies and gentlemen, is Baton Rouge. You will shortly be able to see New Orleans on the same side. We have had the benefit of a tail wind most of the way and we expect to reach Miami in about one hour and fifteen minutes. Thank you.'

Any moment now. He turned the camera on his chest so he could see the square of plaster, and removed his sunglasses. He took out his handkerchief and put the capsule inside it.

The stewardess got it first. She was passing with a tray of drinks and her head was nearer to the air vents overhead than those of the seated passengers. He heard the tray go with a crash, and turning he was in time to see her sprawling and gasping on the floor. He held his breath. The white plaster square on the camera was turning a faint blue, and darkening. He hauled out the handkerchief and knew wild panic for a second when his fingers missed the lump the capsule made. Then it was between his teeth. He bit hard and felt it splinter. He rammed the handkerchief over his nose and mouth and breathed shallowly. The stuff was acrid, but not unbearably so. It would hold out the gas for about a minute, Booth had said. The young man on the bulkhead seat had started to rise to go to the stewardess's assistance, but he hadn't made it, and was now sprawled beside her on the floor.

Hatchman reached up and pulled the emergency oxygen mask out of the overhead trap and clamped it over his nose and mouth. His eyes were watering somewhat, but not to an incapacitating degree. He stood up and looked round. All the passengers in the first class section were unconscious.

Through in the tourist section he could see Booth standing near one of the rear seats wearing the oxygen mask that normally would have been the other stewardess's. Two men, also masked, were standing nearby. All other passengers were slumped inert in their seats. Hatchman waved with his disengaged hand, and Booth acknowledged, and then held up five fingers.

He stood looking at the square of plaster. It was paling again. He looked at his watch. Five minutes, Booth had said, for the gas to be drawn in through the extractor vents, cleaned, and the air recirculated. He hoped that information was accurate. The stuff was odourless, he had been told, so there was no way of detecting its presence other than by the litmus-soaked plaster. He tested the length of the thin plastic tube of his mask, but it was not long enough to allow him to move to the flight deck door.

He waited. The plane, obviously straight and level on automatic course, was as steady as a rock. The litmus was now pure white again, but he forced himself to wait the further fifty seconds that would make the full five minutes that Booth had stipulated.

He looked down the plane. Booth removed his mask and sniffed cautiously, then gave a thumbs-up sign and walked towards him. Hatchman dropped his mask, turned and shot into the flight deck. The crew were lying back in their seats as if asleep. The captain had his seat belt on as regulations prescribed. Hatchman unbuckled it and pulled the man sideways, but he jammed between the seat and the console. Booth came in then and helped him.

Hatchman slid into the seat and took over the headphones. There was a mush of signals coming through but he disregarded them and ran his eye expertly over the instruments. Height three-six-two-five-zero. Course one-zero-five. Smack on for Miami. He had worked out his corrections in advance. For Havana he wanted Course one-six-five from New Orleans. That would be it ahead and to port. The plane would undoubtedly be on their scopes—in fact he could hear them calling its number now. The hell with them—he had too much on his plate to put *their* minds at rest. He flicked off automatic and pushed the control column forward and felt his speed increase accordingly. Five-eighty-five miles—just under the hour. He pulled round on to course. They'd have seen that even as it occurred, and would guess what had happened. Just another skyjacking in the pattern the world had got wearily used to—right where it started originally. Already the wires would be hotting up, and he could see tomorrow's headlines. How had this one happened? All passengers electronically frisked. Those machines could detect a pin in a woman's bra. Armed skymarshals travelling on every plane. How? How? How?

Booth said something, and Hatchman raised one phone from his ear.

'What's that?'

'They'll have the fighters scrambling and up after us about now, won't they?' Booth said.

He nodded. 'Guess so—but there's damn-all they can do about it. How's everything back there?'

'Fine. The boys have frisked the skymarshals and handcuffed them to seats with their own jewellery.'

'*You* have any difficulty?'

'Not a bit. Just like I said. The inlet vent is behind a panel in the john down aft. Just had to unscrew it with my penknife and tip the stuff in.'

'As a matter of interest, where were you carrying the stuff?'

'In a plastic tube down the seam of my pants leg. Quarter of a pint—more than enough. It gasses on contact with the air.'

'What in the name of God is it? A new invention?'

'Hell no. L728—they've had it on the secret list since World War Two but it's never been used.'

'How long does it last?'

'In this concentration it will knock them out for anything up to two hours. Varies with the individual, of course—but they're all safe for an hour or more—and they'll be too shaky to be troublesome for some time afterwards.'

Hatchman nodded. 'Fine—but even so I'd be glad if you'd have the boys shift the crew out of here. I think I've met the second pilot somewhere. I'd rather not meet him again when he comes round.'

'Sure. I'll do that,' Booth said. 'Put your sunglasses on and keep your handkerchief up to your face when we get in. They're going to hustle us into a car and away immediately we land.'

'What happens to the crew and passengers then?'

'They'll fly on to Miami—less the three the Cubans want.'

'Who are they?'

'Does it matter?'

'Not particularly. Just idle curiosity.'

'Three top boys in the Free Cuba movement. They're worth half a million bucks on the hoof in Havana. That's all that concerns us.'

'I see. But there's one thing that worries me.'

'What's that?'

'Well, obvious, isn't it? "Hatchman" won't be on the plane when it gets to Miami—and the stewardesses and the skymarshal got a good look at me. The F.B.I.'s going to do some fairly easy checking.'

'So what?' Booth said. 'Grow a beard and keep away from airports for a while. You and your hundred thousand bucks will be dropped any place in the world you care to name. You don't have to worry about a thing.'

'I'm not really,' he answered. 'Okay—I'll have to ask you to scram now. I want to cut out all this crap that's coming in on the radio and tune into the Havana frequency, and it calls for concentration.'

Booth nodded and peered out into the darkness. 'Seems to be a couple of aircraft out there,' he said. 'Coming up fast.'

'Bound to be,' Hatchman grumbled. 'They know bloody well where we're going now.'

'Think they'll try to buzz us?'

'With eighty-plus passengers on board? Not a chance. Just riding herd, that's all. They'll sheer off when we enter Cuban air space. Now suppose you beat it?'

The lights of Havana were ahead and below them, and he came in on the beam smack on, and green-clad bearded soldiers swarmed aboard before anybody was stirring. They smuggled them both away in a closed car, and Hatchman slept a solid eighteen hours. Booth was standing at the foot of the bed when he awoke.

'How are you feeling?' he asked.

'Splendid. Do they run to bacon and eggs and English marmalade here?'

'Maybe. I'll ask.'

Hatchman looked at his watch. 'Good God,' he said. 'Have I really slept that long?'

'Sure. I told 'em not to wake you.'

'The plane flown on yet?'

'Yeah—but they had a bit of bad luck.'

'How?'

'It blew up fifteen minutes out over the sea. Time bomb.'

Hatchman stared at him.

'Was—was that part of it?'

'Reckon so.'

'But why? They'd got their men.'

Booth lit a long cigar, carefully. He blew the match out and looked at Hatchman through the smoke.

'If they'd got back and talked it would have taken F.B.I. a flat two minutes to guess what had happened. As it is, nobody knows—but nobody. I reckon that can be pulled half a dozen times in varying forms—at anything up to two million bucks a time. No lack of takers. It's Boeing pilots we're short of—Boeing pilots that have been grounded for different reasons—like running a couple of pounds of heroin into London.'

'They never made it stick,' said Hatchman.

'And how glad I am they didn't. You wouldn't have been free and available if they had. But you lost your job, didn't you? And you're blacklisted through all the companies.'

Hatchman nodded slowly. 'Um—see what you mean,' he said.

'So how's about it? Staying with us a bit longer?'

'It certainly has its attractions. I'll think about it.' He

stretched and swung his legs out of bed. 'Now if you can do something about that bacon and eggs and marmalade —oh, and lashings of coffee, old boy—I'd be awfully obliged. Thank the Lord I don't have to be a phony American for a while.'

'No—just your natural sweet self,' said Booth. 'A cold-blooded son-of-a-bitch—like me. I think we're going to understand each other.'

Chapter One

THE GUIDE, a Ludhiana Sikh, was leading. I was on his heels. After me came the client, then Safaraz, then Nadkarni, then Wilbur.

We had one thing only in common; none of us wanted to be there—the Sikh because he was a pressed man and didn't think he was being paid enough—Safaraz because he was a Pathan, with all that peculiar race's distrust of Sikhs—Nadkarni because he was a policeman off his beat—Wilbur because he had been promised leave after his last assignment, and even now should have been with his wife and two kids in Nantucket—I because I thought my briefing had been far too vague—and finally the client because he was scared rigid. And it was raining like hell.

The Sikh stopped, and I walked into his back and the client walked into mine. Safaraz, cat-eyed in the pitch dark, halted the others in time and hissed insults past me and the client at the guide. You can be very dirty in Urdu.

Nadkarni said in English, 'I know this Pathan is your servant, Mr Rees, but when we get back into India I intend arresting him.'

'On what charge?' I asked.

'I'll think of something,' he grunted sourly. 'In the meantime will you please tell him to shut up—or I shall turn back, and take the guide with me?'

'Yes, you do that,' Wilbur said. 'Maybe we'll get on faster—to wherever the hell we're going. How much farther, Rees?'

'I'm the interpreter,' I reminded him. 'That and nothing more.'

'Not two prima donnas on the same trip,' he moaned. 'Isn't this temperamental cop enough?'

'I am a Superintendent of Police,' Nadkarni said with icy dignity. 'Kindly remember that.'

'Then for Christ's sake start superintending this schmuck up front,' Wilbur snapped. 'He's bushed. He's been bushed for the last two hours. He's your man, isn't he?'

'Only insofar that he is receiving recompense from police funds.'

'Then he's gypping you. I want to know where the hell we are.'

'Ask Mr Rees.'

'I just did, and got a brush-off.'

I realized that this could go on indefinitely, so I groped my way forward to the Sikh, who was squatting in the inadequate shelter of a boulder at the side of the track, an ill-used man.

'Where are we?' I asked in Punjabi, which I hoped Nadkarni, a Bombayite, wouldn't understand.

'In Nepal,' he answered sulkily.

'I know that. But where in Nepal?'

'The Pathan called me the son of my elder sister, who coupled with an ape.'

'I heard him. He shall be dealt with.'

'Then deal with him. I rest here.'

'And the policeman will deal with *you* then—when you return to India. Come, save yourself six months on the road gang and tell me where we are.'

'Near Khumbar,' he mumbled, and that didn't reassure me at all. Khumbar was right on the frontier—Indian guards one side and Gurkha the other, and this fellow's brief had been to lead us in a long detour round it.

'When did you lose your way?' I asked.

'When we crossed that thrice-damned river. You saw yourself—the bridge was down, so I had to take you five miles upstream to the nearest ford. I should have forked right, but it is confusing in the dark——'

'How far are we from Khumbar, and in what direction does it lie?'

'I am a poor man, forced into this by threats—and a promise of fifty rupees which will now be withheld from me.' And he started to weep into his beard.

I went back and translated to Wilbur and the policeman.

'It's no good,' I finished. 'He's lost, and if we try to force him we'll end up in a guard post. Best wait until daylight, then go back to the ford and try again.'

Wilbur sighed and said he should have been eating broiled lobster about now. Nadkarni spat, which was unusual for a Brahmin. The client whispered to me for the tenth time that he had eighty-five thousand dollars in the Ottoman Bank, Beirut, and what about it? And Safaraz saved my life.

They must have had three portable searchlights hidden among the surrounding rocks and they opened up simultaneously with half a dozen burp guns, or almost simultaneously. There may have been a split second between the light and the first blast, or perhaps a sound audible to none of us except to the Hill-conditioned ears of Safaraz, but it was sufficient for him to leap straight at me, grab me in a bear hug and then continue the leap over the edge of the track into the river that ran beside it, and we surfaced, three-quarters drowned, under a waterfall half a mile downstream.

The lights were coming down the track towards us, stabbing and darting into the river, so we inched back under the curtain of water and braced our feet against the current with just our noses clear. They passed, went on a couple of hundred yards and then, thank God, gave it up and turned back.

I don't think we could have lasted more than another few minutes, because this was pure melted snow, and very recently melted at that.

We crawled out on the other bank and wrung what water we could out of our clothes and then put them on again. I figured that since this was a classically arranged ambush they would have blocks set out up and down the track, in case anybody had managed to make a break, and if they were really doing it per textbook they'd comb both ways at first light, looking for two frightened men on foot, or two dead ones in the shallows, because corpses wouldn't float far in that rockstrewn stream. That being the case, our safest place was well under cover somewhere near them. I told Safaraz this and he nodded his agreement. He was quite impassive about it all—he'd been bushwhacked before—but he was glumly regretful that he hadn't followed his natural instinct to slit the Sikh's throat earlier on.

'Treachery has a smell, sahib,' he told me. 'Just like fear has, though they are different. The Sikh and the Arab stank like a jackal and a hyena caged together.' He may have been right at that, but I was in no mood for hillman's imagery so I told him to belt up, and we pussy-footed back to a spot I judged to be roughly level with the ambush and went to ground among the loose rocks.

They were still there in the morning—half a dozen of them huddled in sheepskin robes—and they had a Tibetan butter lamp going and they were brewing tea. My guess had been right, because six more joined them later on—three from each direction. They were Kampas, outlaw Tibetans who, since the Chinese takeover, tended more and more to drift into Nepal and India itself. They had a short pow-wow. We were near enough to hear what they were saying but it didn't help much because neither of us understood Tibetan. I could see bodies lying around, but loose rocks cut off full view. Wilbur I could make out, sprawled face downwards, and the legs of Nadkarni, and there was a third who I assumed was the client. I wondered where the Sikh was, but not for long, because one of them dragged him out from behind a rock by the feet, as dead as the others.

They stripped the bodies of everything, clothes, boots and packs—then they just left them staring at the sky where already the 'sentry' vulture was poised on motionless wings. When all movement had ceased and the Kampas departed, the sentry would dive, and other vultures, each watching his own area for just such largesse as this, would converge and dive and join him. We didn't like leaving them there, but what could we do? We certainly couldn't bury them in that terrain, and then there was always the possibility that the Kampas would be watching the skies as they marched back up into the hills, and suspicion would be bound to grow if the vultures didn't swoop. No, we had to get out of it, and fast.

We crossed back into India that night, not a difficult task even in these uneasy days, because neither country can guard every yard of their common frontier so they settle for the few roads and a pretty thorough overall aerial watch linked to ground patrols. Both countries are perfectly friendly towards each other, and the Indian government, like the British before them, enlist Gurkha troops in their army and frontier police—but that in no way relaxes their mutual vigilance. Nepal looks into India only to the west. To the east is Tibet—and today Tibet is China.

We bumped into Bareilly in a battered mail truck, and travelled by slow train from there to Ferozepore, third class on a foot-wide wooden bench because I was dressed, like Safaraz, in the miscellany of garments that has become a uniform along the Indo-Pakistan border—Moslem in general but with Hindu undertones—the clothes of poor men who just wanted to get by without being pushed around by either side, the meek ninety per cent of the population of those parts. The other ten per cent are the guards and petty officials who man the crossing points, and they are *not* meek. We dodged the latter by taking a long midnight walk waist deep up an irrigation canal, and a quick duck under a rusty barbed-wire fence that marks the frontier proper. The wires are ostentatiously insulated with heavy porcelain cups and the supporting posts carry sudden death warnings in Urdu and English with red skulls and crossbones, but the current has been cut off since their last war in 1967, when each side blitzed the other's power stations.

Safaraz said, 'When I was a boy a man could travel from Afghanistan to Ceylon without being asked for papers. Now one crosses two different frontiers in one day. Ee-ai—it is good for smuggling, if for nothing else.'

We went to Lahore then, slowly by foot, bullock cart and finally by a mail truck which had been converted to charcoal gas at some date back in the mists of time, travelling on the roof with the fuel.

Yev Shalom's shop, where you can buy anything from a tenth-hand camel saddle to a brand new fire engine, is in the Anarkhali Bazaar. It has a frontage of eight feet, but once you get past the old Kashmiri who repairs prayer rugs in the entrance, and the even older Bokhara Jew who runs a money-lending business inside, and finally the two Baluchi wrestlers who sit in the gloom at the back doing nothing, apparently, but contemplating their navels, you find yourself in a small courtyard amid piles of assorted junk from every corner of Asia, and a medley of smells which run from attar of roses to plain honest-to-

God donkey shit, which, with exquisite logic, is collected, bagged and sold from here to the growers of the roses, who pay for it in kind—with attar. The attar, shipped in bulk to Grasse in the South of France for blending with their local perfumes, is a seven million dollar a year business—and is one of Yev's many minor sidelines. So now I don't need to tell you any more about him. He's versatile. Anybody who can run one eye over a hundred bags of donkey droppings and pick out the one with an admixture of buffalo ditto, which weighs heavier but induces mildew in roses, while checking a tender for the supply of hydro-electric equipment for a major irrigation scheme with the other, has got to be.

Nobody announced us, but he met us in the courtyard. It took me years to worry that one out. Actually the Bokhara gent had a hidden bellpush, the memory of a computerized elephant, and a simple code. One ring for somebody he thought Yev might want to welcome personally, two for somebody he'd maybe prefer to take an all-appraising squint at from an upper window first, and three for the Urdu equivalent of 'sorry, Mr Shalom is out of town and we don't know when he'll be back'. If you didn't fit into any of the three categories the bell wasn't pushed at all. A beard was stroked and an eyebrow was lifted, and the two Baluchis rose slowly and stood before the door to the courtyard. They never spoke, but somehow they got the message over. Possibly the fact that they were about the six feet six mark and were built accordingly had something to do with it; anyhow, I've never heard of anybody who wasn't at least partially welcome ever busting in—and Yev's callers ranged from top Government officials to charcoal-grimed bums like us.

He made the sign of fraternal greeting. You probably know the one I mean—small tradesmen in suburban London, poor camel dealers up the Khyber Pass, and rich oilmen in Dallas make it on certain specified occasions—if you don't know it, it doesn't matter. Actually I was rather a lapsed brother, but Yev was top man on the tracing-board in these parts, and the only one I've ever known who kept the code rigidly and punctiliously, in spirit as well as letter—the hardest driver of bargains in Asia, but the only man I'd trust life, wife, purse or secret to without a split second's hesitation.

He said, 'Someone awaits you here, Idwal Rees.'

'I know,' I said. 'I'm sorry to use your place as a caravanserai, Yev—but he named it. I didn't know you knew him.'

He smiled dryly. 'One knows the monsoon, floods, fire and famine.'

'As bad as that?'

'Not necessarily. I was referring to inevitability. These things come and one cannot deflect them—but a wise man takes precautions. Let us call him a precursor. I have never known this one to appear without trouble being hard on his heels. Take an old man's advice and say no.'

'To what?'

He spread his hands and hunched his shoulders. 'His proposition.'

'What is it?'

'Do you think he confides in me?'

'If you really wanted to know, he wouldn't need to.'

'I *don't* want to know, but thank you for the implied compliment.'

'It wasn't meant as a compliment, you bloody old rogue,' I said. 'Just a plain statement of fact.' Actually it was both, and he knew it. It was his one small vanity, this appreciation of his perspicacity. He grinned like an ageing Puck and chuckled throatily, face screwed up and orthodox elf-locks bobbing. Behind me Safaraz joined in the laugh and Yev's ceased immediately.

'Has this Pathan of yours learnt some English since we last met?' he asked, nettled.

'Not a word,' I told him. 'He just likes to get in on the act.' Which was true. Safaraz spoke his native Pashto, Arabic and Urdu, sometimes running all three into a bastardized patois, but English, except for the dirty words, eluded him, though he loved to give the impression that he understood it like an Oxford don.

'Tell him to go to the men's quarters, bath, get clean clothes and eat,' Yev said, and added in Pashto as I turned to translate, 'And also tell him that if he as much as looks at a woman on the way, my Baluchis will cut his balls out and throw them to his brothers, the tom-cats.'

Safaraz went off bellowing because this was an implied tribute to his masculinity, dearer to the bawdy heart of a Pathan than the offer of hospitality couched in flowery language that one of lesser understanding than Yev would have made.

Yev took me by the elbow and led me through an archway into another courtyard more cluttered than the first, then up some stone stairs into a big workroom where men were handstitching some of the best polo saddles that ever came out of the whole sub-Continent, where the game was born—and through it into another where other men were looming carpets that would eventually fetch more in Bond Street and Fifth Avenue than the original articles from Persia that they were copied from—and on through storerooms piled high with Oriental antiques that would have been worth many fortunes in any market in the world, mixed with the most appalling junk: a fretted ivory screen studded with cut lapis lazuli alongside an old hand-cranked corn-husker with a broken hopper; a seemingly genuine peacock throne rubbing shoulders with a barber's chair on a lop-sided pedestal; Mogul armour and a pile of moth-eaten soldiers' tunics, circa Kipling. You didn't need to name it, he had it.

I knew the general layout, of course, though not the detailed geography of the place. No man knew that except Yev himself and his son, Solomon. It takes up the whole of the north side of the Anarkhali Bazaar and is probably greater in area than two full city blocks, but it is surrounded by a labyrinth of shops, eating houses, Sikh temples, mosques, caravanserais and brothels, all of which back on to a thirty foot high, six foot wide stone wall that encircles their whole empire. The wall was started by Yev's great-grandfather and has been constantly added to and strengthened by those who came after him so that now it is as near impregnable as a place can be, short of modern warfare tactics. It has three gateways to the outer world besides the one I came through, but only a favoured few know of them, I being one of the privileged, but one is not expected to use them except in extreme emergency.

We reached the centre of the maze after fifteen minutes brisk walking, suddenly and dramatically. One moment we were in a huge vaulted chamber that held camel saddlery, the next we had come out into a courtyard that had a fountain playing in the centre and dwarf palms round the sides, and it was cool and quiet except for the plash of the water and the twittering of bright birds in a large aviary.

It was high noon by now, but the place was shaded overhead by wide-meshed camouflage netting that admitted light and air, but would have cut off the view of even a very low-flying aircraft. This, I knew, was the heartland. Yev's house was the one that faced us as we entered through an archway, Solomon's was to the right, with next to it their small family synagogue, and facing that, the guesthouse and servants' quarters. He showed me into a suite on the upper floor—bedroom, sitting-room and bathroom one would have said in England, no doubt—but here those homely terms didn't fit. All were walled, paved and ceilinged in marble—but different marble for each room—the pink of Siwalik in one, blue of Udaipur in the next and a cool leafy green in the other—all polished so that the light that came in from the courtyard through the deep balconies was reflected softly but without glare.

Yev said, 'Your friend is next door, but bath, change and eat before you see him, Idwal Rees. As you stand now you are at a disadvantage.' This was the first reference he had made to my appearance, which was typical of him. If I had turned up in a top hat and a kilt he would not have remarked upon it directly.

I nodded and sat down on the floor because I would have soiled the Queen of Sheba-sized bed or the silk damask chairs. 'You're right,' I said. 'You're always right, Yev. This time maybe I'll take your advice and turn him down. The trouble is, I've taken some of his money already.'

'Give it to him back,' he said. 'You know I'll take your note—at five per cent compound.'

'Sure,' I agreed. 'I also know you'd tear it up afterwards. But we haven't reached that stage yet, have we? I don't borrow from my friends. I just batten on their hospitality.'

'You're tired,' he said, 'or you wouldn't have said that. "Friends" and "batten" in the same speech don't make sense, Idwal Rees. If I advanced money to Solomon would he be "borrowing"?'

'No, he'd be performing a bleeding miracle. Money off the old man? Cor, feavvers off a flaking frog!' Solomon had come in behind us. He advanced towards me, beaming all over his battered pan, hand outstretched. 'How are yer, cocker?'

Picture it if you can. Yev, small, neat, aristocratic, something like Haile Selassi, without the grandeur but with all the dignity—orthodox in his immaculate kaftan and skullcap—his son, round and fat, like a smalltime light heavyweight turned smaller time promoter, which was exactly what he was when Yev traced him in the East End of London and brought him out here. He, Yev, had been sent to England to school by his father, and then had gone up to Oxford. Leah, Solomon's mother, had been just one of those things—albeit a pretty one, with some strength of character. In fairness to Yev he didn't know he had left her with child when he came back to Lahore to take over the business, and she didn't tell him. Thirty years later, on a trip to London, he looked her up, just for old times sake, but she'd been dead for ten years and the little Jewish bakery where she had worked had given place to a highrise office block. But there were some still around who remembered her. Solomon, when the old man found him, told him to go to hell in the ripest Cockney, but Yev persevered and eventually pulled off a Prodigal Son in reverse and brought him back. Now there was love and respect between them, it's something that's in the blood and bone of the Jews, but two more unlike than these I've never seen.

He nearly wrung my right arm off, buffeting me on the shoulders with his free hand and insulting me as grossly as only a Cockney can, when he really knows and likes you.

'Jesus!' he roared. 'You look like an Aden brothel tout, after a hard night drumming up business round the coal wharves—and you stink like a billy-goat. Who are you working for now? The wogs or the commies?'

Yev, who disapproved of buffoonery, told him sharply to go and order breakfast for me and arrange about clean clothes.

'Sure,' said Solomon. 'Goy or local? We can do you anything except bacon or an Irish priest's cassock.'

I settled for mutton pilau and loose Punjabi shirt and pants, and when I reluctantly crawled out of a hot bath half an hour later it was all ready for me, together with a bottle of scotch, but I didn't enjoy any of it, because the Gaffer came in then.

Chapter Two

HE SAID, 'You're losing your touch.'

'I'm alive,' I told him. 'Your people are dead.' I helped myself to a stiff drink, then sat cross-legged on the floor in front of the brass tray that held my meal and started to eat, native style with my right hand, as if the food was the only thing on my mind. Childish perhaps, but it meant that he would have to start questioning me now, which put him at a disadvantage, and anyhow I was hungry.

'What happened?' he asked after a long pause.

'You probably know all about it already, since you've just told me I'm losing my touch.'

'I was referring to timing. You were supposed to meet Wainwright here the day before yesterday.'

I balled buttered rice into mutton gravy, dipped it into chili sauce and stuffed it into my mouth. Nobody can talk under those circumstances so he had to wait, fuming, for the full minute it took me to masticate, swallow, belch, take a drink of water and start preparing the next mouthful, which is the only polite way to eat in these parts.

'Come on, Rees,' he said angrily. 'Balls to the inscrutable Oriental act. What happened?'

'Is this a debriefing?'

'You know bloody well it is.'

'Then suppose you conduct it as such.'

I make no apologies. It always had to be this way with Henry George Gaffney. Let him get the upper hand in any dialogue whatsoever and he rode you into the ground.

'Sorry,' he grunted. 'Go ahead from the beginning——' he almost choked, then added, 'please'.

'I met Wainwright in the Great Eastern Hotel, Calcutta, on the twenty-fifth of last month, in response to a letter I received from him two days previously. He offered me a job.'

'Doing what?'

'I understood that he was acting on your behalf. Do you want me to go into it fully?'

He nodded, and I realized that he was checking on Wainwright's side of it as well as mine.

'I was to liaise with a Detective-Superintendent Piralal Nadkarni, Indian Special Branch, and certain others, and arrange to cross the Nepalese border on the thirtieth.'

'Did he name the others?'

'No.'

'Go on.'

'He stressed that although we had this Government of India man with us, it was top secret. No local co-operation this side or the other. If we were caught we were to say that we were collecting botanical specimens for the Bombay museum and that we had strayed over the line—then leave the rest to Nadkarni.'

'Did he give you any hint of what it was all about?'

'None—other than that we would be leaving one of the party that side and bringing somebody else back.'

'What was your specific part of the job?'

'Dogsbody. I'm supposed to know the border country and the local language.'

'*Do* you?'

'I take it that you believe I do, or why were you engaging me?' A small triumph, but one which I had the satisfaction to note annoyed him. He hated things to be turned back on him in a debriefing.

'Go on,' he grunted.

'I met Nadkarni as arranged.'

'Where?'

'The Sarosh Hotel—a native flophouse in Bareilly—on the twenty-ninth.'

'Cover?'

'I and my Pathan servant were dressed as Punjabi Mussulmans—Nadkarni as a westernized Mussulman.'

'Why the difference?'

'Nadkarni was a southern Hindi speaker—a big city type—his Urdu was heavily accented—so he was fronting as a university lecturer.'

'Did he give you any further particulars?'

'Not at that stage. He merely confirmed what Wainwright had told me—that we were taking somebody across the Nepalese border and bringing somebody else back. He stressed the need for absolute secrecy as strongly as Wainwright had done.'

'Did you ask him to elaborate?'

'Naturally not. It was obviously a "need to know" proposition, and that was all I did need to know at that stage. I did, however, ask where the rendezvous was to be. He showed me on the map. It was a spot some miles the other side of the border, up a mountain track.'

'Who had picked the spot?'

'I have no idea. I didn't like it though.'

'Why not?'

'Too vague. We were to go there in the dark. It's impossible to judge distances to within a couple of miles under those conditions.'

'Did you voice your objections?'

'Yes. He agreed with me but said that there was nothing we could do about it. The spot had been arranged and we couldn't change it.'

'All right. Go on.'

'Nadkarni then gave me instructions to meet him and

the rest of the party at a dâk bungalow a mile short of the Nepalese border an hour after sunset that evening. I did so, with my Pathan, and found that the others were an American called Wilbur, an Arab, whose name I never learned, a Sikh guide and two Federal plainclothesmen.'

'Had you any previous knowledge of these people?'

'Only of Wilbur.'

'What did you know about him?'

'That he was C.I.A.'

'Did he tell you that?'

'He didn't need to. I'd worked with him before.'

'Where?'

'Sorry, that doesn't concern you. I'm engaged by the job, and the fee carries a three-monkey pledge afterwards—as you very well know.'

'Go ahead. What happened then?'

'Nadkarni sent the plainclothesmen back and the rest of us set off in the dark, and the guide lost the way.'

'If you were the Johnny Know-all why did you need another guide?'

'I have a general knowledge of that part of the country, not a particular one. I made that clear to both Wainwright and Nadkarni right from the start.'

'Who engaged him?'

'Nadkarni presumably. I certainly didn't. Things went badly from the moment we set off. The Arab, who I gathered was the one we would be leaving the other side, was an unwilling party, and he was dragging his heels and slowing us up. He tried to buy his way out.'

'How?'

'He propositioned Nadkarni in the first place. He offered him twenty-five thousand dollars to let him make a break.'

'What was Nadkarni's reaction?'

'Nil. Nadkarni didn't speak much Arabic—so the client had a go at me. I shrugged it off, so he raised the bidding —right up to eighty-five thousand.'

'And then?'

'Not much more to it. We eventually got back on to what the Sikh thought was the track, and then we were suddenly jumped and blasted.'

'And you say rubbed out—with the exception of you?' He looked at me quizzically.

'And Safaraz, the Pathan.'

'Lucky people.'

'You could put it that way. Actually it was a case of reflex conditioning on the part of Safaraz. He obviously sensed something a split second before they opened up, and he jumped straight into the river, taking me with him.'

'So he must have been expecting something?'

'*All* Pathans are *always* expecting something. There are only two categories in the part of the Tori Khel where he was raised—the quick and the dead. If you're not the first you're automatically the second.'

'You trust him implicitly?' He was trying to needle me, but I'd been debriefed by the old devil before, so I didn't fall for it. With the Gaffer you needed the temperament of an honest and phlegmatic cop being cross-examined by the defence. One flash of temper and he'd turn it back on you like a counter in judo.

I inclined my head gravely and said, 'Implicitly.'

'So the others were caught flatfooted?' he went on.

'I'm afraid so.'

'Including the Arab?'

'Including the Arab. I can vouch for that. Nadkarni, Wilbur, the Arab and the guide were all dead next morning.'

'Which rules out collusion on any of *their* parts.'

'I should say so.' He obviously wanted me to react indignantly to the emphasis on 'their', but again I didn't rise to it. He lit a cigarette and I reapplied myself to my food.

'Get a look at the ambush party?' he asked after a long pause.

'Yes—they were Tibetan Kampas.'

'Pretty smart of you—in the dark and all.'

'It wasn't dark when I saw them next morning. Safaraz and I went to ground the other side of the river, close by. Quite clearly they realized that some of us had got away, so they scouted up and down stream, but didn't look for us right under their own noses. They gave it up after a time, stripped the corpses and headed back into the hills.'

'What did it look like to you? Just an ordinary case of banditry—or a carefully planned stake out?'

'Definitely the latter. Kampas do go in for banditry, but they pick their marks—mule trains, trading caravans, that sort of thing. These people were after *us*, not loot.'

'I see. Right, so they made off. What did you do then?'

'Carried out Wainwright's instructions as far as we were able, which were to bring the exchange here since Nadkarni, an Indian policeman, couldn't risk crossing into Pakistan. Well, here we are, though without the exchange.'

He nodded slowly, thoughtfully, gazing through his cigarette smoke at the ceiling, then he felt in the inner pocket of his grubby white drill jacket and pulled out a thick wad of notes. He flicked them across to me and I grunted my thanks and slipped the wad inside my shirt without checking it. This, I knew, was my fee and expenses, less the advance Wainwright had made me when I accepted the job, and I also knew that it marked the end of the debriefing. Anything that came now would be off the record.

He said, 'Who fingered the deal, Rees?'

'Obviously the man who named the rendezvous,' I answered.

'That was Wainwright.'

'I don't particularly like him,' I said, 'but I'd find that pretty hard to believe. Anyhow, he's your man. You deal with him.'

'I can't. They're holding him.'

'Who's "they"?'

'Let's just stick to "They" for the moment. Capital T.'

'So They put the screws on Wainwright, and he talked. Can't blame him for that. I'd do the same myself under certain circumstances—and so would you.'

He nodded ponderously. 'You're telling me,' he said. 'I'm not the stuff heroes are made of, and I don't expect anybody who's working for me to be either. Gent advancing on me with a pair of red-hot pincers in one hand and a wire loop in the other gets a gush of girlish confidences, fast. Matter of common sense. No, that's not the point. If Wainwright had been snatched this side of the border and carried over, I'd have expected something like this to happen. But he wasn't. He went over after the ambush, I think.'

'You mean he's defected?'

He shrugged. 'I'd have put my money on the sun rising in the west before I'd have believed that—normally—but——' He trailed off and pursed his blubbery lips. 'Here,' he said, as if coming to a decision. 'Do you want the background?'

I said, 'No,' firmly. I'd carried out my contract, as far as I was able, and I wanted no further part of it. If the Gaffer, archpriest of the 'need to know' persuasion, was proposing to tell me more, it was because he wanted me to stay on the job.

'No strings,' he promised. 'You want to walk away from

it afterwards, I won't try to pressurize you. But I *would* like a second opinion. Come on, Rees, you're the only man in the business I'd ask a favour of. I think you know that.'

I didn't. I couldn't imagine his asking a favour of anybody at all, but it made interesting hearing nevertheless—and let's be honest, I was curious. I have no illusions about espionage or the weird characters who earn a living by it, but Wainwright was one of the few I'd have backed as straight. I'd just told the Gaffer I didn't like him. That wasn't strictly true. *He* didn't like *me*, because he imagined I'd put a knock in against him on a previous job we'd been engaged on. I hadn't, actually. This mischief-making old bastard had twisted something I'd said at my debriefing and had fed it back to Wainwright—who had never forgiven me for it.

The Gaffer reached out for the bottle and topped up my glass, generously, then poured a scant half-inch for himself. He caught my eye and grinned wryly. 'It's all right,' he assured me. 'I'm not trying to get you pissed. I can't take it myself. Bloody ulcer.'

'Get on with it,' I said. 'I'm going back into India tonight, and I've got some walking to do as I haven't got a passport.'

'Palinovsky mean anything to you?' he asked, and I nodded impatiently. It was a seemingly stupid question because he was headline news all over the world. He was the First Secretary of the Soviet Embassy in Delhi and he had been flying down to Calcutta on an internal flight when the aircraft, an ancient D.C. 3, had been hijacked and flown up to a spot on the North-East Frontier and landed on an old wartime strip in the jungle. The plane had then been blown up and the passengers and crew had been allowed to make their way back to civilization on foot—less Palinovsky, who had been carried off. He had been a bargaining piece since then against twelve Chinese political prisoners held in India. Negotiations were still going on, but it was widely believed that the Indian Government, feverishly anxious not to offend a foreign power, were bowing to these demands.

'All right,' went on the Gaffer. 'So you know it all. Who do you think snatched Palinovsky?'

'Maoists, acting without the official cognizance of the Chinese Government, so we're told,' I said.

He shook his head. 'Not well enough organized for that sort of caper yet. You need more than a pure heart and a copy of the Thoughts of the Chairman to hijack a plane these days.'

'Hired somebody to do it for them?'

'Going rate to knock off a plane nowadays is something in the region of two million dollars. You think the Chinks, desperately short of foreign currency as they are, are going to give that sort of dough for twelve small-piece bums like that?'

'So who?'

'The Russians themselves.'

'Snatched their own man? What the hell for?'

He looked as smugly triumphant as a conjuror at a children's party who had just pulled a large rabbit out of a small hat. 'He was about to defect to the Americans.'

'Surely to God they could have dealt with him themselves without going to all this complicated nonsense,' I said.

'You tell me how?'

'Recalling him to Moscow would seem the obvious thing.'

'He'd been under recall orders for a couple of weeks,' he told me. 'He'd been stalling his departure off with stomach trouble. It wasn't all stalling either. They'd been hocusing his grub. He guessed it, and had been feeding on canned stuff he bought himself in the bazaar. But it was only a matter of time. They'd have got him in the end.'

'So what did he do?'

'Got in touch with the Yanks and told them to hustle things up. They did. He was to have been shipped out from Calcutta on a Pan-Am flight. They told him to come out over the wall of the Russian Embassy at night, and that there would be a car waiting for him. He was to go to Meerut and travel by night-flight to Calcutta, where he'd be picked up and whisked off. The night flight was hijacked.'

'How did they get on to it?' I asked.

'His wife. She decided that she preferred Moscow to Washington—and blew him to the resident K.G.B. man.'

'So all this exchange talk is so much baloney?' I said. 'They've probably knocked him off already.'

'At the risk of appearing flinty-hearted,' he said, 'I wish like hell they had. It would have saved a lot of trouble all round. No, he's still alive—and I believe some other mob is holding him at present.'

'Which mob?'

He shrugged hopelessly. 'Wouldn't we love to know that. Look, try not to interrupt and I'll tell you what happened.' He started to count on his fingers. 'One—to the Indian Government it's a straight-cut proposition. A Chinese crowd has snatched a foreign diplomat and are holding him against twelve minor politicals in Indian prisons. All the Indians want is the diplomat back in his embassy with a minimum of skin off anybody's ass. Right? So they agree to release these bums, and the handover is being arranged. Two—they don't know of the American involvement—but the Yanks are bending over backwards to get hold of him. He'd be the biggest catch for the West since Petrov skipped in Australia. But there's nothing they can do about it at this stage. This is something between the Indians and an alleged Chinese minority faction. Three—one night this C.I.A. man, Wilbur, is called on the telephone in Calcutta and Palinovsky speaks to him. There is no doubt that it *is* Palinovsky, either. Wilbur knew him. It was Wilbur who had been handling the American end of the whole thing. Palinovsky says he's not where Wilbur thinks he is—he's somewhere else—being held. He says they can forget about the twelve Chinese politicals. These people he is with now only want *one* man—an Arab by the name of Ib'n Shakoor, who nobody has ever heard of up till now. He's just a little two-bit crook serving an ordinary criminal sentence for theft in Israel. Not a damn thing known about him politically at all. Hand him over and they'll slip Palinovsky to them quietly. Just like that. Pure horse trading. Well, Wilbur's on the hot line to Washington within minutes —and before morning a deal is arranged.' He sighed wistfully. 'I wish our bunch of shiny-assed desk commandoes could move as quickly. Six fighters and a couple of ground-to-air missiles to Israel for one unremarkable con. Bloody good business for somebody. So Ib'n Shakoor comes out and is whisked down here. Wilbur didn't know much about up-country India and Nepal, where the swap is to be made, so C.I.A. asks for our co-operation. I put Wainwright on to it. Wainwright calls you in. One of our geniuses insists on the Indians being told, to put their minds at rest, so they detail Nadkarni on a watching brief. Now you've got the whole thing.'

'The Arab we were taking over——?' I began.

'Was Ib'n Shakoor.'

'And they rubbed him out.'

'As you saw for yourself. And the bastards are still holding Palinovsky, and they've upped the bidding to five million dollars to the Americans—for the gent on the hoof—or they can have his head in a hatbox for nothing. Take it or leave it.'

'Complicated.'

'Like you said—complicated. For Christ's sake leave that curry alone, will you? It's making my ulcer spin in circles just watching you.'

'Too bad,' I said and took another mouthful.

'Well—are you going to take it on?'

'Take what on?'

'Don't play silly buggers, Rees,' he said wearily.

'I'm sorry,' I said, 'but I don't see what it's got to do with us. From what you've told me it appears to be strictly an Indian-American affair with Russian and possibly Chinese undertones.'

'Wainwright.'

'What about him?'

'Oh, for God's sake. He's over that side—willingly or unwillingly—or he's dead. I want to know which.'

'Just Wainwright?' I asked.

'Well—if you can pick up anything else in the way of a lead I'd be grateful,' he said, and grinned sheepishly. 'The Yanks have been very polite about it all, but I know they think we've made a cock-up of things. I'd like to set the record straight.'

'All for the honour of the Regiment,' I said. 'You hypocritical old bastard.'

'Honour of the Regiment plus fifty per cent—and no beefs about the expense sheet.'

Against my better judgment I nodded.

He pulled out the wad of notes again but I wouldn't take it at that point. I sat on chewing rice and mutton until he couldn't stand it any longer, and he left swearing dirtily.

Chapter Three

I SLEPT AFTER THAT—twelve dreamless hours—because we'd been on our feet for the previous three nights. The Gaffer had wanted to get on with the briefing immediately, but I'd stuck my heels in. That's the best of freelancing; you can do it your way, or quit—right up to the time you take your advance—which is why the old devil was always trying to recruit me in on a regular basis. 'Five thousand pounds sterling a year,' he used to wheedle. 'Slipped to you under the table, so you don't have to pay tax on it—and expenses on top of that. Christ, you might go a year or so at a time without us calling on you, so you can moonlight all you like on the side.'

But I wouldn't wear it. This way I could take a job or leave it alone—and the part about not calling on you to earn your keep for a year at a time was baloney anyhow. Once on their permanent payroll they got their money's worth, and you were on call twenty-four hours a day, seven days a week.

I lay on my back, hands behind my head, and looked up at the marble ceiling next morning and knew that I was kidding myself. Take a job or leave it alone? You always took it. Your way or quit? There was only one way at the final reckoning—the Gaffer's—for the simple unarguable reason that he was the best man in the Business, Their side or Ours. Like him, I'm using capitals, because, although there are lots of splinter factions, there are only two sides in today's world. You are born on one side or the other, and usually you stay there. People *do* cross, of course. The Philbys, Burgesses, MacLeans and Blakes from Ours to Theirs—and a roughly equal number of faceless 'ovskys and 'oviches from Theirs to Ours. Sometimes it is for personal gain—sometimes through genuine change of heart—and sometimes, the really clever ones or the badly frightened, because they are planted. Sometimes you get a wild joker who drops into more than one category.

My father was one of these. A Welsh Marxist from the starvation-haunted Rhondda Valley, planted by Them as a 'sleeper' in Shanghai after the First World War. He 'slept' for ten years establishing a perfect front as an underpaid sub-editor on a Right Wing paper before he was activated. But he had done a lot of reading and even more thinking in that time and he wasn't enthusiastic about some of the earlier jobs They gave him—snooping on his friends with view to possible recruitment, in the main. Then he was upgraded to straight blackmail, and he was even less enthusiastic after one of those friends committed suicide—so he quit cold—and They disciplined him through my mother, a White Russian, whom They kidnapped one night on her way home from her job in a department store. I won't go into details. I was seven at the time and I only saw her once after the old man got her back—a pretty little woman with large dark eyes, in a hospital that had bars on the windows—and she didn't seem to know either of us. So the old man was on this side thereafter but he wasn't much use in the Business, for the simple reason that he hated too fiercely. I hate too, but I was recruited young enough and trained so thoroughly that I can be rather more objective about things.

I didn't know I was being trained at first. The old man was by way of being an Oriental scholar by this time, and he taught me classical Mandarin, and let me pick up the Shanghai dialect, and later Cantonese, from the ragged-arsed Chinese urchins who were my friends in those days. Then came the war and we were evacuated just ahead of the Japanese occupation, and the old man worked in the Translation Branch of the Combined Intelligence Bureau in Calcutta, and my friends were then equally ragged-arsed Indian urchins—so languages came to me naturally, together with the way that men of diverse races dress, and walk, and eat. I'm dark, like my mother, and I was always on the skinny side, and I remember the old man once betting me five rupees that I couldn't beg for an hour round Sealdah Station without being rumbled by the professionals. I did, in a filthy dhoti and half a shirt, whining in Hindi, Bengali and soldiers' English, for a whole morning—collecting seven annas from the travelling public and several boots up the backside from the railway police in the process. I think I was about ten at the time.

We went to Hong Kong after the war, and the old man died, and I was just old enough to get into the Korean show. They commissioned me into an infantry battalion after O.C.T.U. but I did very little regimental soldiering before being seconded to the Intelligence Corps, where I stayed for the whole of my Short Service term of three years. Then I was picked up by the Gaffer. They gave you two or three jobs at first before inviting you to sign up or just dropping you.

I decided not to sign up, mainly because of the two-year course one had to undergo at a school in the Wirral. I'm always vaguely uncomfortable in England. They offered to skip the course, but by this time I'd started a small commercial intelligence office of my own, and I preferred to keep my independence. But I still work for the old bastard on an *ad hoc* basis.

I often wondered what made the Gaffer so indissolubly Ours. With his background he would have seemed to have been a natural for the other side. He was about sixty now, which put his childhood back in the days of the First World War and the Depression that followed it. With three juvenile convictions for larceny to his discredit he shook the dust of London from his heels at the age of fourteen and stowed away on a freighter to Montreal, and drifted down over the border to Chicago. At sixteen he was driving a beer truck in the dying days of Prohibition, and he was carrying a gun for one of the minor gangs before he was twenty. He left America, speedily, with several notches on that same gun, and found himself in Shanghai where he was recruited into the European bodyguard of General Chang Tso Lin, one of the gorier of the warlords who came to power in the turbulent days after the death of Sun Yat Sen. That was his post-graduate honours course, and what he didn't know about the seamy side of China by the time World War Two broke out, wasn't worth knowing. He was made to measure, therefore, for the job the Far Eastern Bureau gave him, liaising between Chiang Kai-shek, the Americans and the British. With his inveterate propensity for rising like scum to the top of whatever murky stew he found himself in, he was heading the whole concern by the time the hot war ended and the cold one began, and his sphere of influence extended all over the Far and Middle East. What he was down on the books as, I never knew. Probably he wasn't down on any books at all. Those of us who suffered under him, either regularly or on an as required basis, merely knew him as 'the Gaffer', a play upon his real name of Gaffney, and the amorphous group he ran was 'the Firm', and the Firm, because it *was* amorphous and could therefore be disowned by the more orthodox Government agencies, handled anything pertaining to Intelligence which was deemed too delicate, which means dirty, by M.I. 5 or 6, who have their limits. He was fat, sway-bellied and rotten-toothed. He had the constitution of a bull-elephant, the morals of a sewer rat and the manners of Gadarene swine. He had also, in respect of his job, the dedication of an anchorite and the concentration of a chess Grand Master. In my considered opinion he was the most healthily respected and cordially hated man in the Business—by both sides. Nowadays he ran things from a dirty little apartment near London's Victoria Station, but he had the habit of popping up unannounced in the Field from time to time. Like now.

He came into my room without knocking and stood at the foot of the bed.

'Sleep well?' he asked. He meant it sarcastically but I thanked him nicely and said I had.

'When are you starting?' he demanded.

'When I'm ready,' I told him.

He breathed hard down his nose and felt in his pocket and took out the pad of hundred rupee notes again. 'Usual rates plus fifty per cent for quick results. Here's three hundred on account.'

He held the money out to me.

'Hang on to it,' I said. 'I'm not under orders yet.'

'I said *quick* results, Rees.'

'What do you think I am, a bird-dog? I want to know a lot more about things before I start haring off into the blue.' Behind him Yev had come to the door and was making signs to me to turn the whole thing down. At that moment I felt like taking his advice, but I pretended not to see him, and he went regretfully away.

'I'm putting you in the picture,' the Gaffer snarled. 'What are you trying to do? Jack the price up?'

'I've got some questions to ask,' I said. 'If I take a straight briefing from you at this stage, those questions don't get answered. What's it to be? My way, or not at all?'

He sighed gustily and sat down on the edge of the bed. 'Come on—let's have it,' he said.

'Who's this new crowd that you think have got Wainwright?'

'I told you—I just damned well don't know. It's not the Russians, that's for sure.'

'*Why* are you sure?'

'Figure it out for yourself, Rees, for God's sake,' he said impatiently. 'Why the hell would they be stirring things up—complicating the issue—with this crazy Ib'n Shakoor deal if they were holding Palinovsky?'

'We're not talking about Palinovsky. We're talking about Wainwright.'

'I think the same mob has got them both. Somehow or other they've managed to snatch Palinovsky from the Russians—Wainwright blundered in on it and they got him too—or rubbed him out.'

'What was the last you heard of Wainwright?'

'I saw him here the night I arrived from London. He was as sore as hell.'

'About what?'

He sat considering for a while, and then he said, 'I'd better tell you the lot. He was sore about *you* He'd laid the whole thing on with Nadkarni and Wilbur and he assumed he would be running the show—but then I stood him down and told him to hand over to you.'

'Why did you do that?'

'He made the plan and laid on the admin side of things, and had done it very well, but I considered that you would be the better man on the actual ground. He reacted the way he always does—prickly as a hedgehog. He threatened to quit and I had to get tough with him. I told him to remain here and take over Palinovsky from you when you returned—then hand him over to Wilbur. I went to bed then—and in the morning he had blown—scrammed.'

I stared at him.

'You mean he *had* quit?'

'Hardly. Not even Wainwright would pull anything quite as raw as that. No, I think he went down to where you people were meeting in order to make sure that everything was Go before you crossed—and that he had no doubt every intention of returning here and carrying out my orders when you got back. But he must have got on to something, and was following it up—because, as I told you, he was seen crossing the frontier—on his own feet—alone.'

'Who saw him?'

'Nadkarni's two plainclothesmen who were coming back from the dâk bungalow. They saw this lone character—got suspicious and shadowed him—then realized it was Wainwright, and withdrew. That report came in just ahead of you.'

I told you—we live with suspicion. The sickly-sweet stink of potential treachery is always in our nostrils. Just suppose Wainwright *was* doubling, the Gaffer had stymied him by this last-minute switch. He would have to get down there and warn somebody in that case. I felt the old familiar cold empty sensation in the pit of my stomach. I don't think my face was showing anything, but the Gaffer knew damned well what I was thinking.

'No,' he said. 'Even my dirty mind boggles a bit at that. At the same time, what do you know of him? Really know of him?'

'He's all right.'

'Don't bust yourself,' he said dryly.

'I said he's all right,' I snapped. 'Well trained, intelligent and his guts are in the right place.'

'You know bloody well what I'm referring to,' he said. 'Background.'

'Why ask *me*? You recruited him, didn't you?'

He said in Mandarin, which was more grammatical than his English, 'He who sees the dropping of the foal knows more than the rider of the mare.'

'Yes,' I agreed. 'I knew him as a kid in Shanghai. His father was a cop—an Inspector in the Concession Police. But we were never particularly friendly. There's an age gap. He's about ten years younger than I.'

'When did you first know he was working for us?'

'About two years ago, when you told me yourself—in Calcutta.'

'You never suspected in Hong Kong?'

'Never. He was just a pen-pusher in the Hong Kong and South China Bank to me. Somebody from the old home town who I would nod to in the Club.'

'Which shows he knows how to cover his tracks, at least,' he said. 'You were both on the active list there at the same time.'

'I'm bloody certain *he* didn't rumble *me*, either,' I said, stung in my professional pride.

'I wouldn't have expected him to,' he grinned. 'Don't *you* start getting hedgehoggy. Hm—"well trained"—"intelligent"—So were old Kowalski and Carter and a lot of other doublers out this way. All the buggers came from Shanghai originally too. Nothing personal, of course,' he added hastily.

'Don't apologize,' I shrugged. 'You really don't trust anybody, do you?'

'Only myself,' he said solemnly, 'and then strictly on those occasions when I got no other option. I often wonder what would happen if the Opposition ever came up with the offer of a capital sum in Swiss francs bigger than what our bums will laughingly call a pension when they finally send me to the knacker's yard.' He got up and stretched. 'Any more questions?' he asked.

'Yes—let's come back to this new mob. You are pretty certain that they aren't Russians? So they must be Chinese.'

He shook his head. 'I doubt it.'

'Why?'

'I just can't see them going to all this trouble just to keep a Russian defector out of American hands. Anything that upsets the Rusks suits Chairman Mao lovely.'

'What about the five million dollars?' I asked. 'There's a very Chinese smack about that.'

'Yeah—maybe—but lots of other people like dollars too.' He stood rubbing his chin. 'You know something? I've got a feeling that there might not be anything political in this at all.'

'You mean wild jokers playing their own hand, just for the dough?'

'Could be.'

'But what about the twelve Maoists they wanted out?'

'Well *what* about them? Nobody's mentioned them for days now. They're sitting on their asses in Bareilly Jail looking hurt and forlorn at the moment. Nobody wants 'em.'

'Ib'n Shakoor?' I said. 'Where the devil does *he* fit in?'

'I wonder.'

'Anything known about him at all?'

'Open book—dirty pages but very legible. Palestinian Arab—in and out of jail since he was twelve. First long sentence in Beirut last year. He got five years on a heroin smuggling charge. He was an aircraft cleaner. His sentence was remitted after a few months. The Israelis, who checked for us, think somebody put a substantial wad of dough to the right quarter. He went to Jerusalem on release—got into a fight his first night there and was nearly killed. The police found more heroin on him, so when he came out of hospital he went back inside—four years. It was from that rap that we sprung him and brought him down here.'

'Nothing political at all?' I said. 'But somebody wanted him pretty badly.'

'Looked like it.'

'And he was offering me eighty-five thousand dollars,' I went on. 'Big money for an aircraft cleaner.'

'Lot of money in heroin.'

'And a lot of heroin in these parts. I wonder if that's what we're up against—like the Bowyer business?'

'Again—could be,' he said. 'But let's get our priorities right, shall we? It's Wainwright who's my prime concern at the moment. I've got to know whether he's alive or dead—and if he's the former, what the chances are of getting him out. Anything else you pick up will be completely incidental—but none the less welcome for that. You've got *carte blanche*—write your own ticket.' He took out the money again. 'You've pumped me dry, Rees, so now, will you for Christ's sake take this dough?'

I took it, and asked him how I reported. He told me to contact him here at Yev's place if he was still around when I got back—or to fly on to London if he had returned. Yev would be my banker for any further funds I required. He shook hands then—a thing he rarely did, and for which I was thankful, because it was like handling a pound of liver out of a refrigerator that hadn't been working for a couple of days.

'Just one thing more,' I said as he reached the door, and he turned impatiently. 'The dead men? How are they being explained?'

'The C.I.A. are making their own arrangements about Wilbur—cholera—cremated. Nadkarni will have had an accident in the mountains. Actually he *was* an amateur botanist, poor bugger. Nobody knew of Ib'n Shakoor's presence down here—and as for the Sikh guide, who's going to enquire?'

Yes, who? I wondered—and added Nadkarni's epitaph.

I spent the rest of the afternoon with Solomon, outfitting Safaraz and myself. We were Punjabi Mussulmans again, but with heavier outer clothing this time, and packs containing cheap Indian tobacco, with a little contraband local rum underneath it—the normal trade goods of the border country. We took hardware with us, a flat .38 apiece and a couple of wicked Khyber knives, which made Safaraz drool. A Pathan without a knife feels like a butler without his trousers. We also took a little food —hard barley loaves and parched gram, and finally I routed out an ancient but accurate army prismatic compass and the map sheet of that area. These worried me because if we were ever searched they would be highly compromising, but I had to take them if I was to bring back an exact location from that wilderness. Then, as I was puzzling over the best way to hide them on our persons, Yev came to light with a little gem. It was an American survival compass that fitted innocently into a brass button. They wear things like that—army badges and buttons—in belts as a decoration—in those parts. The map he dirtied up and wrapped, with old newspapers, round the tobacco. He felt I had let him down, and myself, in taking any job whatsoever under the Gaffer, but he was helping for friendship's sake, which was typical of him. And he wouldn't take payment.

We left as the sun was setting, and travelled back to Ferozepore, first class on the mail trucks, as befitted small but prosperous peripatetic traders, which meant that we rode inside instead of on the roof, and got less charcoal dust on our shirts, but more bugs inside them. The border we crossed as before, walking through the irrigation canals, with our sandals and baggy pantaloons bundled into our packs—and we finally rattled into Bareilly on the morning train.

Safaraz, with the mountain air once more in his nostrils, was enjoying it.

I was glad *somebody* was.

Chapter Four

WE CROSSED into Nepal openly, by daylight. The Gurkha frontier guards pretended to be doubtful about our trade goods, but a small roll of tobacco leaf and half a bottle of rum fixed that. We padded along steadily for a couple of hours, heads bent and shoulders hunched against the pack straps, and when we rested it was in the squatting position with the weight of the packs being taken on a convenient rock. White hikers walk upright with their eyes lifted to the hills, and when they halt they throw off their packs—and it's hell to resume them. We talked little, and spat often, and drank sparingly only from each third spring, cupping the water in our right hands, and so avoiding the belly cramps as the air got thinner. Only at high noon did we halt for more than a few minutes, and then it was not to eat, as infidels would have done, but to rinse out our mouths, wash our feet, spread our tattered prayer mats and kneel towards Mecca. And no doubt I sound theatrical and pedantic, but this is the only way I can do it. Talk, breathe and think the part you're acting and crêpe hair and dark stain become futile nonsense. Besides, in the East you never know who the hell is watching you.

We recognized the spot at which the guide had gone wrong, but we didn't turn aside then as that would have meant our leaving the main path for no sufficient reason, so we went on another three miles or so and then, as the sun was sliding down behind the western ridges, we camped. I studied the map in the fading light and fixed our spot fairly accurately by three surrounding peaks, then I ran a pencil line across to where I judged the ambush to have taken place. We were closer to it than I had thought—in fact a short but steep climb over two intervening ridges would bring us to it—a mile and a half as the crow flew, against six or more if we retraced our way back along the paths.

I discussed this with Safaraz. He's no good with a map, six years' army service notwithstanding, but his nose and eyes and ears more than make up for that. He sniffed and peered up into the gloom and said it shouldn't be too difficult, but we'd have to be careful going down the other side in the dark, as there were people camped in the next valley. *I* certainly couldn't smell smoke or hear sheep bells, but I didn't argue with him. We heated water in a brass cup over a twig fire that two hands would have covered, then washed down barley bread with alternate swigs of hot rum and brown sugar. Safaraz, as a Mohammedan, is supposed to eschew hard liquor, but the army, plus his subsequent service with me, had overcome his inhibitions to a point where he could outdrink a Gurkha —and that's quite a claim. I think I mentioned that he's a Tori Khel, the toughest of them all. They are Trans-Frontier Pathans, technically neither Indian nor Pakistani subjects, so, like the Gurkhas, who fall into the same category, we have been able to continue to recruit them in limited numbers into special units of the British Army since Independence. He had just come out from a short hitch in the military prison, Hong Kong, when I arrived to start my service, and the Adjutant, who didn't like me, detailed him as my batman. He's been with me ever since, for which I owe the Adjutant a debt I'll never be able to repay.

The climb was hell. We were linked together by our two knotted turbans so that only six feet separated us, but

I couldn't see him in that pitch darkness, which meant that he shouldn't have been able to see me either, but even so, he led me straight up to the first crest in a bee-line that had me sweating and gasping, cold though the night was. I could hear him chuckling and making cracks about sahibs with big feet who climbed like pregnant camels, and all I could do was to curse filthily in return.

He was right, there were people in the next valley, but we passed their camp downwind, so that not a single dog barked, although we were close enough to hear their hobbled sheep snuffling nervously at our unfamiliar smell. We crossed the stream and climbed the second ridge, which wasn't quite such a killer as the first, then, when we could hear the main river below us, Safaraz halted and said with certainty, 'Down there, sahib, a little to the left, is where we came out of the water. To the right is where those sons of whores ambushed us.'

And this time I did argue. He was good, but not that damned good, I told him and he laughed and said, 'Does the sahib not value his house, his cattle and his wife?' which is the Pathan way of saying, 'You want to bet on it?'

Since I didn't own any of these three stakes he mentioned, I took him up on his next month's pay—double or quits—and when the sun rose I saw I'd lost again. I'll never learn.

We went down carefully after scanning the path, both ways, for fifteen full minutes. I expected to see the bodies, or what would have been left of them, lying where we had last seen them, but there was no sign of them, and for a moment I thought that Safaraz was bluffing and that I'd saved my bet, but he pointed out bullet splashes on the surrounding rocks. Yes, this was the place all right. He started questing round like a bird-dog, and I had the sense to leave him to it.

'The Kampas went that way, sahib,' he said, pointing up-track.

'We saw that.'

'But others have come and gone since.' The path was rocky, but here and there were small pockets of sand and he was reading the signs like a printed page. 'See—Kampa boots—yak hide with felt soles—they leave their mark here—and here—and again here. It was raining, so the wet sand has held the marks. Now here are other marks, sahib—chaplis with heavy nails, like the ones on our own feet. They are later than the others, because they overprint them in places—See? Here—and here. They are the ones that have moved the bodies.' I didn't need to question that one. Kampas, bad bastards though they are, are still Tibetans, and no Tibetan will dispose of corpses. That is for the Outcasts and Untouchables.

'Which way did they take them?' I asked, and he pointed up-valley, so we set out but we had only gone a few paces before he stopped and sniffed the wind, then he led off the path and we found them—bones, stripped clean for the most part, but still retaining the sickly sweet smell of recent death. They had been pushed under a shelving boulder, and smaller rocks had been piled over them to keep the jackals from unearthing them again. This was a little-used path, in fact it could hardly be called that at all. It was little more than a natural line following the rocky bank of this brawling river. Who would have taken the trouble to clear these bones? And why? Violent death, by accident or design, was common enough round here. The sparse population of these barren hills was too preoccupied with the mechanics of living to bother unduly about the dead. A devout Buddhist might spin his prayer wheel a little faster and throw a couple of extra stones on to the next chorten, but the average passer-by, Hindu or Mohammedan, seeing a heap of bones, would skirt round them without a second glance —unless he had particular reason to be interested in them. It was a pretty safe bet that none would go out of his way to report them to the police. A wise man minded his own business up here.

Safaraz, watching me, seemed to follow my line of thinking. 'Some thought that others might follow, sahib,' he said.

'In which case some may be watching us now,' I said uneasily, and started to scan the surrounding hills, but he shook his head.

'Who but a fool would set an ambush here, except in the dark?' he asked. 'The slopes are too bare to shield a rabbit. There is scrub on the next ridge, but look—wild goats are grazing on it. No—none watch within sight of where we stand now.' Which was comforting for the moment, but I was still worried. This track had been cleared, therefore it was a reasonable surmise that somebody was expected. I wondered what might lie in the next valley, but decided against going up to the ridge in daylight. Those goats would take off if we approached too close, and that would be a warning to anybody staking out the other side.

'We stay here until it is dark,' I told Safaraz. 'When we move it will not be along the line of the river as it was last time, but two hundred yards to a parallel flank.' And he clucked approvingly.

'A Pathan march,' he said. 'Like when I used to steal cattle as a boy. If that damned Sikh had listened to me that night he mightn't be fanning himself now in hell.'

We crossed the river then and went to ground in the same spot we had used last time, which was about the only one that gave all-round cover, and we were just settling down among the rocks when we saw the Kampas again.

They were coming down the valley, four of them. One moment the path had been bare, the next there they were, not two hundred yards away, across the river from us, shuffling along in their peculiar flat-footed mile-eating gait, bare-torsoed, with their dirty sheepskin robes rolled about their waists. They had burp guns slung across their backs, and two of them were carrying a blackened iron pot between them. Safaraz had just risen to go to the river to get water, and his head was above the surrounding rocks. He froze, and they passed without seeing us, and I started breathing again.

'Where the hell did they come from?' I asked, and Safaraz, for once being unable to come up with a slick answer, swore and said that they certainly hadn't come over the top, because the goats were still there.

'They have not come from far, sahib,' he said with certainty, 'nor do they *go* far. There was food in that pot, and it was still steaming.' He felt he had lost face over this, and begged of me to let him go and reconnoitre, but I thought it was too risky, and while we were getting as near to arguing as I'd ever let things go, we saw four more —coming back the other way. I thought at first that these were the same ones, until he pointed out that two of these were armed differently, with rifles, and that they hadn't got an iron pot with them. It seemed fairly obvious then. This was a guard being relieved, which meant that their headquarters were up-valley and their post somewhere down to the right. But *where* up-valley? As I have said, the path was plainly in sight right up to the scrub-crowned ridge—except for fifty yards or so where both it and the river were hidden by a fold in the ground.

'That's it, sahib—that's it,' Safaraz was chattering. 'If I hadn't been as blind as an earthworm I'd have seen it before. They camp in that dead ground.'

'They had hot food,' I pointed out. 'Where in hell were

they cooking it? Even a dry dung fire gives *some* smoke.' But he was right. The returning four went out of sight behind the fold—and didn't show up again. It was needling me as badly as Safaraz by this time. The guard-post, if guardpost it was, was down-stream from us. If we'd stuck to the path the night before, we'd have run smack into it. Yet the spot where they'd ambushed us was right opposite. Why had they changed it? I voiced this question aloud, and Safaraz looked at me somewhat askance. 'Do you stake out for a tiger twice in the same place, sahib?' he asked. 'Particularly for a tiger who has smelt the first trap? These people know that two got away—and therefore might return. Let me go down-stream, sahib. We've got to know—we've *got* to.'

So in the end I let him. He slid out of cover like a snake, and although, once clear of the patch of boulders we were holed up in, there wasn't a rock more than a foot high, within thirty seconds I had lost him. He was back in half an hour, grinning triumphantly, because once again he had been right.

'A place like this, sahib,' he said, 'but with slightly better cover by day, and they can see further down the valley. They lie among the rocks, three of them sleeping, and the hubshi who should be watching is scraping the last of the filth from the pot and stuffing it down his ill-conditioned throat. Allah was watching over us when you decided to come over the ridge instead of following the path.'

I hadn't decided it, and he knew it, but he always became exquisitely polite when he had scored over me, knowing that it made me writhe. He kept extolling my wisdom until I let him go upstream in sheer self-defence. He was away longer this time and he was quivering with excitement when he came back. It was a trick in the contour of the ground he told me. The fold was longer than it appeared from here because we were viewing it obliquely, and it bent back into a narrow, deep little side valley—and until you got right up to it you couldn't see the cave the other end.

'That's where they go, sahib,' he told me. 'Like rats down a hole. It goes in a long way because the mouth of it is dark, like a tunnel.'

So this was the local H.Q., I decided as I marked the spot on the map. Right, the Gaffer had got something for his money. I wondered what he'd do with it. It seemed a natural for the Nepalese police. A posse of tough little Gurkhas would enjoy smoking a nest like this out. There wouldn't be much they could bring to court, of course, particularly if they had already smokescreened the deaths of our party—and I couldn't see the Gaffer allowing *me* to give evidence. Anyhow, who could I give evidence against, other than the most circumstantial? Still, they had means of gathering information out here that didn't figure in the law books further West. *Something* might come of it under interrogation—including what had happened to Wainwright, I hoped. The main thing was that I had discovered the ambush H.Q.

I said, 'All right, let us eat, and when darkness falls we shall return the way we came.' And it was while we were eating that we saw this party coming into sight from behind the fold in the ground.

There were five of them—three on foot and two on mules, and they turned right—up the valley and away from us—towards the scrub-crowned ridge.

Safaraz said, as casually as if he were discussing the weather, that the two men on the mules were Ferenghis, which means Europeans—and that one of them was Wainwright-sahib. I stared at the receding column until my eyes ached, but to me in the failing light they were just figures in Kampa sheepskins.

'Are you absolutely certain?' I demanded.

'On the head of my mother,' he answered. 'And Wainwright-sahib has his hands tied in front of him.'

I received this with mixed feelings. If he hadn't had his hands tied I'd have felt fully justified in returning to the Gaffer with the bare information that Wainwright was with the Opposition. That and nothing more. His would be the assessment. As it was, Wainwright wasn't a willing guest of theirs, so in decency I had at least to go on further to pinpoint, if possible, where they took him to. I hoped it wouldn't be too far. So I was a bit fed up about it—although I did feel a certain relief. Defection doesn't surprise these days—but it does tend to sicken.

The sun went down as they reached the crest, and darkness fell almost immediately as it does in the hills, where the very clearness of the air defeats refraction. We swung round the valley of the cave in a wide detour, and went on up the slope, keeping a good hundred yards away from the river, which was here a series of rapids. It was easy at first, while we had the sound of the water to guide us, but I had doubts and misgivings when the path debouched from it at the head of the valley. The going was rough here, with nothing to orientate on at all, but Safaraz, thoroughly in his element, wasn't fazed for a moment. We were still a hundred yards from the path and proceeding parallel to it, he said—and I had to accept that.

The next valley was wilder than the one we had left, but in the distance we could see pinpoints of light, which, when we got closer, turned out to be a rukh, which means a village occupied only in the summer while there is some sparse grazing for the hill sheep. I sat down thankfully and let Safaraz go on up nearer for a nose round. It probably seems that I was leaving a hell of a lot to Safaraz. Have no doubts about that whatsoever. I was. He was incomparably better at this sort of thing than I, so I left it to him. I'd have been a fool to do otherwise. You don't try to flush game yourself when you've got a superbly trained bird-dog with you.

He came back very quickly, and if he'd been a bird-dog in reality, he'd have been wagging his tail and expecting a pat.

'They were resting here when I sneaked in through the sheepfolds, sahib,' he told me. 'I got close enough to hear them talking—but the three Kampas were gibbering in their own barbaric language so I cannot tell you what they were saying. They have gone on now, and they are about ten minutes ahead of us.'

I climbed stiffly to my feet. We'd been pounding the trail for hours and I'd had about enough, but Safaraz was already loping away into the darkness, so I groaned and followed. We detoured round the village and lost a lot of ground thereby, but we made it up before long because led mules move slower in darkness than men walking alone. We heard the clicking of hoofs on the path, and Safaraz judged them to be a couple of hundred yards ahead of us. I hoped he was not over-estimating it, as now we had to stay right in their track, because the terrain had narrowed into a funnel and we couldn't march to a flank as before. I decided that the interval was too small for safety and I quickened my pace to catch up with Safaraz, who was now about ten yards ahead of me, in order to tell him to slow down a little and I caught up with him just as he ran into somebody.

There was a muffled yelp, a brief struggle and a nasty little gurgling sound, and Safaraz muttered apologetically, 'Sorry, sahib. The bend in the path hid the fool until I ran into him. He had stopped to piss.'

We stood listening for a few moments. The rest of them were still moving forward steadily, the sound of the hoofs receding. We bent over the figure on the ground. It was one of the Kampas. I thought that Safaraz had knocked him out, and I wondered what we were going to do with him, then I realized he was dead, and Safaraz was tucking his Khyber knife back into his belt. I said, 'Move him off the path quickly. Somebody will come back to look for him.'

'Who comes back to look for a straggler in the dark, sahib?' Safaraz asked with earthy, trailbred wisdom. 'You imagine him to be following on at his own pace.' But I was taking no chances, so we lifted him like a limp sack and dumped him behind some loose rocks, and Safaraz crowed with satisfaction as he relieved him of his rifle and cartridge belt. 'No problem now, sahib,' he said. 'We follow on, and when daylight comes I pick them off—two Kampas, one sahib—ping, ping, ping—and their pissing friend is no longer lonely.' This was a beautifully simple bit of Pathan logic, but we had no opportunity of putting it to the test, because then we heard someone calling softly from up the path, so we sank down beside the corpse.

This character came on slowly. We couldn't see him but we could read unwillingness into every lagging footstep. He called again as he passed us, and added a querulous phrase which I couldn't understand but was obviously the Tibetan equivalent of 'Where the hell are you, you stupid bastard?' Then Safaraz, without orders from me, glided away, and after a short interval I heard a sound that was no more than a sigh, and I went back to the path.

'No need to follow now, sahib,' Safaraz chuckled. 'They come to us.'

'And you're two months' pay the poorer,' I told him angrily. 'Act without my orders again and you'll be one *job* poorer.'

He said he was sorry, but didn't mean it. We dumped

this one down beside the first and I tried to figure out what would happen now. The 'sahib', whoever he was, would hardly send the third Kampa down when these two failed to return—not unless he was a complete idiot. No—he'd be halted some little distance ahead, a very worried man. If he had any sense at all, and I had no reason to assume that he hadn't, he'd hole up beside the path now until daylight, which I reckoned was no more than an hour away. He might send the other one down then—or he might execute that tried and trusted old military manœuvre of getting the hell out of it, quick—if necessary, once mounted, galloping off with his prisoner and leaving the last Kampa to follow as best he could. That's what I would have done in his place, if the prisoner was a valued asset, as I assumed Wainwright was to them. That way I could still lose Wainwright. What I needed to do was to get up closer to their position before it was light—but the advantage in that case would be with the waiting men.

Then an idea came to me, and I told Safaraz to help me get the big sheepskin chubas, which are half coat and half robe, off the two dead men.

We dumped our packs and got into these things, and pulled the hoods over our heads, then, as the sky paled we went off up-track.

Chapter Five

THEY WERE WAITING a quarter of a mile further on and they saw us long before we saw them. I was limping badly, using the rifle as a walking stick, with Safaraz pretending to help me the other side, the second rifle in his right hand. The remaining Kampa came out of cover at the side of the path and shouted at us angrily in Tibetan when we were about a hundred yards short of their position, and Safaraz, head down, made an answering gesture with the rifle, in the manner of a man too weary to argue. The Kampa turned away, slinging his burp gun over his shoulder, and called to the others. They came out on to the track, already mounted, but I couldn't see them clearly because we were facing into the rising sun and they were in shadow. I thought for a hopeful moment that we were going to get right up to them before uncovering, but the Kampa turned back towards us and shouted again, and whatever it was seemed to call for an answer, Safaraz gestured again, but this time it didn't work and the other guy repeated his question, and there was a rising note of suspicion in his voice—and he was starting to unsling his burp gun. I jerked my rifle up and fired from the hip, and missed—but Safaraz didn't. He got the Kampa as he started to throw himself flat—and again before he hit the ground. The two mules were bucking and rearing and one of the riders was thrown heavily and the other took off at a stretched gallop up the track followed by the riderless one, and vanished round the next bend. Safaraz cursed and raced up the slope to get him in sight again, but I couldn't tell which of them was which so I roared at him to come back. He did so, miffishly, like a bridge player baulked of a grand slam, and we went up to the one who had been thrown.

It was Wainwright, out cold. His wrists were tied in front of him, cruelly tight with a length of leather thong, and they had evidently kept him like this for a long time, because they hadn't been able to put his arms through the sleeves of his chuba, which he was wearing secured round his shoulders like a cloak. We sawed through the thong carefully and I tried to chafe some circulation back into his wrists. The pain of it brought him round and he started to babble questions and struggled to sit up, but I wouldn't answer any until we had lugged him back to where we had left our packs and had given him a stiff slug of rum. He was a pretty tough youth and he had recovered within ten minutes, although he looked like hell.

Like us, he had been wearing Punjabi clothes, and they were indescribably filthy and he was thoroughly lousy from the chuba and had a flourishing ten-day beard. He looked at me rather coldly and said, 'All right, who starts?'

'Please yourself,' I told him. 'I haven't got much to tell. Our party was shot up, with the exception of Safaraz and me. We went on to Lahore, and the Gaffer asked me to come back and look for you. We were lucky.'

'And modest as always,' he said sourly.

I said, 'Suppose we skip the rancour until later? Our immediate concern is to get out of this before that fellow brings somebody back. Have you any idea where you were making for?'

'No, except that it was two night marches from the place we started from. We were supposed to have camped at the top of this pass by dawn, but he lost two of his goons during the night, and that slowed us up.' He nodded at the two bundles behind the rocks. 'Are those they?'

'Yes.'

'Clever of you. We didn't hear a thing up there.'

'One of them stopped for a leak, and Safaraz dealt with him. Then his pal came back looking for him. I told you —we were lucky.'

'And modest,' he said again, then, as I turned away abruptly to pick up the packs, he added, 'I'm sorry, Rees. I was just thinking of that old bastard sharpening his claws on me when we get back.' He got up, wincing, and started to stamp some of the stiffness out of his legs.

I said, 'We'd better get off this track and rest up for a few hours.' And his hackles rose again.

'I'm quite fit,' he said shortly.

'Well, we're not,' I told him. 'We've been padding the hoof for the better part of the last week.' I tossed him the burp gun we had taken from the third Kampa and started to climb the slope away from the track. I could hear him making heavy weather of it behind me—a night on a mule isn't the best preparation for a stiff mountain climb—but I didn't slow up, and when Safaraz tried to help him he got a sharp brush-off. He was in a muck sweat when we got to the top, and his face was grey under its coating of dirt and blood from a cut he'd got on his head when he was thrown. I didn't pause, but set off at a smart clip over the plateau to the next valley. We went down into it and up the other side, then down into the next before I called a halt. I wasn't working off any spleen on him, it was just that I knew that while we were within a couple of miles of those corpses the vultures wouldn't dive. We settled down at last in a clump of rhododendron near a small stream, and he went out like a light. I took first watch because I wanted to try and fix our position on the map.

Imagine a hand, palm down and fingers spread. The back of the hand and the wrist was the massif running north-east to the main Himalayan range. The fingers were the ridges we had been crossing, and the gaps between them the valleys. We had come into Nepal up the valley between the index and middle finger, and were now in that between the third and little finger—hard up against the knuckles. Our way out into India lay somewhere near the tip of the middle finger. That's it in its simplest form. It didn't look too daunting on paper, even when you realized that the fingers were something better than thirty miles long, but the valleys weren't straight, and I reckoned we had a sixty-mile hike before us. Twenty miles a day would be a fair thing for fit men, and Wainwright, while pretty battered, should be all right after a good day's rest. I checked on our food. We'd finished the barley bread, but there was a couple of pounds of gram left. Chewing gram is like trying to cope with a mouthful of lead shot, but it's sustaining stuff once you get it down. It's what the Tibetans grind to make their staple food, tsampa—and that gave me an idea and I searched the pocketlike sleeves of the chubas we'd brought along, livestock notwithstanding, for warmth at night—and found two leather bags of the latter, about four pounds in all. It is normally mixed with tea and yak butter, but I experimented with the last of our rum and brown sugar and made six flat cakes that had set as hard as rocks by the time I woke Safaraz at mid-afternoon. I told him to wake me at sunset, and then I drifted off for six blissful hours.

Wainwright had managed to clean himself up a little and had even had a dip in the icy stream, so he wasn't quite as objectionable when Safaraz roused me. I gave him the general plan I had worked out, and showed him the route on the map and he nodded his agreement without any snide remarks. There's a certain protocol about these things. We had no seniority grades as such, but regular incumbents normally ranked the casually employed for the simple reason that they were still around after a job to bear the slings and arrows of the Gaffer's inevitable displeasure, while we took our hire and went our way, so nominally Wainwright was in charge.

I said, 'I thought it better to make this first one a night march, just in case they fan out and start looking into the parallel valleys. You wouldn't know how many Kampas they've got, would you?'

'There were twelve in the place they were keeping me,' he said. 'Four were always on guard somewhere outside, in eight-hour hitches, then there were some Indians who used to come and go—and of course, the German. That was the fellow who buggered off on the mule.'

'He was the boss?'

'Only locally. He used to get his orders by radio from somebody else. Unfortunately I don't know much German, and in any case I couldn't hear what the other fellow was saying because this one was using headphones. He was pretty subservient though. It was all "Jahwohl, mein Herr so-and-so—nein, mein Herr so-and-so".'

'Did he speak any English?'

'Not that I ever heard. Actually he never spoke to me directly at all. I don't think he spoke Tibetan either. He used to brief the Kampas in Urdu, through an Indian interpreter. That's how I knew where we were going and how long it was going to take us.'

'Did they realize that you were a European?'

'They didn't give any sign of it, one way or the other. They just carted me into the cave the night they caught me, tied me up and dumped me down in a corner. They shoved some filthy food and a can of water down alongside me at intervals and left me to cope with it as best I could.

Twice a day one of the Indians would untie my ankles and lead me out to a latrine. Ever tried to get a pair of these bloody Punjabi pants down with your hands tied together?'

'How were you caught?' I asked. 'Or would you rather keep that for the debriefing?'

'It doesn't matter a damn now,' he said gloomily. 'I was acting without orders. I intended tailing you to the handover place, wait until you'd taken Palinovsky back, and then tail the others to wherever they holed up, and then make my way back to Lahore with some useful information. Dead simple. I thought it would be easier to move ahead of you than try to follow—but I found I was being tailed by a couple of Indians the other side of the crossing point, so I led them a dance—and lost my way in doing so. When I got my bearings again, time was running short—I'd been aiming to get there two hours ahead of the handover and hole up. As it was, I wasn't ten minutes in front of you when I ran smack into this ambush. Two Kampas dropped on me and knocked me cold—or not quite cold because I heard the shoot-up that must have been your crowd getting it, just as they jumped me in the cave. So now you know.'

'Who picked that point?' I asked him.

'I was never told, but I rather gathered that the C.I.A. were dealing with a go-between in Katmandu. Anyhow, Wilbur gave it to me and Nadkarni. Just the map coordinates. We had to figure it out then from the relief map at the Survey Office. Neither of us was happy about it—far too vague—and Nadkarni told me he was going to engage a local guide when I was pulled off it.'

He lapsed into silence then. I was genuinely sorry for him. It was ever thus with poor bloody Wainwright. Nobody could call him stupid, and he certainly didn't lack guts. He was just plain damned unlucky.

I said, 'The point that puzzles me is why they didn't just knock you off like the others.'

'I think they realized that you were close on my heels, so they couldn't risk shooting at that stage—then having got me in the bag they decided to keep me for questioning.'

'But why keep you there at the site of the ambush for three days?' I mused.

'Probably to let the trail cool off. They obviously expected somebody to be sent in to look for us. How you managed it without being rumbled I'll never know.' He bit into a tsampa cake savagely. 'Don't say "lucky" again, for Christ's sake.'

I woke Safaraz then and gave him something to eat, and we started off down the valley in single file, with Safaraz in the lead, then Wainwright, then me in the rear. There was no semblance of a path herc, just a small stream running through tumbled rocks, and Wainwright and I were stumbling badly. I told Safaraz to slow the pace, and Wainwright thought I was doing it for his sake, and got prickly again. I'd had enough of it by this time so I called a halt.

'Listen,' I told him. 'I'm as tired as you and I don't want to be exhausted before morning. Now, are you going to get that chip off your shoulder, or do you want to make your own way back?'

He started to argue, then, suddenly, the fight went out of him and he mumbled an apology and we went on. I hoped that it would be plain sailing all the way to Lahore, because I was convinced that Wainwright was finished as far as this job was concerned. It was a pity, this complete inability of his to accept a temporary set-back without imagining that people were getting at him. It was dangerous too, because it had a tendency to make him take unnecessary chances as a result, just to prove himself. I hoped that the Gaffer wouldn't give him too rough a ride over this one, but whether he did or not, I made a mental resolve not to work with Wainwright again. This business is the very last one for oil and water relationships.

The rest of that night's march passed without incident but we were well short of the twenty-mile target. We were still in the valley at daybreak, and the sides were too steep for me to get a fix on the surrounding peaks. Wainwright offered to climb up with the map and compass but I turned it down. We were much lower here and there were scanty stretches of grass, which meant that there was always a possibility of running into herdsmen with their flocks. I got this over to him without argument for once. Our last exchange seemed to have cleared the air a bit.

We slept in turns throughout the day, trying while awake to quell our rumbling bellies with the last of the tsampa cake, then we set off again, and by dawn we had come out of the foothills and were in the semi-cultivated area which runs along the actual frontier. We ditched the rifles, burp gun and chubas, because they were no part of a peaceful Punjabi trader's equipment and we'd have been pounced on with them if we'd run into a Gurkha police patrol. The going was easier here and I was able to fix our position. We were on course and were, in fact, only a few miles from the frontier, but it wouldn't have benefited us to have crossed right away because we'd have had about sixty miles of trackless hill forest to traverse on the Indian side before hitting the Bareilly road.

There was no need to march by night now, so we kept going well after dawn towards a village which the map showed some six miles ahead, and for the last part of it we were able to thumb a lift on a bullock cart. The village consisted of a score or so of mud-plastered stone huts set round an open maidan, and there was chai-khana there.

That's a teahouse where you can sometimes get a heavier meal than the normal tea and chapattis they sell, but they don't have sleeping accommodation. The old Mohammedan who ran it killed a couple of scrawny chickens and plunged them into the big pot of curried vegetables he had simmering over an open fire, then, when we'd gorged ourselves into distension, he directed us to the caravanserai which was some distance down the dusty road the other side of the village.

We reached it, almost asleep on our feet, at mid-morning. It was just an open square bounded by four high walls with a strong teakwood gate in one of them, and we'd have been more comfortable sleeping out in the fields, but the Indian traveller is a creature of habit and the police look askance at people sleeping in the open near the fringes of civilization. It was empty now and there was no watchman on duty—normally they are only used at night—so we went in. I didn't feel the necessity for keeping watch here, so we burrowed into a pile of loosely baled hay under a lean-to shed in one corner and just went to sleep.

I woke up suddenly as I felt the lobe of my ear being pinched, and Wainwright was bending over me. He whispered, 'A car's stopped outside.'

'That can only be cops,' I said. 'Routine check. Just sit tight if they come in, and let me do the talking.'

But then there was a warning hiss from Safaraz. 'Indians, sahib,' he called softly. 'Three of them coming this way.' He was on the roof of the shed above us, peeping over the wall. I got up as if I'd been stung, tugging my gun out from under my arm, and darted outside the shed and clambered up beside him. The serai was about a hundred yards off the road where I could see a dusty car standing, and half-way between us and it these three were approaching, their eyes glued on the gate. Safaraz had already got his gun out and he said hopefully, 'We can get them as they come in,' and added politely, 'If the sahib takes the first, giving time for the others to enter after him, then I can——' But I shut him up with an elbow in the ribs. A shoot-up near a village in full daylight was the last thing I wanted—and anyhow, these might have been *bona fide* travellers. Wainwright had joined us now, so I said, 'Over the wall, quick—and into the ditch,' and led the way. We went along the ditch, which ran right round the ten-feet-high walls like a dry moat, until we came to the angle of the wall where the gate was, and I peeped round cautiously. The first one had just come up to it, and he was getting a gun out from under his shirt. Safaraz, rubber-necking past me, said in prissy 'I told you so' tones, 'It is as I said. Now if the sahib will take the first, as I suggested——' This time my elbow got him under the chin.

They were dressed, like us, in Punjabi clothes, though considerably cleaner, and the other two now had guns out. They argued in an undertone before going in, and none of them seemed keen on being the first. Eventually they shoved the smallest guy through and watched him for quite a time before following. They were out of sight now and we were safe for the moment because the only place they could look over the wall from was the roof of the shed, which was the other side of the square. But there was always the chance of their coming out for a look round, so I motioned to the others to follow, and led off to a clump of cactus near the car, which was the only cover within a couple of hundred yards. We got down on the blind side of it just in time, because an old Gurkha came along the road then, wearing a tattered army jacket and a brass armband. He stopped and looked into the car, muttering to himself—then the Indians came out and, as I had expected, had a swift looksee round the four sides of the wall. I hoped our footprints wouldn't have been too evident. They came back to the car then.

The old Gurkha said, in bad Urdu, 'The serai does not open until sundown, and the tariff is a rupee per gharry and half for a man. Women, children and cattle are free. No dogs.'

'Peace, babu,' said one of the Punjabis. 'We look for three men—Punjabis, like ourselves. They have been here —and recently.'

'None since last night,' said the Gurkha positively.

'Liar,' said one of the others. 'The keeper of the chai-khana told us——' But he got no further, because the Gurkha cut loose with a beautiful stream of vituperation.

'Who are you to call me a liar, you Hindu bastard?' he roared. 'I, Parta Dhansing, police pensioner, keeper of the serai. We know how to deal with brothel scum in these parts.'

'Peace—peace,' soothed the other. 'We merely look for our friends——'

'What friends does a lousy Punjabi have? Be on your way. You are in Nepal now, not in your own damned country. Enter my serai again without permission and I'll have your ears off.' He whipped his kukri, the deadly Gurkha chopping knife they all carry, out of its scabbard and made a token pass at the nearest of them. They retreated hurriedly and piled into the car and drove off. The old man howled abuse after them, then turned and stalked off towards the serai, muttering angrily. He was about half the size of the smallest of them, but nobody who knows the breed ever attempts to mix it with an angry Gurkha with his knife out—not unless he's prepared to shoot, which these types obviously weren't, certainly not out in the open.

'Three left to plague us,' gloomed Safaraz. 'We should have dealt with them inside, as I said.'

I turned on him and gave him particular hell because he was showing signs of getting out of hand, which is the weakness of the Pathan once he has killed. Safaraz will normally take a chewing out from me quite cheerfully, but this was in front of a third party and he hated it. He sat hunched and sullen when I ran out of breath, and because this involved loss of face I relented a little. 'But you did well to hear that car,' I told him. 'I was at fault not to have set a watch. You saved us, Safaraz.'

But he didn't want any hand-outs and he mumbled that it was Wainwright who heard it first, and Wainwright, who was reading the situation perfectly, was suitably modest and said that that was purely because he was having trouble with his bowels and had risen to go to the latrine at that moment.

'I heard the car pass, going towards the village,' he explained, 'and ten minutes later it came back and stopped outside. I aroused Safaraz who leapt as silently and skilfully as a mountain panther for the roof of the shed and saw them in time. I, personally, am grateful. I wouldn't want to fall into the hands of those bastards a second time.' And he solemnly shook hands with Safaraz, who grinned shamefacedly and became even more modest, and things were back on an even keel—and I, personally, was grateful to Wainwright. Pathans are the slickest operators in the world in this sort of situation, but, Christ, they take some handling.

We were in a quandary now. These three goons had gone off in the direction we wanted to go and were now between us and the crossing point I had been making for. What had brought them here? I wondered. We certainly hadn't been seen coming down the valley, or they'd have dealt with us there. Were they watching all the valleys, every exit, and patrolling this frontier road? It appeared so. 'Three Punjabis' they had said. They knew who they were looking for. They'd have got that from the German. He already knew how Wainwright was dressed, and he'd seen Safaraz and me when we'd thrown our chubas off.

Wainwright said, 'Do you think we ought to get other clothes?' But I knew that would be useless. The only other ones we could get this side of the border would be Gurkha. The average Gurkha is five-feet-six—a stockily built little man—and he has Mongolian features, and, apart from the occasional wispy moustache, he doesn't grow hair on his face. We were six-foot, wildly bearded Caucasians.

We had to move because people were now arriving at the serai, and the cactus clump didn't give us all-round cover. We set off in the gathering dusk, walking separately but keeping each other in sight. I tried to put myself in the opposition's place. They knew that we were somewhere in this area and that we would be crossing into India, but they didn't know that we knew they were tailing us—therefore we might reasonably be expected to make for one of the easier crossing points, preferably one close to the main road to Bareilly, which was the first big communication centre on the Indian side. We would make, in actual fact, for the one we were heading for now. They would try to jump us this side, but, if they failed in that they would no doubt try the other. That they were well organized and had good communications was self-evident. Obviously, therefore, our cue was to keep away from the easier routes and to continue moving at night. I hated the idea, but there seemed nothing else for it.

I sighed and led off the road and struck due west across the sparse cultivation that lay each side of it. Behind me I could hear the others cursing, because even the indestructible Safaraz had had a bellyful by this time.

Nothing actually marks the frontier at this point, but I reckoned we were across it by dawn and we were down to the level of the plain in thick jungle. We hit a track after a hellish period of crashing through rhododendron and bamboo, and we followed it for a couple of miles until it ended at a Dogra village that was not shown on the map. I left the others on the outskirts and went in and bought food. It was market day and one Punjabi, albeit a very dirty one, didn't seem to be drawing too many curious glances, so I nosed around trying to get my bearings, and here we had a break. There was a truck, mail, passengers and anything else that could be crowded on to it, which ran each day down to the main Bareilly road. I asked an old man outside the freight office when it left, and how far the main road was. He said midday, fifty miles and, he added, the trip took five hours if Allah was compassionate. Still, it was better than walking. I went back and collected the others and after eating we came in, again separately, and bought tickets. We also bought different clothes in the market—countryman's kaddar shirt and beaded cap for me, babu's jacket and dhoti for Wainwright, and again Punjabi khamis and pantaloons for Safaraz, but different in colour from his old ones. Then we cleaned up at the washing ghat and got ourselves shaved by pavement barbers.

There was a slight contretemps with a rear wheel, which delayed our departure until two o'clock, but Allah *was* compassionate thereafter, and we did the trip in just under the five hours, sitting as far from each other as thirty other passengers, eleven goats and an unspecified number of crates and bales would allow. We were lucky again at the main road in that we found ourselves only about five miles from Bareilly and we hitched rides in on different buses. Safaraz bought all three tickets to Ferozepore and brought them outside the station to us, and we split up and boarded the train on the blind side, and didn't meet again until we reached Lahore.

So that was the end of that one. A job—just a job—rather more unsatisfactory and inconclusive than most, and distinguished only by the success of the fog of mendacity that followed it. Two alleged luggage coolies swore that they saw Nadkarni fall over a cliff and disappear under an avalanche of scree. They brought back a boxful of the specimens he had collected, a well-merited eulogistic obituary appeared in the Hindustan Times, and his name was inscribed on the police roll of honour. The C.I.A. made their own highly efficient arrangements to explain Wilbur's death. Anonymous 'well-informed sources' leaked contradictory stories about Palinovsky. The skyjackers, shortchanged on their end of the bargain, had shot him; his own people had caught up with him and knocked him off; he had been seen in Washington, Peking, Moscow, alive and flourishing. Take your pick—if you were interested. I wasn't. I just took my pay and went back to Calcutta—the Gaffer grinned wryly, said you couldn't win 'em all, and departed for London. I don't know where Wainwright went—I wasn't interested in him either.

Yes—just a job—D.C.F. Do. Collect. Forget.

Chapter Six

AND I *had* forgotten it, completely, when the telephone rang weeks later in the three a.m. dark of a Calcutta monsoon morning. It was a bad line, made worse by a thunderstorm at the other end, and the caller obviously wasn't used to our modern marvels and he wasn't pitching his voice very well, and I was still muzzy from sleep, but finally I realized it was a very old friend of mine, one Miraj Khan Bahadur. He said, 'Come quickly, sahib, taking care not to be seen, because there are watchers here. My sahib is troubled.'

Miraj Khan and his sahib, Old Man Culverton, are two of a possible five people in this world that I wouldn't want whys and wherefores from in advances, so I said I'd be there that night and I flew up to Delhi on the midday flight from Dum Dum Airport, and as it is easier to accept the expense of an extra ticket than to argue with him, I took Safaraz along. Since Miraj Khan had said there were watchers there, and a European, other than the Old Man himself, would have stood out like a sore thumb in Ramabagh, once more I was back in P.M. clothes, and we reached the farm late that night after a long and dusty ride by train and bus from Delhi.

The Old Man met me in the very English drawing-room. It was as chintzy and bright as when I'd seen it last, some years before, and the big Kashmir bowls of flowers were there—too many of them—but the blooms were rammed in tight with roses, sweet williams, stocks and others of the gentler ones in uneasy juxtaposition with flame of the forest, frangipani and jacaranda, and the silver-framed family photos I remembered all seemed to be lined up stiffly on parade on bookcases and piano top.

Yes, the feminine touch had gone all right.

The Old Man came forward, stepping unerringly over footstools and moving past furniture as if he could see it. He stopped an exact two feet in front of me and his hands found my shoulders and gripped hard for a moment, then he turned away abruptly and went to a drink table and poured two stiff scotches. There was a slight stoop to those once straight shoulders, and more lines in the rugged face, but otherwise he was little changed. He turned and handed me my drink.

'I didn't ask you to come, Idwal,' he said. 'That was that old fool Miraj Khan. But thank you all the same.'

'That's all right, sir. What's the trouble?'

'Do you know a fellow called Wainwright?'

One didn't have to worry about facial expression when dealing with the Old Man—just one's voice. I sank a good half of my drink and said, 'Hah! That's better. Wainwright? Yes—I've met him once or twice in Calcutta. Works in a bank. Hong Kong and South China I think. Why?' It sounded all right in my own ears.

'Is that all you know about him?' In casual conversation the Old Man always faced one directly, and since there was no trace of opacity in his flinty blue eyes, it was hard even after long acquaintance, fully to realize his blindness. When he was really studying one, however, he was apt to turn his head slightly obliquely in order to bring his better ear into alignment. That one missed nothing. He was doing this now.

I said, 'As far as I know,' but it didn't get over.

'I'm not asking you to tell me anything you're not at liberty to, Idwal,' he said. 'Just the fellow himself—not what he does, or who he does it for. Is he—is he all right? You know what I mean.'

I said, 'Again—as far as I know.'

He was silent for a long moment, then he gave a slight shrug and found his way to a chair. 'Sit down,' he said. 'You must be tired. You've had a long trip—part of it, at least, sitting next to a gent smoking native tobacco in a huqar. I know you're wearing a kaddar shirt. What else?'

'Punjabi pagri and pants,' I told him.

'Why?'

'Miraj Khan hinted that it would be better not to be too noticeable.'

'Silly old devil,' he grunted. 'Actually there have been one or two strangers from over the Pakistan border hanging about—but nothing that called for your going into fancy dress. Got their eyes on some of our cattle. This place is now the exact equivalent of the old American Wild West a hundred years ago—rustlers, gunslingers—the lot.'

'But no U.S. Cavalry.'

'No cavalry of any sort—more's the pity. I wonder why I keep the damned place on. There's nothing for me here any more. Not since Sheila died.'

'I was sorry to hear of that, sir.'

'Yes—yes. Thank you for the letter—and the English flowers you had flown out. Arrived in splendid condition—packed in dry ice or something. Good God—flowers from England in twenty-four hours. Took me old great-grandfather six months to come out here originally. Sailing ship round the Cape to Bombay—then horse and bullock cart up here to his Regiment. We've got that irrigation scheme running now, by the way. Had we started it when you were here last?'

'You were just about to.'

'Hm. Dam's the other side of the border, unfortunately, and those buggers blow up the pipes from time to time. Told you—just like the Wild West. Police are no damned good. Afraid of the politicians. Now in me grandfather's day, or even me father's, we'd have had the troops out after 'em.'

And that was the pattern of things until he realized that I was sleepy, and had me shown up to the guest room. An old man lost in the present and constantly groping back to the past. It was an act, of course. There was nothing geriatric about *this* Old Man, but he had the pride of the devil and he thought I'd snubbed him over Wainwright, so he was putting up a smoke screen. But each of us knew that the other was avoiding the subject that was uppermost in our minds.

The guest room hadn't changed. There were even flowers there, again rammed hard into a vase by an untutored masculine hand, and the atrocious oil painting of a long dead Culverton in cavalry uniform still loomed over the very English fourposter bed. But the mosquito net was dusty—something that it would never have been in Lady Sheila's day.

Tired as I was, I couldn't get off to sleep. I lay staring up through the darkness for hours. A job—Do—Collect—Forget. I was usually successful in this—certainly in the second and last. Why had Wainwright come back to upset the comfortable axiom? And what was his connection with Culverton, to whom I knew anything that remotely touched upon espionage in any shape or form was complete anathema? Damn it all—it was that which had smashed things up between Claire and me. Wasn't it Claire herself who said——? But I wouldn't let myself follow that one up. It had taken me too long to forget. Instead my thoughts went back to Culverton.

His great-grandfather had come out here as a subaltern

in an East India Company cavalry regiment, had risen to command it and had gone on to a generalship. He obviously had more of a social conscience than was entirely usual in those days, because he didn't like what happened to his Indian troopers when they were old and worn out, so he retired in India and started a farm where he trained these men to scratch a living for themselves from the tired soil instead of begging in the bazaar. The scheme succeeded and the Government plied him with land grants and the Ramabagh Military Farm grew to immense proportions, largely because the old General quickly became a legend in his own time and was able to keep the dead hand of officialdom out of it. It was said, apocryphally no doubt but with possibly a trace of truth, that he had warning notices in five languages set up round his boundaries to the effect that tigers, hyenas, moneylenders and Government babus would be shot on sight. His male descendants followed in this tradition, each serving his time with the Regiment and then taking over the management of the place. But it looked as if the tradition would end when this, the last one, was blinded by a mortar blast in some stupid little Frontier skirmish that should never have happened. Actually he succeeded beyond the others and was probably the first man ever to take a First Class Honours Degree in Agricultural Science—at Cambridge—entirely in Braille. And he wasn't an armchair farmer either. He knew his way over every square inch of his thousands of acres, by touch and smell. He could price a crop by pulling a handful of grain from it, and his marvellously sensitive hands run over a horse, steer or sheep told him much more than eyes alone could have done. His 'eyes', when he really needed them, were those of his former senior Indian Officer, Rissaldar-Major Miraj Khan Bahadur, M.C., Indian Order of Merit, 3rd Rangar Cavalry (retired). To see these two old gentlemen galloping flat out across country, stirrup to stirrup, with not so much as a leading rein between their horses was a sight which never failed to make the hair on the nape of my neck stand upright. Yes—Miraj Khan, and, of course, his wife, the redoubtable Lady Sheila Culverton, now dead these two years. And Claire—but again I shied away from this.

A wonderful old boy. The greatest of his line. I think the Gaffer would have given his own eyes to have got him on the payroll. He was ideally placed here—right on the Indo-Pakistan border—Nepal one way, Kashmir the other—two back doors into Chinese Tibet—and not such a hell of a distance from the southern fringes of Asiatic Russia. A natural cross roads. God, if he'd been inclined that way he'd have been a better sounding board than Yev Shalom himself. But he wasn't inclined that way. In *his* simple lexicon spying was dirty—so were politics. All he was interested in was training farmers and raising the agricultural standards in these parts. That and nothing more. When Independence came in 1947, and the British marched out, some members of the new Indian Government voiced doubts as to the advisability of an Englishman remaining in such a delicate area, and it is said that Gandhi himself spoke for him. No—you'd never get Old Man Culverton even remotely to touch anything tainted by the Business.

Then how the bloody hell did Wainwright come into it?

It was no good. I couldn't sleep. I climbed from under the mosquito net and crossed to the french window which opened on to the flat roof of the veranda below. The monsoon, never heavy in the Upper Punjab, had not reached here yet, and the air was heavy and flat. I leaned on the parapet, lit a cigarette and looked down over the surrounding farm buildings, white in the light of a quarter moon. The bungalow was L-shaped. Claire's room had been across there in the shorter arm, but there was a break between the veranda roofs. I remembered the death-defying leap I'd had to make one night when Lady Sheila had been on the prowl.

A stone clicked sharply on the concrete floor beside me. I looked down and made out the foreshortened figure of Miraj Khan just below. He came up the lattice as silently as a cat and dropped down beside me and saluted.

I said, 'Salaam, Khan Bahadur,' and took his right hand between both of mine.

'Let us go inside, Idwal Rees,' he whispered. 'The Old Sahib's room is below this, and he has ears like a chital.'

We went in and I looked at him in the light. Like Culverton he had aged somewhat, but was still ramrod stiff, dressed, as always, in high-necked, knee-length black coat, white jodhpurs and immaculately polished chukka boots. His beard and fiercely upbrushed cavalry moustache had much more grey in it than hitherto, but his turban was just as smartly tied and cocked. He had joined the Regiment as a raw recruit when Culverton was first commissioned, so there would not have been more than a year's difference in their ages one way or other, but they always referred to each other as 'old'. Age carries merit in the East, and transcends personal vanity.

He said, 'How did you arrive, sahib, without my knowing?'

'Quietly,' I told him. 'As you asked. Across the fields dressed as a Punjabi Mussulman.'

He grinned. 'And that thrice-damned Pathan thief of yours——?'

'Is still with me.'

'He'll cut your throat one night—while you sleep.'

'I doubt it.'

'So do I. A joke.'

'What is the trouble, Miraj-ji?' I asked him. 'Can you

tell me without the betrayal of a trust? The Brigadier-sahib has told me nothing—nor will he.'

He pondered for a while, then said, 'To talk with a friend, in the interest of a friend, is not betrayal, sahib.'He turned away and walked to the window and stood looking out for a full minute, then he turned back towards me. 'I said a *friend.* Can a friend be forgiven a great impertinence?'

'*You* could—because an impertinence would not be intended. What is it, Miraj?'

'Why did you and Claire-miss-sahib, not marry?' he asked, and it was my turn to be silent. When I did answer I was dissembling like hell.

'She had her work,' I said. 'Her hospital in the hills. You know about that, Miraj.'

He grimaced. 'Is she a dried-up missionary memsahib who couldn't find a husband in Berlaiti? Aren't there a thousand other than a young and beautiful woman who could dole out soup and wipe the noses of bazaar brats?'

'That is not true, and you know it,' I said sharply. 'She runs a very big hospital for Tibetan refugees who would otherwise be worked to death by the Chinese.'

'I never knew a Tibetan who could be worked—to death or short of it,' he snorted. 'A woman on marriage should leave all else and stay with her husband.'

'Does yours?'

'All three of them, worse luck,' he said, and grinned again, which eased things a little, but he wouldn't drop the subject.

'So Claire-baba wouldn't leave her damned Tibetans? You wanted her to, didn't you?'

'With our race a woman has freedom of choice,' I said.

'In *all* races women should sometimes have their minds made up for them—with sweet reason, if it works.'

'And if it doesn't?'

'With a stirrup leather.'

'You try it some time—on *her*—if you find life weighing too heavily on you.'

'I have—as a cheeky little bitch of a larki—many a time. She used to climb that nim tree by the forage barn when denied her way, where the sahib and memsahib couldn't reach, and hurl filthy abuse at them in sweeper's language. I'd go up after her with a piece of rattan cane for the good of her manners. She wouldn't sit in comfort for two days after that.'

'As you said—when she was small, Miraj,' I said. 'Those days are past. We don't beat our women.'

'A pity. Even a horse needs a touch of the whip occasionally to knock some sense into it.' He looked at me directly. 'We are talking round the subject, sahib—and we both know it. Why did you not marry—truthfully?'

'Our ways lay along different roads,' I told him. 'Kismet.'

'And she didn't like your road?'

I shrugged. 'It would seem so.'

'You could not join her in her work up there?'

'Am I a doctor—or a woman, to wipe running noses?'

'No, thank Allah the Compassionate. So *you* did not like *her* road?' He threw his hands up. 'Shaikh mati.' Which is the same as our 'Checkmate'. 'So, for that you both live in sadness.'

'Not so. Both have now forgotten.'

'Which is why she still keeps your picture—and asks me quietly when she comes here if I've heard of you?'

'All right then,' I said angrily. '*I* have forgotten.'

'Which is why you were looking across at her room just now like a bull camel in rut.'

'That is too much, Khan Bahadur, even from you. You mentioned impertinence just now.' I felt red around the ears.

'And I ask the sahib's pardon. I don't mean it as impertinence. I am an old man—and I've seen many generations of young cockchafers of British officers—and Indian. They don't differ so much. None thinks the worse of another for stealing a little fruit from the future father-in-law's tree. Is a man the less for that?'

'Let us drop the subject,' I said with finality.

'Verily—if the sahib really wishes it. But we have not come yet to the real reason. It was your work really that she could not stomach.'

'I don't know what you're talking about.'

'Sahib, sahib, sahib,' he said reproachfully. 'I who took you across the frontier once when budmashes were behind you—and you and your Pathan were nearly killed. You were a friend in danger. Did I ask the colour or the politics of those budmashes? I don't ask now. I don't care. *I* have no politics or colour, other than that of my skin, any more than has the Brigadier-sahib. But I'm not a fool. I know what your work entails—whichever side pays you. It is that which I want to talk about.'

'It is that which I *cannot* talk about.'

'Even if both the Brigadier-sahib *and* Claire-baba were now mixed up in it—and were in danger?'

So *that* was it? I felt a cold sensation at the pit of my belly. I didn't want to go on with this, but I had to know now.

'You know what I do,' I said. 'I work for who pays me—but my paymasters are all on one side—*this* side—and I've never worked against India or Pakistan. Yes—that was the reason. The Brigadier-sahib and Claire-baba both hate this work. But I know no other. Tell me what you have to say, Miraj.'

He expelled his breath in a gusty sigh of relief. 'I'm sorry, sahib. We've been talking like women round the village well—and I've made you angry. But that is it.

Claire-baba has been drawn into something up there in that hospital of hers—and her father knows it, but can do nothing.'

'*What* has she been drawn into?'

'I wish I knew. First this man came here and asked for her——'

'What man?'

'A young man—European—Win-light——'

'Wainwright?'

'That is so. My tongue cannot twist round these Angresi names——'

'Go on.'

'He said he had met her in Calcutta when she was down there buying supplies for her hospital, and she had invited him to call her if he should ever be in this part of the country. The Brigadier-sahib made him welcome, as is his custom. Three days later Claire-baba came down from the hills. The Brigadier-sahib was very happy, because she does not visit here very often these days. She and this young man were together a great deal. I thought—I thought——' He tailed off uncomfortably and I had to prompt him again.

'I thought that she had got over her unhappiness,' he went on. 'That the man was a new suitor. I discussed it with the Brigadier-sahib. I don't wish to flatter, sahib, but we agreed that we would have preferred her choice to have been different—but if this *was* her choice—well—kismet. You know how the Brigadier-sahib grieves because he has no son to carry on here after him. He would dearly love a grandson—and time does not stand still. Well, some days went past—then one morning they were attacked while out riding.'

'Attacked by whom?'

'Four armed men, at the top of the southern grazing tract. Win-light sahib was carrying a pistol under his jacket and gave account of himself, but he was hit in the left arm. Some of our herdsmen the other side of the hill heard the shooting and went over, and the four men made off.'

'Cattle thieves?'

'Perhaps, but it is highly unlikely. Cattle thieves thieve cattle—by night. Apart from their thieving they are peaceable folk—even timid. They do not attack with guns—by day. The Brigadier was away at the Karnal cattle sales that day, and Claire-baba begged of me not to tell him of this thing, and against my better judgment I promised. We brought Win-light back here, but they would not let me send for the doctor from the village, and Claire-baba attended to his wound herself. The police had heard of the affray and they came here. Fortunately the sub-inspector is an old friend of mine and I was able to secure his silence—but he told me certain things that worried me. There had been whispers in the bazaar of strangers here. He thought the farm was being watched. He had heard of enquiries being made for this man Win-light. I went to Claire-baba and told her of this. She thanked me, and put her arms about my shoulders and told me I was not to worry—that she and Win-light could handle it—and once more she made me repeat my pledge that I would not tell her father. And then, in the night, they left.'

I stared at him. 'Knowing this, you *let* them go?'

'Do you think I would have done, if I had known?' he said miserably. 'I am an old fool, and these nights I sleep heavily. No, Win-light I'd have let go to hell, and gladly, but I'd have held her by force if necessary until the Brigadier-sahib returned next day. But, it was mid-morning before I realized they had gone.'

'Do you know where?'

He shook his head. 'Not for certain, though I imagine

it would be up to her hospital. I went up the trail for some miles, but they had many hours start by this time, and I had to return to meet the Brigadier-sahib.'

'You told him everything?'

'Everything—promise notwithstanding. We sent my son, Habib, up the trail then, with six armed jawans.'

'Did they discover anything?'

'Nothing, the fools. They were turned back at the Kashmir border.'

'How long ago was this?'

'Three days.'

'There is no telephone to the hospital?'

'No—nor will the army permit private radio transmitters any longer. I have begged the Brigadier-sahib to let me go up.' He shrugged hopelessly. 'He thinks I am too old. I then suggested that he should send for you. He said no—we had no right to call upon you. So then I took it upon myself to telephone. He was angry when I told him—but I know he was also relieved.' He took both my hands in his. 'Idwal Rees,' he begged. 'You are her man—she is your woman. Go up there for the sake of Allah—and take me with you, so that I can wipe out this shame that is upon me.'

Chapter Seven

THE OLD MAN SAID, 'Don't say "as far as I know" again, for Christ's sake. If you don't want to answer tell me to shut my mouth—or shut yours. Is the bastard a spy or isn't he?'

'Yes.'

'For Us or Them?'

'As far as—to the best of my knowledge, for Us—if by "Us" you mean the West.'

He sat 'looking' at me across the breakfast table, his head cocked to one side.

'You think like them, don't you? Yes—you've been living and dressing like them for so long that you *think* like a babu. Surely to God you must know which side he's on.'

'Listen,' I said. 'I've been in this business long enough to know that I wouldn't take a bet on my own father. I've known people, lots of them, who worked for both sides—people with far more impeccably English middle-class backgrounds than Wainwright's—or mine. Do the names Philby, Burgess, MacLean and Blake mean anything to you?'

'So you think he's—what's the wretched term?—doubling?'

'I didn't say that. I said I wouldn't bet on anybody. All I know of Wainwright for certain is that he fronts at the moment as assistant manager of the Calcutta branch of the Hong Kong and South China Bank. Prior to that he worked at their head office in Hong Kong. I also know that he works for British Intelligence—as do a hell of a lot of other people.'

'Including yourself.'

'Including myself, periodically.'

'Then it should be a reasonably easy matter for you to find out what he's doing now—and what the hell he's dragged my girl into.'

'It wouldn't. In the first place I wouldn't even know who to ask. When they want me they get in touch with me. In the second, they wouldn't tell me anyhow.'

'So you can't help me?'

'Not that way. I could go up to the hospital to see if everything's all right there—willingly.'

'You know the Kashmir frontier is closed?'

'She apparently made it.'

'She's a special case. They trust her. She cares for the lot—Indians, Pakistanis, Kashmiris, Tibetans. They also know of my total non-involvement in politics—and hers.' He winced slightly and added, 'Up until now, anyhow.'

I said, 'Don't jump to conclusions. She may be helping him just as—as a friend. She saved *my* bacon once, you know? Then told me to go to hell afterwards.'

He shook his head firmly. 'She didn't. She tried to get you out of this business, and you thought she was putting ropes on you, and you got on your high horse—and buggered off. If you'd had the sense of a louse you'd have pocketed your pride and got in touch with her when the dust had had time to settle. But as I said, you think like an Indian. The little woman is there to cook, clean, bear children and worship the household gods—and keep her trap closed.'

'We're getting off the subject,' I said, when the knife had stopped twisting in my guts. 'I'm ready to go up there, but it strikes me that she mightn't have gone there herself——'

'Where the hell else?' he said impatiently. 'If she were going out into India she'd have taken her car—she keeps it here. They went on the mules she came down with.'

'Did she leave a message?'

He crossed to a bureau and took out a small transistor tape recorder and switched it on. It was the first time I'd heard her voice since that morning three years ago. I was glad that I didn't have to worry about my face.

'Good-bye, daddy darling,' she was saying through the thin static. 'I'm afraid I've got to go back sooner than I expected. I'll get in touch with you as soon as I can, but don't worry if you don't hear from me for some time—we're terribly busy up there at the moment. Look after yourself, my old pet, and give my love to Mamoon—and my thanks.'

He switched it off and turned away from me.

'Tone of the voice mean anything to you?' he asked.

'Should it?'

He almost spat. 'Don't try to pull my ancient leg, Rees,' he said. 'You know damned well it should. *You* knew her. There's tension there. Fear if you like—certainly anxiety. And your nonchalant "should it?" isn't pulling any wool over my ears. That knocked you off your stiff upper lip bloody perch, didn't it? All right then—so you'll go up there?'

I walked to the door and when I spoke I think my voice was steady enough to pass muster even with him. 'I've told you I would,' I said. 'But in *my* time and in *my* way. Now suppose you get off my back, Brigadier-sahib? We're wasting an awful lot of nervous energy this way.'

I walked out into the morning sun. I had told him a half-truth when I said I wouldn't know who to ask. I certainly couldn't call the Gaffer in London—nobody outside a very select circle knew that well-covered number—but I did know that of the Controller in Calcutta, though I didn't want to use the telephone in the bungalow. The Old Man wouldn't consciously eavesdrop, but if he was anywhere within a hundred yards he'd pick up anything I said. There was one in the post office in the village. It was rather public but there were ways of coping with that if one wanted privacy, and had a Pathan with one.

I went out on to the dusty road, and Safaraz, who had been squatting in the shade by the gate, fell into step beside me.

'Mohammed Ishaq wishes to talk with a man in Calcutta,' I told him. 'It is about a horse—a very fast horse—which will be running in a race in Lahore. There are too many outstretched ears around dâk-khana telephones these days.'

He chuckled and twiddled with the hilt of his Khyber knife. He loved anything like this. 'There will be some who will be picking those same ears up from the floor and making fly-flaps out of them if they can't take a hint,' he said, and loped off ahead of me.

When I reached the post office, which in these parts is also the social centre for the idle, there was a noticeable absence of customers round the end where the doorless phone booth stood, and Safaraz was leaning against the counter nearby, delicately manicuring his nails with his knife.

I was lucky that day and it didn't take me more than half an hour to get through. I gave the codeword they always allotted me when I was working for them and said that Mohammed Ishaq would like to discuss gram prices with Wainwright-sahib if they could tell me where he was at the moment. The toneless voice came back with another codeword which I matched, then he asked me how the pilau, which meant security, was in my part of the world, and I said it was reasonable. The voice was just as toneless when it asked me for the number I was calling from. I gave it, and he answered, 'Stay there, Ramree.'

'Ramree' meant that they would be calling me back.

Don't ask me what miracles were performed then. A call to or from London could normally mean anything up to a twelve-hour delay in a backwoods spot like this, but the Gaffer was through in two hours.

He said, 'Pilau?' and again I answered, 'Reasonable.'

'I've been trying to contact you for two days,' he said accusingly. 'Do you know where that bum is?'

'Not the faintest. I want to contact *him*,' I said.

'Why?'

'Personal reasons. Even the depressed classes have them, you know.'

'My arse,' he answered. 'Come on—out with it. What do you know?'

'Nothing I could tell you at the moment. I said the pilau was reasonable—no more. I believe he might need help—but I'd like an idea of where he is and what he's doing before I go barging in.'

'I can't tell you,' he said, and if I hadn't known the old devil I'd have said he sounded really worried. 'We'd like to know—by Christ we would. He's just flitted. Not even the bank know where he is. Not a bloody dicky-bird. You're up the top end now, aren't you?'

'Yes.'

'And you think he's around somewhere? That right?'

'More or less.'

'Then get after him. Write your own ticket—report back to me through this channel. *Carte blanche*—no strings—only find him—and when you do, take charge and bring him back. Like last time.'

'And if he doesn't want to come back?'

'Terminate.' Just the one word, flat and decisive.

'Not me,' I said. 'Get somebody else for that.'

'If he's done what I think he might have done,' he told me, 'there won't be anybody else I *can* get—and that goes for you *and* me. You don't want me to draw it for you, do you? Christ Almighty! He could Blake fifty-plus.'

'Blake', for us, had become a dictionary word—like 'Quisling'. When George Blake went over to Them, forty-three of our agents died, in places as far apart as Hamburg and Hong Kong, and it took us three years to re-establish the network. No, he didn't need to draw it for me.

I said, 'Roger,' which meant that he'd got the message over to me.

'I'd prefer "Wilco",' he answered, which would have meant that I would comply.

'You'll have to let me make my own decisions,' I said. 'I'm not signing any blank cheques. Take it or leave it.'

He said, 'Taken,' and I felt some relief as I hung up—but not much. If he'd left it and stood me down there were a possible three others on the Indian list he could have whistled up—two regulars and another part-timer like myself. If any of those had said 'Wilco', or if, indeed, I, myself, had said it, that would have meant complete committal, and Wainwright would have had to come back without question, or be shot down without a moment's compunction. It could still come to that, but at least this left me some slight discretion.

I walked back to the farm, trying to sort things out without pretending to myself. Why had I insisted on this small concession? Was it because I distrusted the Gaffer's evaluation of the matter? No, it wasn't that. I didn't like him—I didn't know of anybody that did—but equally I didn't doubt his judgment. If he was turning thumbs-down on one of his own men, he had his reasons—and those reasons were sound. I knew with complete certainty that if he had fingered somebody other than Wainwright I wouldn't have questioned it for a moment. Because I couldn't associate Wainwright with this sort of treachery? Nonsense. That was the one thing we lived with day and night in the Business; the ever-present possibility of defection—for profit or genuine conviction. Because I liked Wainwright? Lord no. I didn't actively *dis*like him —although he did me—but he was no buddy-in-arms either.

Why then?

Then I stopped kidding myself. I knew all right. The plainest, simplest and most primeval of all reasons. Jealousy. The bastard had taken my woman. Correction. The woman who would have been mine if, as her father had said, I'd had the sense of a louse. And up to this moment I hadn't the honesty to admit it to myself, and I was bending over backwards to be fair—to convince myself that if I had to pull the trigger on him it wouldn't be for personal motives. Plain expedience—requirements of the Service—to save fifty-plus nameless men and women from getting it behind the ear or between the shoulder blades up divers dark alleys. Interests of State. A job. Do —Collect—Forget. Come out of cloud-cuckoo land, Rees. You know he's up there somewhere with her. Go up after him, and tell him to come back—and hope to God that he'll tell you to go to hell. Then give it to him—with full official approval. The Firm doesn't hand out medals, but they do pay well. The Wild West, the Old Man had said —rustlers and gunslingers. Full house now. He's got a Bounty Hunter as well.

The Old Man was waiting on the veranda when Safaraz and I arrived back. Our chaplis made no audible sound in the powdery dust, but he knew it was us while we were still fifty yards short of him.

He said, with irritability only thinly veiling anxiety, 'Changed your mind, have you? Called back to Town on urgent business?'

'No, I haven't changed my mind,' I told him. 'We'll start out right away if you can let us have mules.'

'Tat ponies,' he said. 'Faster, and just as sure-footed. What men will you want?'

'None—only Safaraz.'

'A guide——?'

'No. I've been up that trail before.'

'Arms?'

'I've got a pistol, but I'd be glad of a rifle for Safaraz—oh, and some field glasses. Ten days' rations—lightest scale.'

He nodded curtly and went off, and then Miraj Khan came out of the shadows at the end of the veranda. 'You're going up, Idwal Rees?' he asked quietly.

'I am going, Miraj.'

'You will take me?'

'I cannot. You know the reason. Let us not hurt each other.'

He grinned wryly. 'I would still be riding when your arse and that of that Pathan bastard were glued to the saddle with blood,' he said, and Safaraz roared his approval. 'But I understand. Give her Mamoon's salaams.'

'Mamoon' is 'uncle' in Urdu, and it was what she always called him.

He turned and went off quickly after the Old Man.

Safaraz, whose pent up curiosity was almost bursting its banks, had not understood the English the Old Man and I had been speaking, but he'd got the drift of things from Miraj's remarks.

'Ha!' he said with deepest satisfaction. 'We go on a journey to see the Miss-sahib. I approve of that one. I also remember some Tibetani women up at the hospital who had been without attention for some time when last we were there——'

I turned and booted him viciously, but he only grinned the wider and winked lasciviously. I'd have given a lot for his earthy and uncomplicated philosophy at that moment.

Claire and Wainwright had gone by night, and watchers, if watchers there had been, would have realized that they were no longer here and would no doubt have been withdrawn by now, but I still thought it advisable to depart by night also. Miraj, by way of a consolation prize, had been given the task of reconnoitring the first part of our route across the fields and into the low foothills five miles away, where the trail proper began, and he mustered his five sons and did it very thoroughly indeed.

The Old Man came with us part of the way. Day and night were the same to him and his perfectly trained Arab-Kathiawar crossbred mare. He gripped my hand hard as we parted, and said, '*Have* the sense of a louse this time, Idwal. Make up her bloody mind for her—and yours.' Then he added, 'God speed,' and turned and cantered away stirrup-to-stirrup with Miraj Khan. I could have wished that he'd said 'Good luck,' instead. It would have been rather more appropriate under the circumstances.

We rode until dawn, the tats picking their way like goats up a narrow rocky path. I had been up and down this trail twice with Claire previously. Two days would see us at the Kashmir frontier, near the alleged cease-fire line across which Indian and Pakistani troops watched each other in fratricidal unease—the eyes of both sides cocked warily towards the unseen but ever present Chinese higher up the slopes on the Tibetan border. An ounce of common sense on each side would have banded them together against this threat to both of them, but the common sense wasn't there, and two sprawling armies had been girding ineffectually at each other and wasting their strength and resources for over twenty years.

The trail was a back door into Kashmir, too narrow for military traffic and closed nowadays to the few traders who used it in happier times. Officially it was closed to everybody. Claire's use of it was winked at for the reasons her father had given me.

I was worried about the consequences of being taken by a military patrol of either side. Each would automatically regard us as spies of the other. The British Government, naturally, just wouldn't want to know us—so this jaunt could, if we weren't careful, easily end in a very rough passage at the hands of the interrogators in either New Delhi or Lahore—*if* they felt inclined to take the trouble to send us back that far.

I conveyed some of this to Safaraz as we ate next morning. He shrugged and said that all armies had gone to hell since we were soldiers, so it shouldn't be difficult to keep out of the hands of these be-wakufs.

I hoped he was right.

Five miles short of the frontier itself, I went to ground in a pine spinney and sent Safaraz forward on foot to see what the form was. He was back in less than five hours, breathing no harder than if he'd just finished a gentle stroll through the bazaar.

'No problem, sahib,' he said airily. 'A guard post at the top of this pass, and a barbed wire fence stretching a mile either side of the path—so who but a fool sticks to the path? We swing round the end of the fence. That to the right is the easier.'

We stayed where we were until darkness fell, then set out obliquely across the slope, with Safaraz, once more in his element, bee-lining it without pause or hesitation, and we hit the end of the fence dead on.

It was my fault, of course. I should have realized that

they'd have posted a flank guard at the end of the fence at night. We were suddenly hit by the beam of a powerful torch and there was a quavering challenge of 'Bas! Roko! Tumlog kaun hai?' Safaraz, leading, put his heels in and galloped straight forward, and I followed, and in a matter of moments we were out of the beam, which continued to stab around impotently in the direction from which we had come. Some zealot cut loose with half a magazine in our general direction, but it was away over our heads.

We reined in then while I considered the position. We were now in No Man's Land, smack between the two lines, and I had no idea how far ahead of us that of the Pakistanis lay. I hoped that their fence would at least roughly correspond to that of the Indians, but I couldn't risk taking it on trust, so this time I went forward, leaving Safaraz with the ponies.

I had only gone about two hundred yards when I ran into a patrol—Indian or Pakistani I never knew, or cared. Fortunately they weren't awfully good at it, and I heard the rattle of their equipment long before I came up with them. I lay sweating, hoping they'd swing away from the line they were now on, and so miss Safaraz.

Apparently they did, because I heard nothing from that quarter thereafter, but another patrol approached from the opposite direction, and they were almost on to me before I realized it. The damned place was like Piccadilly. But at least I was able to place these, as one man muttered as they passed within feet of me, that if those idolatrous Indian bastards were shining lights and shooting, it could only be at enemies—and since enemies of said idolatrous bastards could not fail to be friends of the Chosen of Allah the Compassionate, what in the name of the Noseless Whore of Jehennum were they doing out here with orders to kill or capture anything that moved?

'What, indeed?' grunted another. 'Let us return directly

to our lines, and blankets, my brothers—and this-and-that to the castrated babu who calls himself our Captain.'

I blessed them all silently and followed on their tail. Barbed wire and manpower was apparently lighter on the ground their side, because they only had a guardpost with no flanking screens, so I found my way back to Safaraz with some difficulty and we made a long detour to the right, leading the ponies at a snail's-pace in order to avoid hooves clicking on loose stones.

I felt I'd rather scored over Safaraz this time. I didn't take him to task over it, because mine was the ultimate responsibility for the near mishap—but he shouldn't have come back so soon, and been so airily cocksure about things. If he'd sat watching a little longer he'd have seen the flanking guards go out. Well, fortunately he was intelligent enough to profit by experience. Tomorrow I'd read him a gentle object lesson and this which we were doing now would impress on him in future the correct way of making a night march in strongly-held enemy country.

And then I went arse over head over a trip-wire which set off a flare further along, and my pony panicked, pulled away from me and galloped off into the darkness. Safaraz managed to hold his with one hand and grip my arm with the other, and we ran like hell in the direction in which we had been going originally.

Both sides opened up in earnest now—rifle, submachine fire and tracer ripping the night apart, but fortunately it was at each other and not particularly at us, although some of the wilder stuff was uncomfortably close.

We carried on for the rest of that night, and when dawn came we must have been a good ten miles inside Kashmir. We settled on a wooded hill where surrounding thickets gave us all-round screening, and there was a pleasant splash of water nearby. We were a pony down—mine—

and the half of our rations it was carrying. It worried me. If the military of either side found it, the brands and the smart cavalry-style saddlery would undoubtedly connect it with the Old Man.

I felt glum and miserable, and Safaraz did nothing to help. He made up a bed for me with his own poshteen and saddle-blanket, and didn't look resentful when I snarled at him and told him to stuff it. He then lit a completely smokeless fire of tinder-dry twigs, and brewed tea and made up chapattis with atta and ghee and brought it to me with the air of a kind and understanding nanny dealing with a petulant child. The bastard was very good at that, when he was firmly in the right. I ate and lay down on the bare ground and went to sleep.

I woke a couple of hours later. He was cleaning his rifle and singing softly—well, softly for Safaraz—and he sounded like a camel in labour—and he was very happy indeed, because the other pony was back. He of course wanted me to break into paeans of praise at his bloody cleverness and to ask him how he'd managed it, but I didn't give him that satisfaction. Childish, no doubt—but then Pathans are child*like*, with all their guile and cunning. Let them once get the upper hand of you and they'll ride you into the dust.

He squinted up the barrel of the rifle and said, 'Ha! as clean as my family's honour, and shining like a virgin's eyes on her wedding night.'

'Pathans and Brahmin bulls,' I said, which is the start of a bawdy Urdu proverb.

'Both lazy and randy,' he finished cheerfully. 'Thank Allah the Compassionate for the gift of randiness. It was that which brought your pony back. He's a stallion and mine's a mare.'

I went to the edge of the thicket to get our bearings. Below us, about a mile away, ran a military road along which a convoy of trucks bumped slowly. That would be the Pakistani one to the north-west, I decided—new since I was up here last. I turned and looked to the east. The mountains rose in serried steps, the upper ones shrouded in monsoon clouds, their lower slopes covered in snow down almost to the tree-line. That's where the hospital was—sixty miles away.

What the hell was going on up there, I wondered?

Chapter Eight

IT HAD BEEN an old Gurkha fort originally—a stone blockhouse with a high surrounding wall making a big courtyard on all four sides, with a watchtower rising from a corner of the central building. The Sikhs captured it a hundred and fifty years ago and enlarged it to the proportions of a sizable village—then the British laid it waste in the Punjab Wars and it had fallen into ruins. Claire, coming out of Tibet with a crazy American woman six years ago, had halted here to attend to a group of starving refugees and had stayed on.

With characteristic energy she had set them to work on one corner of the place, cleaning it up and then repairing the sagging roofs with what scanty materials she could scrounge from the surrounding villages, in return for lancing their boils and driving out devils with powerful purgatives, which was about the limit of their combined medical knowledge in those early days. Then she had talked some funds out of the Old Man, and the American, who had powerful contacts back home, had raised some more, and the place grew—first to a fifty-bed hospital, then a hundred, then two hundred.

Out-patients trekked here from an area a couple of hundred miles across, either under their own steam, or carried by relatives who usually discovered something wrong with themselves when they got here, so enlarging the throng. The East adores medicine, particularly the more drastic and volcanic type. Castor oil and scaldingly hot linseed poultices head the list. Splint a broken leg for a hairy hillman and he'll be limping on it in a month. Give him a good clearout with a couple of internal block-busters at the same time, and he'll be on his way rejoicing —and boasting—nimble as a mountain goat in two weeks.

That was the measure of things at first. The two girls fed them and cleaned them up, and did what they could medically, by guess and by God, as they put it, because neither of them had any professional training. They just had plain common hoss-sense and boundless compassion. Starry-eyed do-gooders came up from time to time with offers of help, which they accepted graciously if there were no strings attached to them. U.N.O., W.H.O., the Red Cross, World Council of Churches and other professional bleeding hearts licked their lips and made take-over bids, but all were turned down, courteously but very firmly. The girls just carried on and learned by experience. They usually had a doctor or two around—British, American, Indian, Pakistani and even, on occasion, Chinese, but all who came parked their politics and national prejudices at the gate—and often didn't bother to pick them up again when they left. They didn't bar religion as such providing there was no proselytism with it, but woe betide the ecclesiast who tried to poach a Muslim from the Buddhists or make a Methodist out of a Hindu. Black, white or brindle, he was out of the place and down the trail before he knew what had hit him.

The Indian Government gave them a modern operating theatre, and the Pakistanis, not to be outdone, endowed an electric generating plant and an X-ray installation. Both sides claimed that the hospital was in their territory, as also did the Chinese, who had overrun Tibet. That, and the rest of the confused frontiers round this corner of Kashmir, was what they were fighting over. The girls neither knew nor cared who owned it, any more than did the sick and the hungry to whom they ministered. In short, this was an oasis of sanity and goodwill in a mad dog desert. And I've probably made Claire sound like something between Florence Nightingale and Dr Schweitzer. I'm sorry if I have. She was anything but that.

We rode in under the gate arch, and a young Indian orderly with one leg came out on a crutch. He had a clip-board with him and he asked us our names and what was wrong with us, which was all they ever wanted to know. I gave him phony ones and said my companion had two dragons within his belly which fought continuously, causing him to dismount and retire in decency behind the rocks five times in the hour, so slowing up our progress over the trail.

Safaraz looked sour at this—there's nothing heroic about dysentery—but he played up to it, squirming and moaning in the saddle, and the orderly directed us to the Out-patients' department, telling us where we could feed and water our ponies, and adding that if we could pay anything on departure it would be welcome. If we couldn't, then Allah the Compassionate go with us.

The place had grown since I saw it last. The wards had all been inside the main building of the fort then, but now they had added wings to it, and there was a caravanserai for the families of patients at one side, and a steam laundry and a bakery and a row of kitchens catering for each of the main religions. Yev Shalom had donated all these, someone had told me.

We stabled the ponies and I left Safaraz with them, telling him that the disease I had discredited him with would descend upon him in reality if he got into mischief while we were here, and I went out into the courtyard. It was crowded, as always, with the sick, the halt and the maimed, and the high proportion of free-loading hypochondriacs one always gets round a hospital in the East.

I pulled the end of my turban across my face and fingered my cheek delicately from time to time like a man with toothache, and made a slow round of the courtyard through the mob. I wanted to see her without her recognizing me. Just to see her, and to know that she was all right. I couldn't risk anything more.

After that I had to see Wainwright, and to get him outside, preferably after dark. I'd deliver the Gaffer's orders, and I hoped he would have the sense to accept them without question and come back with us. If he refused we would just have to take him back, hog-tied if necessary. Once over the border I'd leave him somewhere, with Safaraz standing guard, while I contacted the Gaffer by telephone again. It would be up to them then. *I* certainly wanted no part in what followed.

I was hating every minute of this. Why had Wainwright dragged *her* into it? How deeply had he involved her? Would she be safe after we had gone? Was she safe *now*? Wainwright and what was likely to happen to him if he had crossed over, or even just stepped out of line, worried me not at all. He was expendable, as we all were. It had happened before—many times—on both sides. I had had to deal with defectors myself in the past—twice. 'Torpedoing' we called it—a term borrowed from the old Chicago mobs. I hadn't liked it at the time—I didn't like it in retrospect—but I hadn't lost any sleep over it. What was the life of one traitor—confirmed or even doubtful—against those of fifty of our agents or more?

I couldn't think straight. Here I was rationalizing assassination while at the same time making completely impracticable plans to take him back and let somebody else do the dirty work—for the sake of a girl who gave me the gate years ago, and whom I would probably never see again after this. What the hell did it matter? Do. Collect. Forget.

I saw her then. She came through the door of a small detached ward block, locking it after her. I remembered that one. It had bars on the frosted glass windows. It was where they put disturbed mental cases. It was a thing she hated doing and it was used only when they threatened danger to themselves or others.

There was a man with her, tall, fair and wearing a white coat, as she was. They passed within feet of me, and she was speaking rapidly in German. She had been educated expensively in Switzerland, and spoke German and French well.

She glanced at me in passing, but I had my turban tail well up round my face and was holding my jaw in agony. She hadn't changed a day. The superb raven black hair was still pulled back and tied severely on the nape of her neck, but I knew that a quick impatient jerk at the ribbon and a shake of her head would set it free in all its wild glory. Blinding sun and the murderous Himalayan winds had done nothing to wither that flawless skin, and hard work was still taking care of her pencil-slim body. No, she hadn't changed.

They went on towards the central ward block, and round the end of it to where I remembered her own quarters had been, adjacent to those she reserved for such doctors or nurses she might have on her strength at any time. Undoubtedly that's where Wainwright would be. It was going to be hard to get in touch with him because those quarters were out of bounds to patients. It was the one small indulgence she allowed herself and her staff. Outside they belonged to the hospital, but off duty she defended their rest and privacy with almost tigerish ferocity.

I continued on my slow perambulation which brought me up to the corner of the mental block, and came face to face with a big Sikh who materialized from nowhere.

He put a hand in my chest and told me to beat it. Trouble was the last thing I wanted, but for a P.M. to back down tamely to a Sikh would have been completely out of character, so I knocked his hand aside and snarled a reference to his parentage at him and continued on, but not for long.

He jumped round in front of me and his hand shot inside his heavy wool shirt. He pulled out nothing more lethal than a small whistle, but I caught the merest glimpse of the strap of a shoulder holster underneath. I did back down then, and turned and made off, still rumbling insults. I went back to the caravanserai and sat in a corner and thought things over.

I remembered the Sikh. He had been here on my previous visits. He was almost a foundation member—a patient who had been brought in slashed to ribbons in a knife fight and had been stitched up and nursed back into a probably totally undeserved new lease of life, and had stayed on as an employee. He was fanatically loyal, not only to Claire personally, but to the institution. But why the gun? That was something she was rigid upon. Weapons, like politics, were strictly to be left at the gate. The idea of her posting an armed guard on a patient, mental or otherwise, was inconceivable. But he *was* a guard, armed and alert, and the whistle meant that he had reinforcements nearby.

Who, or what was he guarding then? Had Wainwright gone to ground there? If I didn't see him around, and if I ascertained that he wasn't in Claire's quarters, that would seem to be a feasible conclusion. I would certainly have to check on the place—possibly both places—and neither would be easy.

Safaraz was becoming restless. Inactivity was a thing he just could not cope with. Pathans were never good at contemplating navels and Infinity. I set him to work grooming the ponies and cleaning the saddlery, then I sent him to buy food, but these were only stopgaps at best. He started to ogle some Tibetan women outside the bakery and was making rapid headway when some of their menfolk arrived on the scene. Fortunately I'd had the foresight to relieve him of both his gun and his knife on arrival, which evened things up a little, and he got off with nothing worse than a mild beating up and a deflation of his ego, which was all to the good. But it had drawn attention to us, and a deputation of hefty hospital orderlies came round and told us that since we couldn't behave ourselves we'd better leave. Virtue, authority and public opinion being on their side, there was nothing else for it, so we saddled up and got out just as dusk was drawing in.

Actually this was an advantage. Snooping around inside would have been difficult to say the least, but I knew the layout of the place and had once had to make a break from it with a gang on my tail. The surrounding wall abutted on to the rear of the staff quarters, I remembered, so getting in should be relatively easy.

We rode off down the trail, twin pictures of injured innocence, and the one-legged porter yelled after us to take our guts to the veterinarian in future and leave the genuinely sick in peace, and then slammed the heavy teak door on our backs. We went on in the darkness for a mile or so, then led the ponies up a deep nullah and picketed them, and found our way back on foot.

Safaraz was rumbling sulkily behind me. We had come up to see the Miss-sahib, of whom he approved, but all we had done was to sit on our arses in a stinking caravanserai and suffer indignities at the hands of the Forgotten of Allah, and then allow ourselves to be driven forth like beggars. I was thankful that he hadn't seen the Sikh give me the bum's rush. I shut him up in the end by threatening to send him back to wait with the ponies.

The wall was about fifteen feet high, and I remembered that it was topped with broken glass set in cement. I stood on Safaraz's shoulders and threw our sheepskin coats up to cover it, then managed to get a finger-grip and heave myself up. I sat astride and reached down for him to make a jump for my hand, but he disdained it, took a run and made a spectacular commando leap for it unaided and cut his backside badly through his thin cotton pantaloons, which delighted me because it gave him something more tangible to beef about than my apparent indecision. We let ourselves down on to a heap of logs piled against the wall inside and pussyfooted to a line of lighted windows across a narrow yard.

The first three looked into the messroom, plainly but comfortably furnished with locally made dining-table, chairs and Tibetan hide yakhdans covered with bright rugs. There was a log fire burning on the hearth, and over it was a three-quarter length portrait of the American girl who had co-founded the hospital. I remembered her as a cheerful little round robin with a Boston accent and the energy of a beaver, who had been shot by frontier guards one night while leading a party of Tibetan children across. She was another of the many reasons why Claire would never quit this place while it still needed her.

The German doctor I had seen earlier was stretched in a chair in front of the fire, reading, and a young Indian in western tweed jacket and slacks was fiddling with a radio in the corner. Through the glass I could hear faintly the signature tune of Radio Delhi. Two bearers in white shirwanis were setting dinner places on the table. Four of them. These two and Claire. Who was the other, I wondered?

I moved along the wall, with Safaraz, active again and with outraged dignity and sore backside forgotten, alert at my elbow. The next window opened into a pantry, and the next two into the kitchen—then there were four darkened ones which I knew belonged to spare bedrooms. Claire's had been the one on the corner. Heavy curtains were drawn across the windows here, but I could see a narrow section of the room through a chink.

The lights were on but the room appeared at first to be empty, but then she moved into view. She was wearing an orange dress, one that I remembered, or thought I did. Brushed kashmir as soft as spun silk—superb material botched up by the bazaar dressmaker that would have looked a mess on anybody but her. She would have been about the most sparsely wardrobed gal in the world by city standards. Slacks and sweater covered by white overalls when she was working, which was most of the time—jodhpurs and Tibetan tanned leather jacket when she was on the trail—but she usually managed to change into something like this for the blessed couple of hours she allowed herself to relax between work and bed, even if she were alone—just as the simple evening meal would be dignified by the name of dinner, and served on fine china and glass she had filched from her home at Ramabagh.

No, she hadn't changed. I wished to God she had, as I stood there with my nose pressed to the glass, and that the old spell could be broken, and that I'd be free again—or that, conversely, I could accept that it never would be broken, and that I could muster the sense and guts to smash that bloody window between us and step inside—on her terms—without reservation of equivocation. But it was too late now. It would still be too late—even if Wainwright was removed from the board. Claire wouldn't be the one to go back to rebuild burnt bridges—any more than I could. Pride—conceit—wounded ego—call it what the hell you will—but we were both cursed with more than our fair share of it. No—too late.

I dragged myself away. There were two other bedrooms the other side. I crept round and peered into the window of the first of them. There was no light in this one, but some came through the open door from the passage the other side, and I could see that it was empty. In the next one a dumpy, middle-aged woman in a wholly unsuitable floral dress was putting the finishing touches to her make-up. She switched out the light and went through to the passage, and I completed the circuit of the building back to the mess.

Claire had come in now, and the other woman followed her, and the German was mixing gin and tonic at a side table. So that was the foursome. Wainwright, wherever he was, was certainly not here. I remember a totally illogical feeling of relief.

I drew Safaraz away and whispered to him that there was another building that I wanted to look into, and pointed it out to him.

The fort was built on a sloping hillside and these quarters were on the higher ground, so we could see the mental block below us in the light which came from the laundry and generator house opposite. I noticed for the first time that there was a skylight in the flat roof, and I said that if we could get up to it I could probably see all I wanted from there. Naturally he said why bother about that? Say the word and he'd go in through the door, and let any emptier of piss-pots who wanted to stop him, have a try. I kept my patience and explained that there was an armed guard around somewhere—but that only made him shoot a bigger line. Give him his knife back, which I was still holding, and he'd cope with the guard all right. It was no use. He was in one of those bloody-minded moods where he was ready to go off at half-cock, and nothing short of slugging him hard would get him out of it—and this was neither the time nor place for that.

So in the end I sent him off over the wall to get the ponies and to move them up to the trail and wait for me. Even in his present mood he couldn't argue with a definite order, so he went off, grumbling.

I climbed down the hill to the mental block. It was a low, stone-built hut, no more than ten feet high, and about twenty by ten in area, which had originally been an ammunition magazine.

As I came round the end of it I could see where the guard was mounted. There was a lean-to shed on the end of the generator house, with two charpoys in it on which a couple of blanket-wrapped figures were sleeping, and as I watched I saw my old friend the Sikh stroll slowly round the building. Two hours on sentry, four hours rest, obviously. They didn't seem to be taking any chances. He completed three circuits of the building and then halted and leaned back against the wall. It was a cold night and he had supplemented his sheepskin coat with a blanket, draped shawl-like over his shoulders. There was a chill wind coming down from the hills behind the hospital, and he had instinctively chosen the sheltered side to rest in. I timed his rest—it was about three minutes before he started to shuffle and stamp his feet and make another circuit. He only went round twice this time before coming to a halt and turtling back into his blanket—but at least he stopped at the same spot.

I was waiting for him to start again when Claire came down with the German. They both had sheepskin coats over their shoulders, and he was carrying a medical tray with bottles and glasses that I could hear clinking thinly as they rattled. They came up to the building, and the Sikh hurried forward and took the tray while the German unlocked the door. I craned my neck but I couldn't see anything inside, except a white-overalled Indian orderly who came forward as they entered. They closed the door behind them, and the Sikh, conscious of the proximity of Authority, made six or seven brisk circuits in 'a smart and soldierly manner', before coming to rest again, and he had two more spurts before they came out. They locked the door and came away, once more conversing in German, but I couldn't understand what they were saying. Then an alarm clock blasted off tinnily under the lean-to and the Sikh galvanized into life and went across and shook one of the sleepers into wakefulness, and when he had emerged reluctantly from his blanket cocoon, the Sikh hopped into it quickly. I cursed. I'd had a sleepy and bored sentry to deal with previously, but this was a fresh man, theoretically at least, with more on the ball.

I timed this one. He was a small lean Sherpa and was more consistent than his predecessor in that he did four circuits and a four-minute rest in the same spot without varying. I slipped through the shadows to the other side. Four minutes would be ample, but a ten foot jump for a fingerhold was rather too much for me to tackle noiselessly. However there was a plank leaning against the wall of an adjacent building, so I used it as a ladder, and pulled it up after me.

I stepped across towards the square of brightness that marked the skylight and felt the roof sag beneath me, and heard the crackle of dried bamboo, and too late realized that the bloody thing was lepai—that is straw matting over a light framework, plastered with a mixture of sun-dried mud and cowdung.

I tried to jump back on to the top of the wall, but I didn't make it, and I went through in a cloud of dust and landed on my back on the concrete floor underneath.

The Indian orderly was yelling in sheer terror and I could hear pounding on the door. I got up ruefully. I was caught like a rat in a trap—barred windows and the door padlocked on the outside.

There were two beds here, and a table and a chair for the orderly in one corner—and nothing more. Only one bed was occupied. I went across, and the orderly's yelling rose in pitch and volume. There was a European in it—his leg suspended in a cradle swung from a framework and his head heavily bandaged. He wasn't exactly unconscious, but he did appear to be under some sort of sedation.

And he certainly wasn't Wainwright.

Chapter Nine

THE DOOR SWUNG BACK WITH A CRASH and the three guards piled in with guns at the ready. I did the sensible thing and stood facing them with upraised open hands, but it didn't get me off anything.

The Sikh reached me first and let me have it on the side of the face with the flat of his pistol, and then the other two got into the act and I was down on the floor receiving an enthusiastic kicking with heavy hill chaplis. Others crowded in after them and things looked serious. I wrapped my arms round my head and balled up tight but I realized that it would only be a matter of time before I was stamped to a pulp unless I could get my knees under me and raise myself out of the ruckus.

Then it stopped, and risking one eye I looked up to see the German standing astride of me swinging haymakers all round at the kickers. My turban had come off and the Sikh swooped and hauled me to my feet by the hair. He was yelling in Urdu that I was the budmash who had tried to get in earlier, and the gate orderly was confirming that he had booted me out with another thieving Mussulman son-of-a-bitch not two hours before.

The German was bellowing for silence in bad Urdu, but nobody was listening. All they wanted to do was to get me outside in the dark and I was being pulled in a dozen different directions, and the guards were trying to pistol-whip me again but fortunately they were being hampered by the press around me.

Then Claire arrived, and peace descended on the multitude like the balm of Gilead. It was an understanding of mob psychology at its most developed. She came through the press like a small, taut rugby three-quarter, elbows boring into bellies and sharp western heels cracking down on bare eastern toes and insteps, making for the heart of the matter, which was the Sikh, who was now using his pistol like a tack hammer on my head. She grabbed him by the beard and jerked his head down and brought her knee up. His outraged roar of indignation terminated in a slobbering snuffle and he sank to the floor nursing his flattened nose. It was only that that saved me. One moment they had been howling with naked blood lust, the next a shocked and embarrassed silence had fallen upon them. Gently nurtured Miss-sahibs just weren't expected to behave like waterfront cops in this part of the world.

And she didn't make the mistake of berating them. She thanked them nicely for their concern for the safety of the hospital, complimenting the Sikh particularly for his vigilance.

She hardly glanced at me, for which I was thankful. I must have looked a mess. One eye was completely closed, I'd had one boot at least full in the mouth, and I could feel blood trickling down all over my face from a dozen secondary cuts and abrasions.

The German crossed quickly to the patient in the bed, who hadn't seemed unduly put out by the racket, and gave him a swift run over. He turned and said something in German to Claire, and she nodded and then shooed the crowd out of the ward and told the guards to take me across to the dispensary and get a dresser to put some stuff on my face.

I was happy to hear her add a stiff warning against my being beaten up further.

They prodded me out into the darkness with two guns held firmly at kidney level, and the Sikh bringing up the rear, still snuffling but somewhat mollified by his public commendation.

The dispensary was another old ammunition magazine, and they sat me down in a chair while an orderly got to work on me with a handful of lint and raw iodine that had me writhing in agony and the guards grunting with satisfied approval. In the mirrorlike surface of a steam sterilizer in front of me I could see my face looked like a boiled pudding that had been used as a football and then treated with dark brown varnish. The guards squatted each side of me and speculated on who I was and what was likely to happen to me. I was undoubtedly a Pakistani spy said the Sherpa, in which case I'd be handed over to the Indian military police, who would shoot me. The Sikh said no, I was plainly a dacoit—bandit—and it would be a matter for the frontier police, who would hang me. The third, a Tibetan, wouldn't commit himself, but regretted the passing of the old days. The Kampas, apparently, had much more picturesque ways of dealing with garbage like me—such as turning it loose naked in wolf country, manacled to a freshly slaughtered dog—salutary and at the same time highly entertaining, because the more sporting sections of the community could then lay bets on which would be eaten first.

They got so engrossed in this that they omitted to search me. I still had my own and Safaraz's gun and knife under my shirt, and a thousand rupees in a body belt. I wouldn't have used a gun inside here under any circumstances, but I was retaining a flicker of hope that Safaraz would suspect something when I didn't turn up, and would come looking for me. Outside would be a different thing altogether, if I managed to make it.

Then Claire came in with the German. They turned the others out, the German taking the Sikh's gun and laying it on the table in front of him significantly.

Claire crossed to me and examined my face. I closed my sound eye and sat with my head slumped forward on my chest. The light was good, but with my wild hair and beard, the bumps and bruises and the iodine warpaint, I felt I was getting away with it. The man shot a question at me in German and Claire translated it into, 'Who are you and where do you come from?' in Urdu.

I went into a long whining spiel that I was Mohammed Ishaq, a poor man from Islamabad, and that I suffered greatly from an aching tooth but that that was now cured because somebody had kicked it out—and could I go now please, because I had a sick wife and seven starving children awaiting my return.

I could see the German watching me with deep concentration. From his spoken Urdu I guessed that he was just about able to follow the drift of this but no more. He asked then what I was doing on the roof of the mental ward, and when Claire translated I noticed that she had slipped from her beautifully articulated Delhi Urdu into the local bhat, which borrows heavily from Punjabi and Pashtu, and is hell for the Outlander to understand. I matched it and told her that I was looking for somewhere to sleep, which was not as absurd as it probably sounded. Flat roofs *are* used for sleeping on.

She shot at me quickly that there was a covered serai here to sleep in, and I answered that men had been known to be robbed while they slept in serais—even poor men, I added hastily. She fed this back to the German, who had plainly been lost now, and I thought up a fairly feasible answer for what would undoubtedly be the next question. Why had I returned after once having been ejected? I had been turned out unjustly, I would say, and my tooth was still giving me hell, so I climbed back over the wall.

But the question wasn't asked, and I assumed that she hadn't heard the gate orderly or the Sikh beefing about it.

They moved away to the far end of the room and had a long muted discussion now. I got the impression that Claire was more or less satisfied, but that the German wasn't. This was entirely characteristic of her. She wouldn't willingly allow anybody to be pushed around—even a thief on the prowl, as she would no doubt have assumed me to be. She knew and understood the people she dealt with up here, where thieving is more a necessary way of life than a crime. You guard against it, naturally, but you no more blame the thief when caught than you would the fox that takes your chickens. That's for the police and the magistrates and the jailers and others who are paid for it. I heard her voice raised angrily once, and got the words 'Armut und Hunger' and 'wunden', which I had just enough German to know meant 'poverty and hunger' and 'wounded'.

But why the hell did she have to do it at all? This was *her* territory, and she ran it *her* way. Who was this fellow to be calling the shots?—and why was she letting him? Had the place in fact been taken over and was she no longer in supreme charge? Knowing her I doubted this very much. She could no more have handed over command of her hospital than a ship's captain his bridge. I'd seen doctors here before. She would never presume to interfere in their purely medical treatment of patients—but administration, policy and overall control remained firmly vested in *her*.

But it was the German who won in the end. He went to the door and called in the guards and I heard him making heavy weather of questioning the Sikh as to a safe place to put me—and Claire wasn't helping. She leaned against a bench glaring at them. The Sikh thought that the old oil store was as good as anywhere, and the German told him to lead the way. Claire spoke then, very emphatically indeed, to the Sikh. She told him that if I were in any way ill-treated, the knee in the nose he'd received would be a love tap compared with the beating she'd see he got—with rawhide—from a couple of the Tibetans—and that went for the others also.

I felt she'd got the point over. I certainly hoped so. The German, not being able to follow this machine-gunlike spate, interrupted angrily, and got another in German, and the few words I understood were never taught to her in her Swiss Academy for Young Ladies.

We filed out into the night and went along to the generator house. There was a small concrete bunker alongside it that I remembered was where they kept kerosene for the lamps in the past, but they had evidently deemed it too close to the boilers here for safety, so it was now empty, although it still stank like the bilges of a tanker. They shoved me inside, and the Sikh muttered, 'I am a merciful man, budmash, who does not bear malice. Tell no lies to the Miss-sahib in the morning and none will harm you further.' The point *had* got over.

There was a heavy sheet-iron door to the place, with a bolt on the outside. They shot this and then I heard them arguing about a padlock. It wouldn't be necessary, said the Tibetan, if one of them was sitting outside the whole time. It would, the Sikh said, because now they had both places to guard—so eventually the Sherpa was sent along to the gatehouse to get one.

I felt round the walls and the ceiling, which was only about five feet high and didn't give full headroom. There was no joy there, because both were solid concrete, and the door was as unyielding as armour-plating.

I sat down with my back to the wall and drew my knees up and rested my aching mug on my hands. What the hell now? I wondered. What had I accomplished for either the Gaffer, who was paying me, or the Old Man, who trusted me? Not a damned thing. Wainwright wasn't here, and although Claire was, something was wrong somewhere. Who and what was this German? Was he a doctor at all? All I knew of his professional standing was that he had worn a white coat. But he had seemed to know what he was doing when he examined the patient in the mental ward. And who was the patient? And why was he so patently kept drugged? Pain? Maybe. His leg seemed to have been pretty well smashed up—and his head was heavily bandaged. What would they do with me now? If Claire had her way I felt I'd be released in the morning. But what if she didn't get her way? Would they hand me over to the military police? Or would they take me down the trail and deal with me themselves, quietly? Doctors didn't do things like that, I tried to convince myself—but then, again, *was* he a doctor? The way he had jerked the jacket back on that gun and squinted into the magazine had been very practised indeed. The fellow who had been holding Wainwright was a German who had spoken a few words of Urdu but no English. Was there a connection here? I'd only caught a distant glimpse of the other one, but I didn't think they were the same person. This chap was bigger and fairer.

And that brought me back to the real question. Where the bloody hell *was* Wainwright?

I heard the sentry make a shuffling round of the bunker, puffing hard and stamping his feet to keep warm, then he halted and I saw a glow through the crack of the iron door as he struck a match and lit a cigarette, and almost immediately there was a muffled yelp and a thud against the door, and Safaraz whispering hoarsely through the crack, 'Sahib? Sahib?'

Irrationally, my first reaction was one of anger and I called him a murdering bastard, but he assured me that he'd only beaned the sentry with a rock rolled in the end of his turban.

'I've been watching outside here for the last hour,' he said, injured. 'If the sahib had not taken my knife, the matter would have been attended to earlier—with dignity. I do not like hitting people on the head, like a common thief.'

I told him to shut up and have a look at the lock. He did so and said that there wasn't a hope of busting it without raising the whole place, but not to worry. He, Safaraz, now had the sentry's gun, and the Sikh had the key—and the Sikh and the Tibetan were sleeping like lice in a warm blanket and——

I said, 'Kill in this place, and I'll kill *you*. I swear it.' He said, what him? Perish the thought—or words to that effect, and then there was a dragging sound as he pulled the sentry round to the back of the bunker. There was nothing I could do about it now. He would just do things his own sweet Pathan way, and apologize later. I hoped that he hadn't found a knife on the sentry. I was being completely unreasonable, of course. There was really no alternative way out of this—but I was oppressed by the knowledge that I had made a complete cock of the whole thing, and once more had to be dragged off the hook by this crazy devil, who was no doubt extracting every ounce of malicious enjoyment out of it.

I waited for some long dragging minutes that seemed like hours, then there was a rattle the other side as the bolt slid back and the door opened. There was a certain amount of light outside coming from the hospital buildings across the open square—and there were two dark figures silhouetted against it. My first thought was that Safaraz had been rumbled and that the rest of the guard had turned out to check on me, so I dropped flat, Christian forbearance going to the winds, and tugged out my gun, but Claire's voice said coldly, 'Come out of there, quickly, and follow me.' She said it in English, and for a moment

I put it down to strain, and answered in Urdu, whiningly, that I was a poor man who had been harshly treated.

'Drop that nonsense,' she said impatiently. 'Whose leg do you think you are pulling, you idiot?'

I once saw a Guardsman outside Buckingham Palace trip over an untied bootlace and fall flat on his face. The poor bastard must have felt exactly as I did now as he got to his feet.

Safaraz said apologetically, 'I went with caution to get the key, as the sahib ordered—but the Miss-sahib was already on her way here with these idolators.' And then I saw the Sikh and the Tibetan skulking in the background.

I started to mumble something, but Claire said sharply, 'Come on—this way—and for God's sake don't make a noise,' and she led off into the darkness with the rest of us on her heels.

She took us right round the perimeter of the place, keeping in the shadow of the wall, and finally stopped at a small postern gate on the far side. It was let into the thickness of the wall and I remembered it as one that she used herself when she went out on her long solitary walks over the hills. She took a key from the pocket of her sheepskin coat and unlocked it.

'You know your way from here, I think,' she said coldly. 'Straight down the path to the river, then left along the bank for three miles until you come to the Kashmiri village. Where you go from there is your own affair—only don't come back here—ever.'

'But surely to God you're coming with us?' I said.

'No. Take these two with you and leave them there. They're not to return until I send word for them. They understand that. Now go—quickly. I've got to get back before anybody starts looking for me.' She shoved me through and chattered angrily at the other three to hurry.

'But damn it all——' I started to protest, but she cut me short.

'Idwal, will you please *go*,' she insisted. 'You'll find James there. If he's fit to travel you're to take him with you. Tell him nothing's changed. He'll understand.'

'Good for him,' I said, 'because I bloody well don't. Now look here, I don't know what the hell's going on, but you're in some sort of difficulty, or even danger. You don't expect me to walk out just like this, do you?—because I'm not.'

'I'm in no danger at all,' she said. 'The Indian military patrols and the frontier police are in and out the whole time. If anything happened to me they'd want to know the whys and wherefores—and these people are fully aware of that.'

'Who are "these people"?'

'Mind your own business.'

'It *is* my business.'

'Nothing that happens *here* is your business. I thought we'd got that straight a long time ago.'

'Whose fault was that? It is my business, I tell you. Your father sent me——'

And, curiously, that was the only thing that got a reaction from her. She gripped my arm quickly. 'Keep him out of this,' she said urgently. 'Please, Idwal—*please*. Tell him nothing—or rather just tell him that you've seen me and that everything is all right. *Please*.'

'Do you think for one moment that I could get away with that? He'd know immediately I opened my mouth that something was wrong. He knows already. That's why he asked me to come up.'

I heard her catch her breath sharply. 'I give you my word that I'm in no danger personally,' she said.

'Then you'd better come down with me and tell him so yourself.'

'I'm not leaving this place until——'

'Until what?' I shot at her.

'Until—well, until things are sorted out——'

I reached out in the darkness and took both her hands in mine. She let them rest there for a moment, then she tried to pull free, but I was holding them firmly.

'Claire,' I begged. 'Trust me just this once. Tell me what's going on. What have you got mixed up in? Who's that German? How does Wainwright come into it? I promise I'm not on the snoop on my own account—or anybody else's. It's just you I'm worried about——'

'You don't have to be,' she said, but the certainty had gone out of her voice, and she sounded tired. 'There's nothing going on that I can't handle myself—if only you others would stop interfering. Please go now, Idwal—I've got to get back.'

'But don't you see, for God's sake,' I insisted. 'That fellow is going to guess that you've let me out.'

But she had thought of that one. 'I'll tell him that obviously you managed to bribe the guard,' she said, then she suddenly jerked her hands loose and stepped back through the door. I tried to get my shoulder to it before she slammed it and turned the key, but I was too late, and I heard her footsteps receding quickly the other side.

I stood there for some moments, trying to make up my mind to climb the wall and go after her, but I knew that would be no good. She wasn't going to tell me anything, and short of manhandling her I'd never persuade her to leave this damned place.

Wainwright? Well, at least I knew where *he* was. 'Fit to travel' she had said. That meant he had been hurt. That would be the one he stopped in Ramabagh—unless he'd got in the way of another since. Just so as it hadn't affected his vocal cords, I thought savagely, I'll twist something out of him even if I had to do it the rough way.

Safaraz was wrangling with the two guards some distance away.

I told him to shut up and follow me but he said, 'These idolators have guns, sahib, and they will not hand them over.'

He had a point there. They gave them to me without demur, and I unloaded them, patted them over for spare ammunition and gave them back. Safaraz, only partly mollified, said plaintively, 'My own gun and knife, sahib?' I gave them to him, then with me leading and him in rear, we set off down the track.

I hated leaving her here, but for the moment at least, there seemed nothing else I could do.

Chapter Ten

I KNEW THE VILLAGE. It was tucked away up a valley that faced to the south and got the sun all day, while the mountains behind it broke the bitter north-east winds. A stream ran its full length, entering and leaving over waterfalls and after the snows it brought down a rich alluvial silt which the villagers used to dredge out and donkey-load up to little terraced gardens where they grew vegetables, and they had planted peach, nectarine and apple trees. Walnuts grew wild here, even though the place was theoretically above the timber line, and there were trout in the stream that used to be thrown back if they didn't extend from a grown man's fingertip to his elbow.

It was from here that Claire used to buy fresh supplies for the hospital, and since she paid fairly and promptly she had brought prosperity to them—and, of course, she looked after their health, so they regarded her with something not far short of worship. It was a place I used to think of longingly when things got difficult down in the heat and stink of India. Miles off the track—remote—peaceful—safe.

And now this bastard Wainwright had snaked into my secret Eden, I reflected sourly as we walked up the trail.

It was just after dawn when we got there, and we had the effect of a flight of hawks over a chicken run. Women gathered up children and ran for their huts, and men on their way to their hillside gardens stood in timid groups, nervously studying us with half-averted eyes. But fortunately they recognized the Sikh, and when he bellowed to them not to be fools, they came hesitantly down to us, and the old headman, whom I remembered, quavered a welcome and offered us tea, curds and chapattis. But quite obviously he didn't remember *me*, for which I could hardly blame him, because if my face looked anything like it felt it must have been quite a sight. I told him the Miss-sahib had sent us to see the sahib who was staying with them, and got nowhere. His face just became a blank uncomprehending mask. A sahib? Here? No sahibs ever came to the village. Plainly the old man had been well briefed by Claire.

I ran my eye round the other villagers, who began to melt quietly away. No help there either.

Safaraz muttered to me that if there was a sahib here he'd find him, but I shut him up. A search of the twenty or so huts was the last thing I wanted. These people were Muslims, and their women were inside now, and there'd have been hell to pay if we'd tried to burst in. That's the one thing that even the most peaceable of them will fight to the death over.

So in the end I yelled, 'Wainwright! If you're here, for Christ's sake come out. It's Rees.'

And he came out from round the back of one of the huts. If I'd expected a welcome I'd have been sadly disappointed. He looked as happy to see me as if I'd been a tax collector with a final demand note. He was plainly a sick man—white and drawn, and his left arm was in a sling. He brightened when he saw my battered mug, but only marginally. His opening gambit didn't do much to warm things either. He said, 'What the bloody hell are you doing here, Rees?'

The headman, the responsibility now being shifted from him, looked relieved, so I sent the others off with him to get something to eat, and Wainwright and I squatted in the dust facing each other.

I said the Gaffer had sent me up, and he said to hell with the Gaffer. He'd quit, finally and irrevocably.

'You'd better come back and tell him that yourself,' I said.

'I will—when I'm ready.' His face set stubbornly.

'I don't think he'll accept that.'

'Too bad—but that's the way it is.'

'You're putting me in a hell of a position.'

'That's too bad also—but I didn't ask you to come.'

'Don't be a damned fool,' I said impatiently. 'You can't quit—just like that. You're a civil servant—like a cop or a postman——'

'Or a garbage collector—but we can all quit——'

'Written resignation, six months' notice and a statutory oath under the Official Secrets Act,' I reminded him. 'And then you've got to let them know where you are, and where you're going in the future——'

'I'm here. Where I'm going in the future is my own affair.'

'Come out of cloud-cuckoo land, Wainwright,' I told him. 'You know better than that. The number of your passport noted in every air and seaport in the West for the rest of your life. Never knowing whether the guy at the next table is watching you. Your apartment or hotel room turned over quietly from time to time. Your mail scrutinized and your telephone bugged. Your job with the bank up the spout—and a little anonymous whisper to every prospective employer you apply to thereafter. How long could you take that for?'

'I lived before these bastards recruited me.'

'It's *after* we're talking about. You know the way they think. You know *what* they think—if anybody gets out of line.'

'Yes—I know,' he said wearily. 'You don't have to spell it out for me. They think of the possibility of that even when we're not out of line. It's that which poisons the whole thing.'

'A vocational hazard,' I said. 'You can't shovel shit for a living and expect your best friends to tell you that you smell of roses. Of course they're suspicious. They've got to be. Damn it all, you get the same sort of thing in commerce and industry—the ever present possibility of the guy with inside know-how going over to a rival company.'

'A man in commerce or industry is given a job to do,' he said. 'If he doesn't do it properly he's fired. They don't put some pontificating bastard on his tail to check on his honesty while he *is* doing it though.'

'Balls. What about accountants—bank auditors?'

'Different thing.'

'All right, Wainwright,' I said. 'I'm not arguing—or pontificating—any more. I was told to deliver a message to you. I've delivered it. The Gaffer wants you back.'

'And I've told you I'm not coming back until I'm ready. What are you going to do about it?'

I said quietly, 'Let's leave it at that for the moment, shall we?'

There was silence between us for a while. He was doodling in the dust with his good hand. He looked up at me, and his mouth was twisted in a bitter grin. 'A torpedoing, eh?' he said. 'Yes, I once heard that that was a speciality of yours. Do you do it yourself or leave it to your Pathan? Bullet in the back of the head—or one's throat cut while sleeping?'

He had stopped doodling and his hand went inside his shirt. I caught him under the point of the chin with the heel of my left hand, grabbed his wrist with the other and hauled it out—and found he had been reaching for a handkerchief. There'd been a hell of a lot of leverage under that poke, and he was out cold—and he'd gone over backwards on to his bad arm.

I looked around quickly, but only Safaraz, who had been bringing me some tea and bread had seen it. We lifted him to his feet and Safaraz, shocked, said that the headman had given us the guest hut. We got him across to it and laid him down on a charpoy.

He stirred and then tried to sit up.

I mumbled, 'I'm sorry, Wainwright—Christ, I'm sorry. I didn't know what you were reaching for.'

He didn't answer. He just sank back on the charpoy and closed his eyes. I could see fresh blood staining the bandage on his upper arm but when I tried to examine it closer he pulled away.

I stood looking down at him, wondering what the hell to do now, then my eye fell on a small white-painted wooden box with a red cross on the lid, on a shelf above the charpoy. I opened it and found bandages, gauze and some bottles and a piece of paper with scribbled directions in Claire's handwriting about treatment.

I sent Safaraz for hot water and when he returned with it I bent over Wainwright and tried again. This time he didn't raise any protest, or indeed even evince interest.

The arm was in a bit of a mess. It was a bullet wound that at some stage had turned septic and was taking a long time to heal. Following the directions, I cleaned it up and put on fresh dressings.

His skin felt dry and feverish. There was a thermometer in the box, still in its sealed container, which he evidently hadn't bothered to use. I took his temperature and found it to be 102 degrees, but whether that was from the effects of the wound or a go of fever that he'd picked up since, I wasn't qualified to tell. Anyhow, there were some tablets there which he'd been instructed to take, but hadn't, so I got a couple down his throat and left him, and soon he went off into a deep sleep.

There was a trail pack standing beside the charpoy,

which I went through as a matter of routine. I found nothing beyond the few simple necessaries of a man travelling on foot through these hills until I came to the bottom, and there I unearthed a Browning .38 in a shoulder holster. I mulled over this for a time. He was coming back with me—of that I had no doubt whatsoever—but I was hoping that I'd be able to talk him into it sensibly, and I didn't want to humiliate him by taking the gun, but at the same time I couldn't neglect elementary precautions. I thought of unloading it and replacing it, but that wouldn't have deceived him for a moment, so in the end I removed the firing pin.

I carried out a few running repairs on my own face then with the aid of his shaving mirror. It certainly needed it. I could see through my right eye, but only just. It was the size and colour of an avocado pear, and my mouth was swollen and lopsided. Then I ate, without particular appetite, and finally I flopped on to another charpoy and passed out like a light.

Safaraz shook me gently hours later. He said, 'It is almost night, and the sahib hasn't given me any orders.'

I felt bad about it. He had been as tired as I, but he'd obviously stayed awake while I slept. I told him to go and sleep through the night as we wouldn't be moving on until the next day at least—and then I saw he was holding my trail pack, and I stared at it. That had been tied to the saddle of my pony. He grinned from ear to ear. Yes—he'd hiked all the way to where he'd picketed the ponies before climbing back into the hospital and brought them up. He was looking very pleased with himself, as he had every right to be. That had been a twenty-mile round trip. He went off jauntily, but walked blindly into the doorpost, and I called him a bat-eyed weakling and advised him to womanize less, which tickled him mightily.

I went over to Wainwright. He was awake and the fever

seemed to have abated, so I found the headman and got some boiled rice and hot milk from him. I brought it back and managed to get him to swallow a few spoonfuls of it.

'We're going back as soon as you're fit to travel,' I told him. 'When we get to a phone you can talk to the Gaffer. That's the end of it as far as I'm concerned.'

'How did you know I was up here?'

'I just followed a lead.'

'Liar. *She* sent for you, didn't she?'

'If you mean Claire Culverton, no.'

'Oh, for God's sake—she was the only one who knew I was here.'

It looked as if we were going to be together for some days, so I thought it better to clear the board of at least one potential source of strife. There seemed no harm in my telling him now, and there was always the chance that if I tipped my hand a little, he might reciprocate and let me know something of Claire's involvement.

'Her father sent for me,' I said. 'He was scared that she was getting into deep water over something.'

'I see. Purely personal?' There was disbelief in every syllable of it.

'Call me a liar again if you want to, but until he mentioned your name in Ramabagh I didn't even know you knew her.'

'I happen to be her bank manager. We administer the hospital trust funds for her.'

'So you're just up here arranging an overdraft? A pity the Old Man didn't explain that. It would have saved me a trip—and a beating up.'

'Clever bastard. But your story doesn't jibe. You told me the Gaffer sent you.'

'Quite true. Naturally I didn't want to horn in on something that might well have been official, so I called him to clear it first.'

'You're a higher man on the totem pole than I thought. *I* wouldn't know where to call the son-of-a-bitch.'

'Neither would I. I called Calcutta in the first instance. They asked for my number and he got through to me.'

'Never stuck for an answer, are you?'

I was screwing down tight on the safety valve. Wainwright was one of those people who could make my hackles rise even if we were only discussing the weather. Calling me a liar when for once I was telling the plain truth was putting a strain on things.

'Believe what the hell you like,' I said. 'But that happens to be the truth.'

'Nice work. Two briefs for the same job. Is old Culverton paying you too?'

'Sure. But actually it's three briefs. She told me to get you off the premises also. I'm collecting off her as well.' I thought I'd scored, but he bounced it right back at me.

'A fee's about all you ever would collect off her,' he said. 'She hates your guts.'

I said, 'You're a gutterbred little bastard, Wainwright, and whatever missionary society paid for that entirely phony English accent wasted their dough.'

It delighted him as much as it belittled me in my own ears. He lay back on the charpoy smiling beatifically. 'That's rich,' he said. 'Coming from a Shanghai half-chat. You know something, Rees? You've been in this scene much longer than I, but one of my first jobs happened to be that of checking old records in the Hong Kong office. Confidential reports and all. I've been right through yours. Jee-suss! No wonder you never got on to the permanent roll. *I* wouldn't trust you either. Not with your background. Torpedoing is just about your ceiling.'

'Save it until tomorrow,' I told him. 'I'll collect up some horse-shit and we can really plaster each other.' I picked up my trail pack and a blanket from the charpoy and moved to the door. 'In the meantime,' I added, 'I'd get as much rest as I could, if I were you. Because you're going back—every step of the way—in the saddle or across it. It's all one to me.'

I sat outside in the darkness, shaking with sick rage, not at anything he had said, but at myself for letting him get through my guard. So much for the training of years. So much for the professionalism I'd always imagined I'd acquired. One schoolboy jibe and I'd reacted like a hysterical whore in a brothel brawl. Why? Christ, I'd been around long enough, hadn't I? I'd been insulted by experts in the past, countless times, but I'd never let myself be drawn like this before.

Of course I knew the answer, even though I wouldn't admit it to myself. It was that one reference to Claire, and his inference that they had discussed me between themselves. *Did* she hate my guts? I wondered dully. She hated everything I represented, admittedly, but surely not me, personally? What had I ever done to her? What was I doing now, except trying to get her out of the very morass in which I lived, moved and had my being? Well, I'd shot any chance I ever had of that now. I'd get nothing out of Wainwright—and the job just boiled down to a squalid bit of policing. I'd take him back and he'd be fired and slapped under tight surveillance until anything he could leak at the moment was old and unsaleable—or, if he was really a hot number, he'd find his books fiddled at the bank—it was crawling with 'our' people—and they'd have something really tangible to hold over him like the sword of Damocles—or, in an extreme case, he'd just disappear, and people would say, 'Poor Wainwright. Decent young chap, you know—but he'd been drinking heavily.' Calcutta is one of the easiest disposal points in the world, where uncounted charred corpses go floating down the Hooghly from the burning ghats every day.

What had he done? I wondered. Or what did they think he was *going* to do? Did they really have the dirt on him—and was he on the scoot across the border, either to China or Russia? This was one of the logical routes. No passports needed up here. But how did Claire come into it? Had he told her some plausible story and enlisted her aid? But that only brought me back to the unassailable fact that she hated anything to do with the Business. Why would she tolerate in him what had smashed things up between *us*? There was a possible answer to that, of course, but it was one which didn't do my *amour propre* the least bit of good. And finally, what sort of clamp was she in at this moment at the hospital? And who and what was that German?

Well, I wouldn't find out from Wainwright. That was for sure. I was tempted to send him down with Safaraz, and to go back to the hospital, but I knew that wouldn't work out. The people I would have to contact down there would talk to me alone. No—I'd take him down—and then, having handed him over to somebody, or turned him loose, if those were the orders, I'd come back under my own steam—and probably get nowhere, fast—like this time.

I rolled up in my blanket then and tried to sleep, but I wasn't successful. My thoughts kept squirrelling round and round the subject, and I was glad when daybreak came.

I went in to Wainwright. He looked somewhat better but he wouldn't let me examine his arm.

I said, wearily, 'Cut it out, Wainwright. I'm not doing you any favours. We've got a long march ahead of us and I don't want this thing to blow up again. Are you going to be sensible, or do I have to get Safaraz in to sit on you?' He gave in then and when I'd finished the dressing I said, 'We've got a couple of ponies. I'll try and get a third from these people, and we'll start off tonight if you feel up to it.'

He didn't appear to hear me. He sat staring ahead of him, so I got up and made for the door, but before I reached it he said, 'Just a minute, Rees.' I turned and he added, 'Can I ask you a question?'

'Go ahead,' I told him. 'But I'm not guaranteeing any answers in advance.'

'Have you seen Claire—or did you come straight here from Ramabagh?'

'I saw her the night before last. She sent me here. I told you—she asked me to take you back to India.' His eyes were fixed on my face, and I could see that he was weighing my every word, trying to sift a few grains of truth from the chaff, so I went on, 'Just that, and nothing more. She gave me no information—but I drew a few conclusions of my own.'

'Such as?'

'There's something going on there. She's not a free agent any more—and strangers definitely aren't welcome.' I pointed to my face. 'I've got this to prove it.'

'What happened?'

'I was caught snooping round at night.'

'By whom?'

I shook my head. 'Sorry. No dice. You said "*a* question". That makes four.'

He was silent for a time, then he said, very quietly, 'How much does she mean to you, Rees?'

'That's five,' I said, 'and the answer to that one is "mind your own goddam business".'

'It *is* my business,' he said, 'and if you feel the way I think you do, it's yours too.'

And now I was searching *his* face. Was this the prelude to a deal? Was he offering me information in return for my not taking him in? Make no mistake about it, I was open to a deal, but I wasn't buying a bag of nails sight unseen.

'Tell me what you know,' I said. 'No promises on my part, but if she's in any sort of trouble I'll do what I can to help.'

'Not good enough. This could be dynamite. You might follow it up on your own account—and leave her out on a limb.'

He said it with finality, but I felt that he was still bargaining.

'I said no promises,' I repeated, 'but I'll amend that. I'll give you my word that I'll put her interests first—always provided that she's not willingly working for Them.'

'She is working for Them,' he said very quietly. 'But the operative word is "willingly" or rather "*un*willingly". You said it yourself—she's not a free agent.'

And that was it. Confirmation of what I'd been fearing all along. I managed to shrug.

'You know the rules,' I said. 'She's only to come clean, and she won't be hurt. That goes for you too.'

'Yes, I know the rules,' he said bitterly. 'The Gaffer makes them—and busts them when it suits him. Listen to me, Rees. If that bastard knew the ins and outs of this one he'd make some more rules—and you'd feel obliged to play them his way, even if it meant that she went to the wall. You're one of the dedicated. Well, I'm not—not in this particular case, anyhow. That's why I went into this without telling him. Yes—I've made a balls of it again—and you're going to take me in for it—but whatever happens to me I'd rather be in my shoes than yours, because I did try to do something that you'd never have the moral guts to do. I stepped out of line to help somebody who—who means more to me than the bloody rules. No, I still wouldn't want to swop places with you, Rees. You rule-abiding, self-righteous prick.'

Chapter Eleven

IT WAS A PURE MENTAL CATHARTIC. All his pent-up spleen in one burst—like the relief of a lancet through an abscess. And it convinced me. Lies will sometimes get past you in this business, but never a rare glimpse of the naked truth. Wainwright wasn't a good enough actor to have faked that one up. There was too much feeling there—feeling that I could understand, and even sympathize with. Twice he'd bungled a job in the past—and each time I'd been sent in to take over. I'd drawn no personal satisfaction from it, because in neither case did I consider it was his fault. He was just plain damned unlucky. But the Gaffer didn't think that way. To him a boob was a boob—and God help the boober—and I know that Wainwright took a severe caning at each debriefing, even though both cases were ultimately successful.

And now here he was up to the neck in a personal involvement—and he'd boobed again—and I was on the scene once more. Could you blame him for not loving me like a brother?

I said, 'All right, now that you've got that off your chest, suppose you give me the whole story?'

He lay back on the charpoy with his eyes closed. 'I'd want guarantees first,' he said.

'Don't talk like a bloody fool,' I told him. 'What guarantees could I give that I couldn't walk away from later?'

'Your word.'

'You flatter me. What do you think we're in? The Boy Scouts?'

'I dislike you, Rees,' he said. 'Very much indeed—but I don't think you'd walk away from your word. That would tarnish your image in your own eyes—and you couldn't stand that. That's part of your fish-blooded omnipotence —your—your——'

'All right, don't start again. What do you want my word on?'

'Two things. One, that if I tell you the whole story you won't just take me in and leave Claire up here without protection. Two, that whatever you decide to do about it, you'll help me get her out of that damned hospital and away to a place of safety—whether she agrees to go or not.'

'I'll take you up on the first,' I said, 'but I'd rather leave the second open until I know more about it. Will you settle for that?'

He nodded and I could see that he was marshalling his thoughts.

'I met her two years ago,' he began. 'It was when I was transferred from head office to the Calcutta Branch—of the bank, I mean. She came down about an anonymous donation she had received to cover a new building programme. She was as pleased as Punch about it, but at the same time, bursting with curiosity. She tried to get me to tell her who the donor was, but naturally I wouldn't. Actually it was Yev Shalom. She stayed in Calcutta for a week, buying supplies. I took her to dinner twice. I had occasion to write to her from time to time, and I got into the habit of slipping a personal note in with the official letter.

'Well, that's how it all started. She used to come down two or three times a year, and we went out quite a lot. God knows Calcutta's a dead enough dump, but it was high life in the big city to her after these hills. I knew how I felt right away, but this game is dicy enough without a wife, so I kept it on the "just good friends" basis until I couldn't stick it any longer. Then I wrote to the Gaffer and told him I wanted to quit.'

'Did you give him reasons?' I asked.

'Not bloody likely. I didn't want any slimy innuendoes from that dirty-minded old swine. No—I just said I'd had enough.'

'What was his reaction?'

'He told me to take six months to think it over. I wrote back that I didn't need to think it over. I wanted out.'

'And then?'

'He didn't answer. But I considered I'd put my formal notice in, and I felt free to ask Claire to marry me.'

'What did she say?'

'It never got that far. I knew I'd have to give up my cover job with the bank as well, but that wasn't worrying me. I couldn't see her leaving her work here for bridge, hen-parties and ladies' charity committees in Calcutta, so I was going to offer to take over the bookwork of the hospital. That in itself is a full-time job and it was getting more than she could cope with on her own. It wasn't the sort of thing I felt I could put in a letter, so I intended applying for a few days' leave from the bank and coming up here—but then the Gaffer clobbered me with the Palinovsky job. I didn't argue. I was going to make it my swan song—do a good job and bow out gracefully. But you know what happened. The Gaffer's debriefing in Lahore was the most humiliating thing I've ever been called upon to face. I blew up in the middle of it and started to walk out.'

'How did he take that?'

'He never turned a hair. He just warned me what would happen to me if I tried to quit before I was released. He said I was no good as a field man, but I had certain uses in liaison work in Calcutta, and that I'd stay there until I was properly relieved. Then he told me to get out—as if he was dismissing a sweeper.'

I said, 'You *are* sorry for yourself, aren't you? You make me want to spew.'

'That's mutual, you superior bastard,' he spat at me. 'Is it any use going on with this, or shall we call it a day and drop the whole thing?'

'Keep going,' I told him. 'Only soft pedal on the bleeding heart aspect of it. I just want the facts. What did you do then?'

'I went back to Calcutta. I got in fairly late, and there was a letter waiting for me at my apartment, from Claire. It was in answer to one of mine in which I'd said I was going to ask for leave and take up her invitation to visit Ramabagh and then come up here to see her hospital. She was delighted. She'd have plenty of time to show me round, she wrote, because she'd had the most unexpected bit of luck. There had only been one doctor there for some months—an Indian—but now another had arrived—literally from out of the blue. It was lucky that she spoke German, because this chap hadn't much English—only a bit of broken Urdu. He'd arrived at the hospital with a patient, another European, who had met with a serious accident in the hills. She asked me to keep this to myself as she suspected that these two were up there without official sanction, because this chap had asked her not to report their presence to the frontier police. She didn't know what they had been doing. She didn't care. All that mattered to her was that she had another doctor for a few weeks, and she wasn't looking gift horses in the mouth. Well, you can imagine the effect of *that* one on me. I had no doubt whatsoever that it was my old friend from the ambush, and the idea of Claire being up here with him, taking him at face value, scared the living daylights out of me. I just had time to make it out to Dum Dum and catch the night flight up to Delhi. I got to Ramabagh next day and asked her father for facilities to come on up here, but he wouldn't hear of it. The frontier was closed and he wasn't going to break his trust by assisting outsiders to violate it. He did, however, manage to get word up to her that I was there—and a couple of days later she came down.'

So that was it. Things were beginning to fall into place now. I let him rest for some minutes, because I could see that the strain of talking was telling on him. After a while he went on.

'I could see right away that she was worried, but I couldn't get anything out of her for quite a long time—and then only in bits. There had been mysterious comings and goings at night. The German had an undercover radio—a thing that's strictly forbidden up here, as you know. She had compromised herself badly by not reporting their presence to the frontier police. That, in itself, was enough to get the hospital closed down if it were found out. In short, the bastard had the dirt on her. He hadn't actually come out into the open, but she knew the threat was there. She felt that there was even a possibility of his getting at her through the Old Man if she got awkward—and, of course, there was no question of her taking the Old Man into her confidence. He'd have blown his top. I begged her to stay down in safety and let me go up for a look round, but she shot that down in flames. What the hell could I, a bank penpusher, do about it?'

He took a deep breath and avoided my eye. 'So in the end I—well—I told her——'

'You blew your cover, in other words?'

'Yes, I blew my cover,' he said. 'Sneer all you like, Rees—but remember that you blew yours to her once.'

'I didn't actually,' I said. 'It was blown for me. But I'm

not sneering. I think in the circumstances that I'd have done the same.'

'Good of you to say so,' he said, and *he* was sneering now. 'Anyhow, that was it. She didn't believe me at first. She thought that I was just trying to impress her. So then I threw the lot. Your name had come up casually once or twice in conversation in the past, and although she hadn't given you away, I guessed that she knew you were in the racket, so I told her that I'd been working with you, and who I thought the German was. That convinced her —and incidentally shot any chance I ever had with her to hell. I was just another cheap cloak-and-daggerer now earning a little pin-money on the side—just like you, in fact. She told me to stay out of it—that she'd handle things herself. All she had come down for this time was to stop my blundering up there and getting mixed up in things. She was going back on her own, and she would wait until the patient was fit enough to travel, and they took him to hell out of it, and she'd be left in peace—and the hospital would be safe again.

'We were out in the fields at the time, and suddenly we were jumped by a bunch of hairies. I had my gun with me and some of her father's people arrived and we managed to get away, but I stopped this one in the arm. Fortunately the Old Man was away that day and she fixed me up and we got out of it——'

'What did you gather from this attack?' I asked. 'I mean what do you think they were after?'

'From what she told me I have no doubt about that at all. She'd told the German that she intended going down to see her father, and he had said that he thought it highly inadvisable at that juncture. If the police happened to visit the hospital in her absence they might decide to have a snoop around and they'd find both him and the patient. She pretended to agree, because she was pretty certain that he'd have stopped her leaving if it had come to a showdown—and she had sneaked out at night. Obviously he'd sent these thugs after her to get her back before any harm was done.'

'I see—and knowing all that, she still came back?'

'Christ! I don't have to explain that to you, do I? You know her. This bloody hospital is everything to her. She wouldn't walk out on it. You bet she came back—but she had no option but to bring me with her. We came by a round-about trail, travelling by night. She wouldn't let me go into the hospital though. She dropped me here, and I couldn't do anything about it because I seemed to have picked up some infection in this wound, and I was in a pretty ropy condition. She sent out some medicine, and these people have done what they could, but I'm only now beginning to climb back. So that's the lot. What are you going to do about it?' He lay back looking at me balefully.

'I certainly haven't got any instant solutions on tap,' I said. 'I suggest in the first place that we stop fighting each other and try and do a little reasonably intelligent thinking.'

He caught my eye and grinned grudgingly. 'All right—peace for the duration,' he conceded.

'Have you seen the German—up here, I mean?' I asked.

'No.'

'I have. I don't think it's the same bloke—but that doesn't mean a thing. There are a lot of East Germans working for the Russians out this way, as you know.'

'Yes, I realize that,' he said. 'But I think it would be safe to assume that they're both with the same mob, whoever they are.'

'If we could persuade Claire to tip the frontier police off, that would put her in the clear with them,' I mused.

'You'll never do that,' he said positively. 'I suggested it, and she tore me to shreds. The hospital is a sanctuary as far as she is concerned—and one of those yegs is a patient. You might just as well ask a Catholic priest to call the cops into the confessional.'

'But if *we* did it——' I began, but he didn't let me finish.

'Count me out on that,' he said flatly. 'You've written yourself off with her already. I'm still hoping.'

'You haven't a chance,' I told him. 'You're just another cheap cloak-and-daggerer—like me. You said so yourself.'

'I also said I'd quit. Whatever they do to me afterwards, that still stands. I don't want any misunderstandings about that, Rees.'

'If you think they'd let you dig yourself in up here as a ministering angel, you're nuts,' I said. 'This is a sensitive area, you fool. The Gaffer would just pass a quiet tip to both the Indians and the Pakistanis, and you'd be out of here like shit off a shovel, with a deportation chit out of the whole sub-continent slapped across your bracket.'

He sat up and glared at me. 'If you call the police in on this——' he shouted.

'Cool off,' I told him. 'I was only thinking aloud. Calling the police in wouldn't do anybody any good. They'd merely hand those two over to the army, who'd interrogate them, and get nowhere, and eventually deport them to whatever country they came from originally—and they'd be as much use to me then as an autographed copy of "Das Kapital".'

'That's all that concerns you really, isn't it?' he said coldly. 'All you want to do is to follow them up as a lead —and collect your cheque at the end of it. Claire doesn't matter a damn, does she?'

'I gave you my word that I'd do my best to get her out of any danger that she might be in,' I said. 'I'm not going back on that.'

'What do you mean—"I"? I said "we".'

'All right then—*we*. But at the same time, *I* haven't quit, and once Claire is off the hook I reserve the right to follow this up my own way. Yes—just for the cheque if you like. Now, once again, suppose we stop fighting?'

'Who started it?' he growled. 'You and your God Almighty "I"——'

I got up and walked towards the door.

'Have it your own way, Wainwright,' I said. 'It wouldn't have worked anyhow. You just set about it any way you think best—only don't get in my hair while you're doing it, that's all—or you're going to get scratched —hard.'

He muttered, 'I'm sorry—come back. You know damned well that I can't do anything on my own at the moment.'

I walked back to the charpoy. 'All right then,' I said. 'I'm not rubbing your nose in it, but I've got to have an understanding. Either we stop bickering like schoolkids, and work together like adults, or we each go our own way.'

He hesitated for a moment, then shamefacedly put out his hand, and I, as shamefacedly, took it.

'Good,' I said, and sat down again. 'Well—to continue. The patient? Had Claire any ideas about him? Who he was? What had happened to him?'

'He has a badly busted leg and a fractured skull. Why?'

'It just struck me—he *could* be Palinovsky.'

He shook his head. 'No—he's English. I remember Claire telling me that he was delirious when they brought him in. From what he was yelling, she thought he'd been in an air crash. The German is apparently a very able surgeon. He X-rayed him, set his leg and then trephined his skull. He did quite a lot of general hospital work for her apart from his own chap—which is another reason why she wouldn't want to turn him in. You know what these medical bods are like—qualified or not. They stick together like glue. All she wants is for them both to go.'

'A pity we couldn't throw a scare into them,' I said. 'Something that would panic them into beating it. That would take the pressure off Claire—and I'd be able to follow them up.' I cocked an eye at him. 'I take it you don't mind my using the first person, singular, there do you? You'd have us all off the premises then.'

'That would suit me down to the ground,' he grinned. Then he was serious again. 'Do you really think that they'd turf me out of it if I wanted to stay up here?' he asked.

'It would all depend on the circumstances under which you quit,' I told him. 'If it was with the Gaffer's full knowledge and approval they might leave you in peace.'

'I wonder?' he gloomed. 'The bastard would probably want me to do some moonlighting for him on the side.'

'I wouldn't be at all surprised,' I said with malice aforethought. 'Then Christ help you if Claire ever found out.'

'You can't win, can you?'

'Not once you've worked for them, I'm afraid. I'll tell you something else you probably know already, but won't admit to yourself.'

'What's that?'

'You never really get out of the Business. It's like alcoholism. You may hate it—you may kick the habit, or think you have—then one day somebody asks you to do a job, and you say "Not me, brother—I've seen the light. I'm saved". Then you get to thinking about it—reasoning—justifying it to yourself. It's patriotism. It's because you hate Them—et cetera, et cetera—and the next thing you know you're right back with it. You said I did it for the cheque. Well, to a point you're right. I certainly wouldn't do it *without* the cheque. That would be a negation of my professional standing—and that means a hell of a lot to us all. But the cheque isn't everything.'

'Just open the gate for me,' he said with feeling, 'and you can stuff the patriotism *and* the cheque.'

'I wonder.'

'I don't. I'm no good at it.'

'Balls. Why do you think the Gaffer wouldn't let you go? If you were no good at it, you'd have been fired long ago—with due muzzling precautions, of course.'

'Are you trying to boost my morale or something?'

'No, why should I? I don't owe you anything. If it comes to that I don't like you either—any more than you do me. I hate to see good training and experience go to waste though. And I hate to see that old bastard the Gaffer get a man down. That's all it is, you know? You can't take the debriefings. I don't like them either. I don't know anybody in the Business that does. But you've got to keep things in their proper proportion. He's only testing the whole thing—strand by strand. It's a technique they borrowed from the Air Force in World War II. I've talked to old fighter pilots who have been through it. The Brass had to know what the enemy's real losses were. Overestimation would have been fatal, so when a chap came back and said he'd shot down three they'd call him a line-shooting bastard, laugh at him, ridicule him, try and shake him, knowing that if he was in any doubt at all he'd break in the end and mumble "well, one might have made it back"—whereas if he was absolutely dead certain he'd stick to it. He'd possibly lose his temper—some of them have been known to take a swing at the debriefing officer—but nobody but a complete paranoiac would claim a doubtful as a cert once he'd been through the mill.'

He was watching my face as I talked. He said slowly, 'You really are dedicated, aren't you? I meant it as a jibe when I said it before. But you are—aren't you?'

And suddenly I felt acutely uncomfortable, but I managed to nod ponderously and mumble, 'Well—um—probably I am. It does mean something to me. Christ, I'll be saying that the game's bigger than the man next.

Anyhow, you quit if you feel you must, but I think it would be a hell of a pity—and I'm pretty certain that you'd never completely get it out of your system.'

And I really did think it would be a pity if he quit. Because while he was still in the Business he had about as much chance of pinching my woman as he had of shoving butter up a wildcat's arse with a redhot hatpin.

Chapter Twelve

WAINWRIGHT had pretty hefty powers of recuperation. I renewed the dressings on his arm at intervals and insisted on his eating properly twice during the day, so by that evening he had perked up considerably—too much in fact, because his inactivity was galling him and he was getting jumpy.

'What are you going to do?' he asked me.

'Go in and see her,' I said.

'Good. When do we start?'

'Don't talk like a bloody fool. You're not up to it yet.' And that started it all off again and for a while it looked as if our rapprochement was in renewed danger.

'How will you get in there without stirring things up?' he demanded.

'I've got ways.'

'They didn't seem to work last time, if that mug of yours is any criterion.'

'That was sheer bad luck.'

'Maybe—but if your luck gives out again you'll merely force their hands into doing something ahead of the gun.'

'I'll have to risk that. Claire may seem the most self-sufficient female in Asia, but she must be feeling pretty insecure at the moment, and even though she's told us both to get the hell out of it, the knowledge that we're still around will be reassuring.'

'And won't you cash in on that!'

'You're being childish again.'

'Perhaps—but I know you, you bastard.'

'All right then—*you* suggest something.'

'We'll go in together.'

'It's a twenty-mile hike—in the dark. With the best will in the world you'd slow things up.'

'You said you had ponies.'

'One each for Safaraz and myself—and he'll have to stand by them while I climb in.'

'We'll get a third from these people. You suggested that yourself.'

'No dice. I questioned the headman. They've only got donkeys here. They couldn't keep up.'

'You think of everything, don't you?' But he still wouldn't give up. 'All right,' he said. 'So Safaraz stays behind and I come in his place.'

'And go through the whole dreary argument again when we get there—because you'd want to be the one who climbed in.'

'Why the hell shouldn't I be?' He stood up and tried his legs. 'I'm quite fit again.'

'I know the layout of the place. You don't.'

And so it went on, but I wore him down in the end.

'Any messages?' I asked him innocently as Safaraz and I set out at sundown.

'None that I'd care to entrust to you,' he said icily. 'You probably wouldn't get close enough to deliver it, anyhow.'

'Want to bet?' I winked. 'I'll wait until she's turned in and then get into her room. Nothing to it. I've been there before, remember.' And the look of sheer hatred on his pan kept me chuckling happily for the next hour—but only for an hour, because after that I had plenty of other things on my mind.

The trail from the village dropped steadily for some five miles into a wide but totally enclosed valley, before climbing again to the heights where the hospital was, so we saw the fires long before we reached them. There were four of them, pinpoints of light from this distance, equally spaced in the form of a square and it looked from up here as if they were straddling the trail itself. I thought at first that they were shepherds, but Safaraz said no, it was too late in the year for sheep. They'd all be well down below the snowline in their winter pastures by now.

'A caravan?' I suggested.

'Where from and where to, sahib?' he asked. 'This trail ends at the village.'

'Then what?' I asked, exasperated.

'Soldiers,' he said flatly, and my heart sank. We were over sixty miles from the confrontation line here, in a semi-neutral zone that had hitherto been reasonably free from military operations. Small patrols from both sides occasionally visited the hospital, certainly, under an unwritten but scrupulously observed truce, but watch fires over an area as large as this meant something much bigger.

I said, 'How far apart are those fires?' and he considered for a time and said two hundred yards. That meant four hundred square yards assuming that the fires were at each corner—an area large enough to bivouac a battalion, with all its transport. So we were cut off from the hospital, and from what I remembered that meant a detour over the surrounding mountains that would take days. It also meant that these bastards would send out foraging parties, and the supplies from the village that were a matter of life or death to the hospital would be commandeered. I sat looking down at them, cursing in a sick, futile rage.

'And yet—? and yet—?' said Safaraz doubtfully.

'And yet what?' I asked impatiently.

'Listen, sahib,' he said. 'No noise. We should hear even a sleeping camp from up here in this clear air—and get the smell of the mule lines. But there is nothing but those four little fires.'

And he was right, of course—and when I came to think of it, I realized that no commander who knew his job would permit fires to give his position away at night.

'Signal fires,' I said with an assurance that I didn't feel.

'Perhaps, sahib—but to whom?'

'Picket the ponies off the track and let us go down to see,' I told him.

We got our answer before we were half-way down. Safaraz heard it first and gripped my arm. Faintly, from high above us, came the staccato rattle of a helicopter. It became obvious then. These fires were marking a landing ground.

'I was right,' he said with satisfaction. 'Soldiers. Flying soldiers.'

'We'll still go down,' I told him. 'I want to see how many of them there are—and whether this is to be a permanent landing ground.'

We continued on, Safaraz scouting ahead on the alert for outposts, but we saw no sign of life and we were able to get up to one side of the square, into a dark nullah equidistant between two of the fires. The chopper was low overhead now, but I couldn't see it because they hadn't got the winking light that aircraft normally carry at night. Then I saw that somebody on the ground in the centre of the square was flashing upward with an electric lamp. It switched on its landing lights then, focusing down on to the ground beneath it, and the glare reflecting up caught the shimmering circle of its rotor. It hovered for some moments, then settled, and the engine was cut, leaving only the dying clack of the idling blades. There were more lights then, bobbing over the uneven ground towards the chopper, and I heard an English voice call out sharply, 'Keep those bloody wogs clear until the rotor stops!' and there was a babble in Urdu: 'Kabardah! Careful! Do not jolt him, sons of owls! Gently! Gently! nameless spawn of noseless mothers!' The customary accompaniment of any group in the East doing a job in concert.

Then they came into the circle of light, and I saw that they were not soldiers, but a miscellaneous bunch of coolies carrying a heavy burden with exaggerated care. It was a man on a stretcher.

A light snapped on behind the perspex of the cockpit and the pilot jumped down. He reached up and caught the sluggishly revolving rotor and held it to a drooping stop. I nudged Safaraz, and we crept closer.

Then I saw Claire. She was walking with the German, both of them muffled in poshteens against the evening chill.

The pilot went forward and shook hands with them, but I couldn't hear what they were saying because of the babble. The coolies were trying to manhandle the stretcher into the door of the chopper, and making a botch of it, and the pilot yelled angrily and started slapping around at them. Claire took charge then and got them quietened down. She took a couple of packs of native cigarettes out of her pocket and distributed them, and herded the coolies away out of the circle of light, then the three of them got the stretcher aboard and strapped into position. We were close enough to hear them now. Claire was speaking in German, then she turned to the pilot and said in English, 'He should be all right now. Doctor Reutlingen knows what to do, of course.'

'I'm glad somebody does,' the pilot grumbled. 'I've had a hell of a job finding you.'

'How will it be on the way back?' Claire asked.

'Hairy. I'm tight on fuel.' He reached into the cockpit and pulled out a chart on a clipboard. 'I suppose you couldn't help me on this, could you?' They bent over it in the light of a torch. 'This, I take it—bunch of lights about five miles due north of here, would be your hospital? Right?'

'That's it,' she agreed.

'Good. Then this, where I've marked it, another bunch of lights at the foot of the mountains—with no name on it? You wouldn't be able to identify that, would you?'

She studied it for some time, then said, 'Yes—that would be Sitlo. It's a biggish village in the mouth of the valley.'

'Thank God for that,' he said, and marked it in. 'You need to be a clairvoyant on this job. I've got to get over that range at the head of the valley and drop down on to an old airstrip—and you can't rely on these charts.' He put a protractor on to the board and ruled off a line. 'Hm—about ninety miles, course two-eight-five from your hospital—That should do it—*if* I can count on this damned compass. Thanks a lot.' He felt in his pocket and pulled out an envelope. 'They told me to give you this.'

I saw her open it and take out a wad of paper money. She replaced it quickly and held it out to him.

'There's some mistake,' she said. 'The doctor has already paid the patient's bill.'

'Better argue with them, then,' the pilot said. 'I was only told to give it to you.'

'I'd rather you took it back,' she said.

'Sorry,' he answered and climbed into the cockpit, followed by the German, who paused, took Claire's hand and raised it to his lips. She tried to shove the envelope at him, but she was too late. The pilot shouted, 'Stand clear, miss,' and slammed the door. She moved out of the circle of light and I heard the engine cough, splutter, and come jerkily to full-throated life. Then the lights snapped off and the chopper was rising.

We lay there in the darkness while she rounded up the coolies. She called, 'Ag bhujao!' and some of them ran outwards to the corners and stamped out the already dying fires. I was tempted to go forward then to her, but I thought better of it. Our next meeting would, inevitably, end in a battle royal, so I decided that it would be in decent privacy, in a venue of my own choice. I felt an overwhelming relief. Those two were out of her hospital and she was, temporarily at least, off the hook—and I had some rough idea of where they were going. I memorized the words. About ninety miles on a course of two hundred and eighty-five degrees from the hospital—over the range from Sitlo—where there was an old airstrip. That shouldn't be too difficult to find, once I got hold of a map. There were scores of old airstrips along these foothills—relics of World War II—and most of them were marked on the latest charts, even though few of them were named.

We gave them a good half hour's start, then went back for the ponies, and followed on. Who the hell were these people, I wondered? Had they any connection with the Palinovsky affair, or was this something new? There was, after all, only one factor common to both—an Urdu-speaking German. He might still be the same man, of course. I could easily have been mistaken in this. Wainwright would be able to answer that when he saw him. *If* he saw him. Wainwright, now that Claire was no longer threatened, might stick to his resolution to quit. What did I do then? My orders from the Gaffer were to bring him back—or to torpedo him if he refused to come. The latter no longer applied. I had discretionary powers in this, thank God, and I knew now that Wainwright wasn't a potential defector. No, if he refused to come back with me I would just leave him up here, much as I hated the idea. Claire would very soon put the skids under him if she was really sore at him—I hoped. In that case would he withdraw his notice to the Gaffer? Would the Gaffer, on the other hand, finally take him at his word and fire him? Well, that was their affair, not mine. Strictly speaking, the job was over now—both from the Gaffer's point of view and the Old Man's. I'd located Wainwright and delivered the order to return, and ascertained that Claire was not in any danger. I was free to return. D.C.F.

But I knew deep down that I wouldn't be withdrawing yet. Not until I'd been to Sitlo and had another look at these people. Sense of duty? If it was, it was not the sort of thing I'd admit even to myself. For the extra bill I'd be putting into the Gaffer? Not entirely. These last two jobs had amounted to a normal year's income already. I like money, of course, but it's not all-important. Just plain curiosity? Yes, there was a lot of that in it. Did I think that they still represented a threat to Claire? Possible but not probable. It would appear now that she'd served her purpose and they'd gone their way. She'd accepted payment from them though, however unwillingly. That is a cardinal rule in the Business. Always pay for services rendered. It gives one a decided psychological ascendancy if the services of the payee are ever required again. They might come back in the future, but if they did what could I do about it? Not a damned thing—unless she confided in me and asked for my help, and there was little chance of that ever happening.

So in the end I decided that it was just that I disliked unfinished business. I wanted to know if this was part of the Palinovsky thing—and if it wasn't, then who the hell these people were.

The hospital was dark when we arrived, with just one lamp over the gate and a few inside. Once more Safaraz had to wait with the ponies—sourly. He said that he'd come in and rescue me again if I didn't return in two hours, in a tone that convinced me that he was hoping that just that would happen. He helped me over the wall and I dropped down behind the staff quarters. There were no lights showing here so I went along to Claire's window and tapped softly, and kept it up until the curtains jerked back and a torch shone in my face from the other side of the glass. I mouthed at her and she snapped the torch out and the window slid up softly.

'What do *you* want?' she asked very coldly indeed.

'Just a talk,' I told her. 'Yes, I know these people have left, but there are some things I think you ought to know for your own sake.'

'Are you alone?'

'Yes—Wainwright is still at the village.'

She was silent for some moments, then she moved away and I heard a rustle as she put on a robe. She came back and said, 'You can come in, but only for a minute—then you must go—and for the Lord's sake leave me alone in future, will you?'

I climbed in and she carefully drew the curtains again, then switched on the light. We stood regarding each other.

'God, what a mess you look,' she said.

I suppose I did. My face still felt stiff and sore, and the filthy P.M. clothes I had been wearing for some days now weren't helping.

'*You* haven't changed,' I told her.

'I know perfectly well I have,' she said. Her hand went to her lovely tumbled hair in a typically feminine gesture and I saw her eyes slide away to the mirror of her dressing-table.

'I meant your temper,' I said. 'Looks? Oh, well, none of us are getting any younger, are we?'

'You *bastard*!' she flared, then we were grinning at each other. 'Well, what do you want?'

I looked wistfully at the Thermos jug on her bedside table. She always had it filled with strong black coffee in case she was called out suddenly in the night. She followed my eyes, then said impatiently, 'Food, as usual, I suppose. Wait a moment.' She went to the door, opened it slightly and stood listening, then she gestured for quietness and went out, closing the door softly behind her.

I sat on a chair and looked longingly at the bed. It was clean, warm, soft and inviting. She was no Spartan when it came to sleeping. No nun's cell this. I was glad she was getting me some food. I didn't particularly need it as I'd eaten just before setting out, but a hungry man is an object of pity to a woman, and I knew I'd get more out of her if she felt sorry for me. It was a lousy attitude, I know, but one has to use the best tools available in the Business, and I would have got nowhere by straight questioning. She was gone some time and I had nodded off when she returned. She brought a cold chicken, cheese, pickles, a loaf and butter, and characteristically she had managed to give even this emergency meal her own cachet of elegance. Good china, gleaming cutlery, a napkin and a lace cloth on the tray. A small oasis of civilization in the sea of squalor in which I moved. I started to mumble my thanks, but she shook her head and told me to eat, and then turned away and poured coffee—two cups. She sat on the edge of the bed, not looking at me except once when I started to tear the bird apart with my hands. It wasn't an act. It was so long since I'd used a knife and fork that I was really awkward with them—and let's face it, that is the way I always tackle a cold chicken on my own. I looked abashed—and that wasn't an act either.

She waited until I had finished, then she said, 'All right—say what you have to say, Idwal—then I must ask you to go.'

'You know who those people were, I suppose?' I bluffed.

'Not in the slightest,' she said, calling it. 'Do you?'

'The German—Reutlingen—is dangerous,' I said.

'To whom?' she asked. 'I only knew him as a good doctor.'

'Some doctor.' I pointed to my face.

'He didn't do that. That was my own people. He rescued you and then had you attended to.' She stifled a pretended yawn. 'Look—will you please go? I've had rather a heavy day and I'm tired.'

'As you wish,' I said, rising. 'But whether you believe me or not, I'm trying to help.'

'It's very good of you, no doubt, but I don't require your help.'

'I wouldn't be too certain of that. They've paid you pretty generously, but that hasn't got you off anything. It's only put you further into their hands.' I wasn't looking at her directly, but in the mirror I saw her start.

'I don't know what you're talking about,' she said.

'I think you do. They gave you a very substantial sum when they left—a sum far in excess of any bill you would have presented to a patient who could pay——'

'What the hell has that got to do with you?' she demanded furiously. 'All right then—so they made a donation to the hospital. People do, you know. You did yourself once.'

'There were no strings attached to mine.'

'There weren't to this——'

'You want to bet? Listen, Claire—please listen to me. You hate politics, especially undercover politics, but you're involved now—right up to the neck. You're trusted by both the Indians and the Pakistanis, but you have certain obligations. You're supposed to report every patient who passes through your hands to the frontier police. Oh, yes, I know that it's winked at in the case of the bulk of the poor harmless devils you normally help, but you know damned well that that wouldn't apply to two European survivors from a crashed aircraft. You would have been expected to notify the police immediately they arrived.' It caught her off her guard. She stared at me open-mouthed for a moment, then recovered herself and said contemptuously, 'You got that from James Wainwright. What charming people you all are. One is fool enough to take you at your face value, tell you things in confidence, then find oneself threatened and blackmailed. *My God!*'

I felt like a slug being sprinkled with salt, but I had to go on with it now. 'I'm sorry if it appears like that,' I said. 'But whether you believe it or not, it's blackmail I'm trying to protect you from.'

'You bloody hypocrite!'

'All right, I'm a bloody hypocrite—but those people are still in the area. Actually they're in a place called Sitlo——' Again she couldn't quite cover a reaction. '—and some of them are likely to get hurt again, in which case they've got first class hospital facilities right on their doorstep. More than that, the winter's coming on and they might need somewhere to hole up, and if they chose to land on your neck there's not a damned thing you could do about it now.'

'Isn't there? Just let them try, that's all. Let *anybody* try —and that goes for you and your furtive underling also.' It cheered me just a little to hear Wainwright coming in for a bit of it. 'You can die on the doorstep from now on.'

'Big talk,' I said, 'but you've helped them once—and been paid extravagantly for it. They've got you in a clamp.'

'Their word against mine.'

'You're not a good enough liar to stand up against professionals.'

'I've learned a lot from you two.'

'But not enough. It calls for years of practice. Listen, whether you've been made a well-meaning mug of or not, the facts are there, and if *I* know them, other people do also. If they decided to put the crunch on you it would be done very expertly indeed. You probably wouldn't even be questioned by the authorities. You'd just be declared persona non grata in the secret files and this place would be closed down.'

'You people would be far more likely to put the crunch on me, as you call it, than they,' she said.

That one really hurt, but I managed to ride it. 'I don't think even you believe that,' I said, and then, since a pinch of fact in a welter of mendacity can often be more convincing than straight unmixed truth, I added, 'Wainwright has chucked his job with us, by the way—in order to help you.'

'Noble of him,' she said acidly. 'But who asked him to? Who asked *you* to butt in, if it comes to that?'

'*You* told him the facts in the first place—and your father, or rather Miraj Khan, sent for *me*. Nobody was spying on you, Claire.'

She sat staring ahead of her for a long time, then she said in a flat, tired voice, 'It's really a case of "a pox upon both your houses," but I don't seem to have much choice, do I? If I don't deal with one of you, the other will put in anonymous charges against me and I'll be closed down. That's what you're saying, isn't it?'

'Not quite. They would do that if it suited their book. Wainwright and I wouldn't. If you won't believe that, then there's nothing more I can do about it.' I rose and wiped my greasy hand on the seat of my pants and held it out to her.

'Thanks for the supper. Good-bye, Claire.'

She didn't take my hand, nor did she meet my eyes.

'You seem to know it all,' she said dully. 'What more can I tell you?'

'I know a lot,' I answered. 'But some of it is guesswork. Inspired guesswork, if you like—but still guesswork. Whatever you can tell me might help to crystallize things a bit more, and we'll be able to flush them out of this part of the country quicker—which incidentally means that you'll get rid of us also.'

She nodded slowly, considering, then she said, 'They turned up here one night—the doctor, with the patient on a stretcher carried by four Tibetans. Naturally I took them in without question. The patient was in a bad way. They, that is Dr Reutlingen and our own Dr Ram Piyare, worked all that night and the next day on him. I didn't think he had a chance—fractured skull, compound fracture of the right femur and multiple secondary injuries. Dr Reutlingen had been hurt also, but not seriously. He collapsed finally through sheer exhaustion. When he was able to talk he told me that they had crashed in a light aircraft up in the mountains. The patient was the pilot. They had been working on a documentary for a Swiss charitable organization—a television film that was going to show just what these people up here are going through. They had no authorization to be here, and if they had been caught by any of the three governments, Indian, Pakistani or Chinese, they would have been in serious trouble. I could quite understand that, so when Reutlingen begged of me not to report their presence here, I agreed. I can trust my own people, but to save gossip among the other patients we put the pilot in the mental ward, and mounted a guard over him. I didn't suspect that they were anything other than what Reutlingen had represented until——' She trailed off.

'Until what?' I prompted.

'Well—several little things. He told me the pilot was German-Swiss also, but then I heard him babbling in English when he was delirious. Then I found that he had armed the sentries—with pistols that he and the pilot had been carrying—and had given orders that they were to prevent anybody entering the ward without his specific permission. That naturally made me furious—*and* suspicious. I had it out with him. He was apologetic. He made amends by doing a lot of surgical work for us—Ram Piyare is a physician—and I was grateful. A routine patrol came round and I kept quiet and warned my staff to keep their mouths closed also. Then a letter came up the trail for me from James. It was in answer to one of mine in which I had mentioned these people. He said he was coming up to see me. I didn't want complications, so I decided to go down to intercept him at Ramabagh. I told Reutlingen that I was going to see my father, who hadn't been well lately. He raised objections—politely at first—then when he saw I was determined to go, he showed his hand a little more. He didn't actually threaten to stop me, but the hint was there. I got out at night. I met James down below—and we were attacked by a group of people one day. I didn't connect things at first—but then James told me about himself—what his real work was——' She broke off again, but this time I didn't prompt her. There was silence for a time, then she went on, 'You can probably guess my reaction to that. First you, now him, bringing your wretched intrigue up here. I couldn't leave him there, of course. It wouldn't have been fair to my father, who dislikes you people as much as I, so I brought him up here, and sent him on to the village.'

'Didn't you consider you were taking a risk in returning here yourself?' I asked her.

'I certainly wasn't going to be chased out of my own hospital by *that* creature. No, I came back quite openly. I told him I'd met another patrol on the way up and that I thought there had been some gossip about the presence of Europeans here, and that I wouldn't be surprised if we were suddenly subjected to a rigorous search. It seemed to have the desired effect, because later I heard him talking on the radio. They had brought it with them, but it had been damaged and it had taken him some time to repair it. He told me that the patient was now fit to be moved, so that they would be leaving within the next couple of days. He said that a helicopter would be coming for them at night, and asked my advice about a landing ground. We've had them here before, with army personnel, so I was only too happy to tell him about it—and to arrange about signal fires. Then you turned up—and you know what happened.'

'Did he suspect that you had anything to do with my arrival?'

'I don't know. Possibly. I played it down. You were either a thief or a beggar. We were used to that sort of thing. Anyhow, there was more radio activity after that —and finally they left—tonight.' She turned and faced me. 'That is absolutely everything I know about them—except that they paid me well—too well. The money will go into hospital funds, naturally.'

I said, 'Thanks. That ties in with what I already knew. I don't think they'll worry you again, but should they do so, get word down to Miraj Khan.'

'I'm not likely to do *that*,' she said flatly.

'Please yourself, of course,' I shrugged. 'But that would be the quickest way of getting them out of your hair—and we'd certainly counteract any damage they might try to do you as far as the authorities were concerned.'

'Good of you,' she said, and I don't think she meant it sarcastically. 'But no, Idwal. We're still poles apart on that subject. The more I see of your world the less I like it.' She held out her hand. 'Good-bye.'

I took her hand and held it for a moment, trying to look into her eyes, but she was avoiding me—then suddenly I had her in my arms.

'I can come out of that world,' I told her. 'Claire, give me a chance—please, darling, just give me another chance.'

But she was shaking her head from side to side, and her hands were pressed hard against my chest. 'It's too late, Idwal—don't you realize that—*too late*.'

'Wainwright—?' I mumbled, but she wouldn't answer that—and then I caught sight of us in the mirror. She, as lovely as ever, and me, dirty, hairy and stinking. Beauty and the Beast in a wrestling bout. I let her go, and laughed. It was about the only bloody thing I could do. She shoved me to the window and opened it. I climbed through and dropped to the ground. I looked back and saw her face for just an instant before she drew the curtains. She was crying.

I went back over the wall and found Safaraz, and we set off back to the village.

Chapter Thirteen

WAINWRIGHT was sitting at the side of the trail when we rode in at dawn. He looked as if he'd been there all night. I was too tired to face another argument, so I didn't rib him. I said, 'All right, they've gone.'

'How is she?' he asked anxiously.

'Sore.'

'At whom?'

'Both of us.'

'If I saw her I could explain.'

'You go right ahead then,' I said wearily. 'Me? I know a determined woman when I see one.'

'Where have they gone?' he asked, switching to another line.

'Sorry—that doesn't concern you,' I told him. 'Not until I know what you intend doing now, anyhow.'

'What are *you* going to do?'

'That doesn't concern you either,' I said. 'I don't want to be offensive, but you can see my position.'

'Yes, I can see that,' he said bitterly. 'And I can see how much you're enjoying it, you smug bastard.'

I reined my pony round and rode on into the village and went to the guest hut. He came to the door as I was lowering myself down on to the charpoy.

'We'd better have this out, hadn't we?' he said.

'What the hell's the good of that?' I answered. 'You just turn everything into a fight. Look, Wainwright, let's try and forget the personal angle of it for the moment, shall we? I'm following this thing up. You, on the other hand, tell me you've quit. All right then, surely to God you don't expect me to tip my hand to you, do you?'

'I merely asked if you were going back into India.'

'You did not. You asked me what I was going to do.'

'Well, I'm asking you now. Are you going back to India?'

'Part of the way, then I think I'll be turning off. I'll drop you at the hospital if you like.'

'You said that wouldn't do any good.'

'I didn't. You're putting words in my mouth. I told you to go ahead if you thought *you* could do any good for yourself. Now suppose you push off? I'm tired.' I shut my eyes tightly, but he didn't go.

'All right, I'm not quitting,' he said.

'Tell the Gaffer that. It's got nothing to do with me.'

'Let me stay on, Rees,' he begged, and there was despair in his voice.

'What can I do about it?' I asked. 'You've sent your papers in. *I* can't rehire you.'

'I told you—he didn't accept my papers. Officially I'm still in the Department. Damn it all, I *did* give you a lead up here, didn't I?'

And that, of course, was true. If he hadn't followed up Claire's letter I'd still be down in India in complete ignorance. At the same time the position was anomalous, to say the least. Could I, a part-timer, re-engage him, a regular incumbent? I could almost hear the Gaffer's reaction to that. Still, I did have discretionary powers. I looked at Wainwright, and believe it or not, I felt genuinely sorry for him. He reminded me of a prisoner waiting for the foreman of the jury to give the verdict. And most of it was my fault. I'd allowed my personal feelings and petty jealousy to colour the whole thing.

I said, 'I haven't the authority, Wainwright, and I don't know if the Gaffer will back my decision, but if you really want to go along on this, all right. But we'll get nowhere carrying on the way we've been up to now. It's got to be all or nothing. Now, for the last time, are you sitting in or aren't you?'

'I'm sitting in,' he said.

'Good—but somebody has to be in charge. I'm the fitter man at the moment, and I know this part of the world better than you. Do you accept my decisions from now on—without question?'

He nodded. 'Without question—and this time I mean it.'

'All right then. Let's get personalities out of it first. Claire is safe—for the time being. Those two have gone, but there's nothing to guarantee that they mightn't drop back in on her if it suited them. I don't think they'd risk strong-arming her, but she's terrified of being blackmailed.'

'You said she was sore at us——'

'And I'm saying so again. I didn't put in any knocks against you—I didn't need to. It's just that she hates the Business.'

'I don't blame her,' he said. 'She never had any trouble up here until we came along.'

'Exactly. I started it—you've added to it. Still, you don't have to take my word for it. If you want to call in to see her when we pass, that's up to you. *I'm* certainly not going to.'

'Nor me.'

'As you wish. Now, regarding the clients. They were picked up by helicopter last night. British pilot. I got close enough to hear them talking. They're heading for a place called Sitlo. It's about a hundred miles from here, across the hills. I haven't got a map——'

'I have,' he said, and made for his trail bag.

'That's fine,' I said, greatly relieved. 'It might have meant a trip down into India otherwise. I've never been there, but from what little I know of it, it's really out in the blue, and I haven't the faintest idea of the route from here.'

'What the hell are they doing out there?' he pondered.

'God knows. They mightn't even be there when we arrive—but that's a risk we have to accept—unless you have any better ideas.'

'None that occur to me at the moment,' he said. 'All right—so we go to Sitlo. What then?'

'You tell me. I'm playing things by ear. We just pick up what we can about them and bring it back. It's up to the Gaffer then.'

He brought the map to me and we spread it on the charpoy. The hospital wasn't shown, but it was easy to work out its position and drawn a line from it to Sitlo. The bearing, in the absence of a protractor, looked about two hundred and eighty-five, and the crowflight distance on the scaleline was a shade over ninety miles. Yes, it was quite easy on paper, but the closeness of the contour lines in between us and it appalled me. It looked as if we had the whole massif to cross, and there wasn't a sign of a trail. Wainwright whistled under his breath. We studied the map for routes alternate to the direct line, but the only practical one involved returning almost to Ramabagh and branching off north-by-east. I scaled out the distance, and gave it up when I reached four hundred miles.

'What do you think?' I asked him, hoping he'd be sensible and say not a chance, but he didn't. He ran his finger along various water courses and said we'd at least find sheeptracks, even if it meant doubling the distance.

'You're not fit,' I said, still hoping.

'Right as bloody rain,' he said stoutly. 'Look, if you're asking my opinion, I'd say let's go—take it blind—straight across country. Coming back won't be so bad. There's a trail direct from Sitlo back towards Ramabagh.'

'Right through the military zone,' I said gloomily. 'On the face of it I think it would be better to call it off and go back to India and report just what we know already. Let the Gaffer make the decisions then.'

There was a silence for a while, then he said bleakly, 'As you wish, of course.'

'Christ, what else is there for it?' I said impatiently. 'Look for yourself. Parts of this line cross the fifteen thousand foot contour. There'll be snow there now, and it will be lower by the time we arrive—even the valleys will be filled. Not a single village between here and there—so that would mean carrying ten days' supplies at least—and we haven't the necessary clothing. No—sorry—it's just not on.'

There was another silence. He walked to the door and stood looking out into the sunlight for some minutes, and then he came back.

'You're the boss, Rees,' he said. 'I accepted that, and I'm not going back on it—but I am asking you to let me have a go at it on my own.'

I shook my head firmly. 'Sorry,' I said. 'It would be rank stupidity for *three* of us to attempt it and it would be sheer suicide for one. Go if you want to, but it will be right in the face of my advice—and I'd have to make that clear in my debriefing. In fact I'd want a letter from you to that effect before you started.'

He sat down on the other charpoy, looking at the ground. 'You realize that this is my last chance, don't you?'

'Chance of what?'

'Everything. Look, Rees, I've made a balls of every damned thing they ever put me on.'

'We've been over all this before. It's not true.'

'It is. Any minor success I've had has been by accident—or because you've pulled me out of the mire.'

'Aw, hell,' I said exasperatedly. 'That one again.

Wainwright, I'm calling this off because it's just not practical. We wouldn't have a chance. I don't mind sticking my neck out if it's absolutely necessary—but I'm not chucking my life away just to prove to the Gaffer that I'm not chicken. Christ, the Gaffer would never know what had happened to us. We'd just disappear—and what good would that do you? You personally, I mean? Actually you'd be confirming what you are convinced is his opinion of you already. A bungler—a bloody fool—a player of Russian roulette. For what?'

He saw the light in the end, albeit reluctantly, and we started back at sunset. I wanted him to ride the whole way, while Safaraz and I took it in turns on the other pony, but he would have none of it, and insisted on putting in his full whack on foot. I halted when we reached the hospital and looked at him questioningly in the light of the lamp over the gate, but he shook his head and rode on.

We had no trouble crossing the confrontation line this time because, forewarned, I led well round the flanks in a wide detour, and we arrived at Ramabagh without incident two days later. I took the ponies back and saw the Old Man, leaving Wainwright and Safaraz waiting on the road outside.

The Old Man listened intently while I gave him a brief run-through of events. 'Who are they?' he asked when I finished.

'I don't know exactly,' I admitted. 'Let's just say that they're people from over the border stirring up further trouble between India and Pakistan. The main thing is that they've gone now.'

'Good of you to scare them off,' he said. 'But couldn't you persuade her to come down here for a while?'

'Could *you* persuade her to do something she didn't want to?' I asked. 'She's *your* daughter.'

He sighed. 'Time she was married—past time. If only

there was a man around with guts enough to take her on.'

'You find one. I know my limitations,' I told him.

'Where's that feller Wainwright?' he asked.

'Waiting outside. He knows *his* limitations, also.'

'Chucked him, has she?'

'Afraid so.'

He grinned. 'Can't say I'm sorry. Sounded a bit of a pansy to me.'

'He's anything but that. He's no particular pal of mine, but one has to be fair.'

'Well, there's no need for me to forget me manners,' he grunted. 'Bring him in. Stay a few days, both of you. Get some decent food in you, and clean clothes. You stink like a bloody polecat.'

'I'm afraid not, sir. We've got to move on,' I said, with genuine regret.

He walked with me to the gate and mumbled his thanks again. He wasn't good at thanking—or being thanked. I left him standing there—a lonely old figure.

Wainwright said, 'Where do we phone from?' when I rejoined them.

'I called from the post office last time,' I said. 'But I didn't like it. Too many small local exchanges to go through. I've got an idea. Let's go to Yev Shalom's. We're only a few hours from Lahore by bus and train.'

He nodded his agreement. Things were looking up. He hadn't argued about anything for the last three days.

Yev met us in the courtyard, ran an all-seeing eye over the three of us and led us off to the guest quarters without question. I'll not forget the sheer, blissful delight of that first hot bath. And his bounty didn't end there, because when we'd got the surface filth removed he sent a couple of enormous Afridis to lead us to the hammam, the Turkish bath as it was originally designed and before we of the West tarted it up. They ran it up to a temperature that would have killed us had it not been carefully controlled, then whisked us out into an ice-cold needle shower, then back into that searching dry heat, then into the shower again, half a dozen times, before thumping and kneading us and finally swathing us from head to foot in soft Turkish towels. I had just enough resolution to put a call through to the Calcutta controller before flopping on to the bed. He told me he'd call me back. I slept then.

The ringing of the bedside telephone woke me in what seemed ten minutes, but was actually three hours. It was the Gaffer. I mumbled that I had the lost sheep with me and a certain amount of news, hoping to God that he wouldn't want it then and there. He apparently didn't because he grunted to me to stop where I was until I heard from him. I was asleep again before I had replaced the telephone, and this time I didn't wake up until the following morning.

I went through to Wainwright's room. He hadn't stirred apparently throughout the night, although I noticed that he had clean bandages on his arm. Somebody must have been watching me, because when I got back to my room two servants were bringing in breakfast. It needed both of them—a huge steak still sizzling over a charcoal brazier, eggs done four ways, hot croissants, honey, fruit and coffee—and, as always, a bottle of the best scotch and a bowl of ice. It was worth a rugged trip through the hills just to come back to this. A barber came up then and shaved me and trimmed my hair, then I showered again and put on the clean P.M. clothes that had been laid out for me.

I began to feel guilty about Wainwright so I went through to him to wake him, but he was still out to it and I decided to leave him in peace. I went back on to the balcony and stretched out on a long chair with a Churchill-sized Romeo e Juliette from a humidor that somebody had placed on the table beside it. I had never felt so completely relaxed and rested in my life. But it didn't last for long—because the Gaffer arrived before an inch of carefully nurtured ash had formed on that perfect cigar.

He stood grinning down at me sardonically, then helped himself to a cigar, bit the end off it and lit it with a stinking petrol lighter. I shuddered.

'What's wrong?' he asked. 'Fever?'

'No,' I answered, closing my eyes. 'Just watching you handle that cigar. That would cost you two pounds in London—if you could get one.'

'What do you expect me to do? Get old Yev to circumcise it? Some of you dilettantes give me a pain in the arse.' He pronounced it 'dilly-tantees', which was just a pose. His French, like his German, Russian, Chinese and a round half-dozen other Eastern languages, was wellnigh perfect. Obviously this was to be a formal debriefing and he was following his invariable procedure of irritating the victim first.

'I've got very little to tell you,' I said.

'Blessed is he who expects nothing and gets sweet bugger all. The day one of you blokes comes in with a bagful and lets it go in its simplest form without the necessity for a stomach-pump, the sun'll rise in the west.' He expelled a lungful of smoke, coughed wetly, and added. 'Come on—let's be having it.'

'Wainwright's still with us.'

'In a pig's eye he is. I'm firing the bastard for once and for all.'

'That's your business——'

'Bloody good of you to acknowledge it—but suppose you stick to yours and get on with it.'

'If it hadn't been for Wainwright I wouldn't have got a lead at all. He got on to something and followed it up. He didn't have time to report back.'

'Balls. There's an emergency procedure for that—and he knows it. So do you.'

'In this case he *hadn't* time. I know the circumstances—you don't.'

'And won't until you stop crawfishing and get on with your report. What are you running? A mutual aid society?'

I said, 'I've fulfilled my contract in that I've brought him back. I'll put my bill in in the usual way.' I closed my eyes again.

He chuckled and said, 'They've got polyandry in Tibet, I know—but I didn't think it had crossed the Kashmir border yet.'

'I don't know what the hell you're talking about,' I said.

'Polyandry—the practice of a woman having more than one husband at the same time—like in California and London, only it ain't legal there.'

'What do you mean by that?' I demanded.

'Well, you're so goddam pally with him that I assumed you'd settled your differences and you were both screwing her.'

First I felt a complete paralysis, then it seemed as if somebody was pouring molten lead and icewater alternately down my spine. Then I thought I hadn't heard aright, so I repeated, 'I don't know what you're talking about.'

He said, 'Claire Culverton——' and I was out of that chair like a rocket, both fists balled. He didn't turn a hair. He just sat and looked up at me with a nasty grin twisting his blubbery lips.

'You filthy old bastard!' I said. 'Out—go on—*out*!'

He didn't move. 'Oh, come on, now,' he said. 'You don't think I didn't know about it, do you? Nice gal—sensible too. She puts the skids under *you*, anyhow—then Wainwright gets a rush of blood to the fork over her—about two years ago. I always thought that was why you and him never got on. Look, it's no good shaping up to me like Cassius Clay. I hope you're too much of a gent to clobber an old man—because this old man is still spry enough to administer the Pekin chop to anybody silly enough to try. All right—sorry. Little joke in bad taste on my part. Get on with it.'

I said, 'Fuck off, Gaffney,' and sat down again, weak at the knees. No, I wasn't playing the outraged squire of dames. It was just the shock of the thing. I didn't know a soul outside our own immediate circle—Claire herself, her father, Miraj Khan, Wainwright and I—knew anything at all about this—and here I was seeing the most private thing in my life being dragged out for inspection by this obscene old goat.

'Forget it,' he snapped. 'Rees, for Christ's sake, I'd expect that sort of reaction from Wainwright, but not from you. I've apologized. Now come on—I take it that Wainwright gets a lead from this bro—from Miss Culverton and goes belting up there without even letting the bank know, so we could cover him. That so?'

'More or less,' I said dully. 'But I still say that he had no option. He opened a letter from her late at night, and just had time to make the Delhi plane from Dum Dum.'

'All right then—that's not really important. What I want to know is *why* she wrote to him? I mean—had he blown his cover to her?'

'No,' I lied. 'She just mentioned in a general sort of way that two Europeans had called at the hospital—one was a German doctor who spoke Urdu but no English—the other was badly injured. She said that the doctor had asked her not to report their presence as they hadn't permission to be there. They were supposed to be working on a television documentary.'

'I see—so up Wainwright goes——?'

'Yes—to Ramabagh—her father's place. He got word to her that he was coming up for a short vacation, something they had discussed in the past. She came down from the hospital to meet him—or actually to stop him going up there, because by this time she was beginning to have her suspicions about these two. The doctor had tried to stop her going down, but she had slipped out. They apparently sent some people down after her, and she and Wainwright were attacked near Ramabagh. She then smuggled Wainwright back with her, because she didn't want her father to know anything about it, because the Old Man——'

'Doesn't like us—*any* of us. Yes, I know all about that. Go on.'

'Wainwright was shot in the arm during the fight, and was pretty well out of things until I caught up with him—' I went on.

'All right, I accept all that,' he said. 'But how did Wainwright get word down to *you*?'

'He didn't. The Old Man's assistant—an Indian officer—got worried——'

'Miraj Khan?' So he knew all about him too, did he? I had ceased to wonder at anything now.

'Yes, Miraj Khan. He knew I was in *some* sort of business, because he and the Old Man had helped me once in the past. He was worried——'

The Gaffer grinned amiably. 'So was I, by Christ,' he said. 'I thought things were being bruited far and wide. Not by you, of course,' he added hastily. 'Okay—I understand now. Go on.'

He heard me out then without further interruption, while I told him the rest. 'You've got nothing to worry about,' I finished. 'The Culvertons don't talk—nor does Miraj Khan.'

'Are you telling me?' he said sadly. 'I've been trying to get them on the books for a hell of a long time. Bloody handy they'd be up there. All right—so they're in Sitlo——?'

'We hope. They may have moved on by now.'

'We'll have to have a looksee anyhow. Don't worry about walking,' he said. 'If Yev can't whistle up a chopper to do part of the way, at least, I miss my bet.'

I sighed with relief.

'Now about Wainwright?' he went on. 'Do you still want him with you?'

I hesitated—then said yes. But even then he couldn't leave well enough alone. He grinned and said something about at least I'd be able to keep him out of the chicken run if I had him with me, or words to that effect. I swore at him again and went into my room, slamming the door in his face.

Chapter Fourteen

HE LEFT ME ALONE for the rest of the morning while he grilled Wainwright, so I lay on my bed and went through the London and New York papers which he had brought out with him. They were only a day old, because he had caught the London-Lahore plane within an hour of speaking to me on the telephone. The East Pakistan flood disaster which had drowned half a million people, and an alleged invasion of a West African state by Portuguese forces were claiming the main headlines, but the Palinovsky affair had not yet been pushed into obscurity. In a welter of surmise and claims to 'inside knowledge from informed sources', two facts seemed generally agreed upon. One, he was still alive, and two, whoever was holding him had upped the ante and was now trying to jack the Russians out of fifteen million dollars for his safe return. Two papers hinted at American interest and one stated categorically that Palinovsky had been on the point of defecting and that the Americans, also, had been asked for fifteen million for his delivery to them. The first to lay the money on the line got him, apparently. Proof that he was still alive was being supplied by the old gag of making him write messages on current copies of newspapers and sending them anonymously to both sides. The Russians, naturally, were not commenting, while the Americans were indignantly denying all knowledge—and interest—of or in the whole affair, but various people who claimed to know him had been shown the messages and were generally agreed that the Russian writing was in fact, Palinovsky's—thus proving that he was alive, at least on the dates of the newspapers. The last, it would appear, had been datelined ten days earlier.

The Gaffer came in just as I had waded through the lot.

'What do you think?' he asked.

'That there's no shortage of inspired liars,' I said.

'Naturally—but as always, there's a few grains of truth shining through the bullshit.'

'You pick them out for me.'

'Palinovsky's alive for a start. I know his writing. I'm no expert—but it's good enough for me.'

'How did you get to see it?'

'We're working in full co-operation with the C.I.A.'

'So what about these ransom demands?'

'Quite true—only it's not fifteen million. It's twenty.'

'Good God! Surely they're overcalling their hand?'

'They're not, you know. He's worth every penny of that to the West.'

'Then why don't they pay?'

He grinned. 'Because he's worth that to the Rusks also. At least, it's worth that to them not to let the Yanks get hold of him.'

'So why don't *they* pay?'

'Because it's developed into a bloody auction, that's why. Each side keeps upping the other's bid. Christ knows where it will finish.'

'But *why* is he worth that?' I asked.

'For the simple reason that he was K.G.B. Link.'

I shook my head. 'Sorry, you're losing me. What does that mean?'

'Crême de la crême,' he said. 'The milk in the bloody coconut. Wainwright would understand. Palinovsky was like a bank internal auditor. He could, and did, go into every Russian Embassy, Legation, Consulate and Trade

Commission in the world—I repeat, *world*—and demand to see the books. He could check on every agent, sub-agent, legman, torpedo, courier, pick-up and letterbox in the *entire world network*.'

'No man could remember it all,' I said.

'He wouldn't need to. Just a bit of it would still make him worth his weight in cut emeralds to our side. But in actual fact he's got all of it down in coded notes.'

I said, 'Where were they kept?' and he looked at me pityingly.

'I know you've been through a tough time, Rees,' he said, 'but that doesn't excuse bloody fool questions. Do you think we'd be chasing Palinovsky if we knew where his notes were? How the hell do *we* know where they are?'

'So it's just got to be Palinovsky himself?'

He smiled sweetly, like a proud parent whose little boy has come up with a really smart one. 'Just like you said—so it's *got* to be Palinovsky himself—and quick, because the Rusks are working like beavers changing their whole system. The sooner we get him the more of the old set-up we can penetrate.' He sat back and closed his eyes. 'God!' he breathed. 'Can you imagine getting him now?' He held out his cupped hand and snapped his fingers shut. '*Now*—just like that. They just wouldn't *have* a system. They'd have to abandon everything it's taken them twenty-five years to build—and start to build again—another twenty-five years at least. Twenty-five years without adequate Intelligence. Rees—the bastards would be dead. Don't you see?'

I saw all right. ' "Link", you call him?' I said slowly. 'It seems a damnfool thing to entrust all that to one man.'

He shot round and faced me. 'Good! You think that, do you? Right—think about it again next time you wail about not being told enough before you go out on a job. "*Need to know*." That's our Bible—the only one we've got. You can blow any bloody thing you like, by accident or design, but the explosion is contained, and the shock waves don't carry far—not compared with the Russian system they don't. Look, Rees—you've been working for me for five years, off and on, and what do you know of me, eh? Oh, yes—you know a bit of my background, maybe—the five per cent of the iceberg that sticks up out of the sea—but the real me—the other ninety-five per cent? Who *my* boss is? Where I get my orders from? How much authority I've got? Where I work from—where I live? You *don't* know. You don't know a damned thing about me—or about any other agent working in this sector, except Wainwright. You had to know about him, because you have worked together. Yes, think about it, Rees—and tell that silly sunnervabitch Wainwright to think about it too. That's been his trouble—"You don't trust me", he quavers, almost in tears—like a sweet little housewife when her old man starts getting ideas about the milkman. Well, he was bloody nigh finished this time, he was. I didn't think he'd defected. He's not the type—but he knows a bit more about the organization of things than you do—like he's got to pay other agents, so he's got to know 'em—therefore if he got taken by the other side he could blow 'em—and would, under torture—just like you would—or me. I didn't want him taken, for that reason. That's why I cleared him for torpedoing if necessary. Make no mistake about that. I meant it—and I expected you to carry it out if he wouldn't come back—*and* I'd have had you dealt with if you hadn't carried it out—or hadn't brought him back.'

He stopped, out of breath. It was the longest speech I'd ever heard him make, and it reacted on me like emery powder on prickly heat.

'Tell Wainwright that,' I snapped. 'Why blast off at me?'

'I have,' he said. 'That boy's had a rough ride for the last three hours. He'll probably cry on your shoulder about it, so I just wanted you to know the form. Nothing personal —not against you, I mean. That's why I wish to God you'd come in permanent—if you did I'd slide him out of it—out of India altogether, and you'd take over his sector.'

'I've heard all that before,' I told him. 'You can still stuff it up.'

I poured myself a stiff scotch.

'Think about it,' he grinned. 'He wouldn't be around then to roger your woman——' I chucked the scotch straight into his face. He half rose, then sat down again and wiped it off with a grubby handkerchief. 'All right,' he said. 'Let's skip the dramatics. I want you in on this job, as you know. I take it you're still with us?'

'Until you make another crack like that,' I told him.

'I'll watch it. I don't like to see good liquor wasted. All right—fine. Pull this off and the pay-off will be the biggest you've ever touched.' He was still mopping his face, not looking at me. 'You'll need it—because you'll never work for me again after this, you bastard.'

'Fine by me,' I said. 'Call it off now if you want to.'

'I *don't* want to. I need you, Rees—and while I need you I'll cherish you.' He reached for the bottle and poured himself a real slug—the first time I'd ever seen him do it—and his hand was shaking slightly. 'But when the job is over—win, lose or draw—*you* watch it.'

I laughed lightly and said, 'You can't frighten me, Gaffer.' Like hell I did. That one had gone home. He meant it to. No, I just poured myself another one and we carried on as if nothing had happened. I was wishing nothing *had* happened.

'All right,' I said. 'I'm in. What's the form? As you see it, I mean.'

'I don't see it.' He knocked back his drink in one. 'I know no more than you. Let's go over things again. Palinovsky is about to defect to the Americans. Palinovsky is skyjacked. The mob that is holding him demand the release of some two-bit political prisoners in exchange for him. The Indian Government agrees. Then they up their demands and ask for money as well. Again agreed. Demand upped again. They want an Arab political in addition. Again agreed. They shoot the Arab and kidnap Wainwright. Things stop there for a time—then demands for straight cash start coming in—and sky-rocketing. We play along each time. That's how it stands at the moment. Okay—what do we want? First and foremost we want Palinovsky—on the hoof, because only he can give us his lists. We'd like to get him for free, naturally, but it's so vital that we'll pay if necessary. I'm saying "we" because we're in with the Americans on this.'

'Are the Americans working on it simultaneously?' I asked.

'You bet your sweet life they are, but not in this sector—so you won't be crowded. But we pass on anything we pick up—and they reciprocate. Right, to continue—if we manage to locate Palinovsky, but can't get him out, we'd like him knocked off. That would stop this financial whirligig. All clear? Objectives, I mean?'

'Yes—got all that.'

'All right—now what do we know about the crowd that's holding him? Simple answer to that—plain damn nothing. First we thought it was the Rusks themselves, using it as a cover to liquidate him. The demand for the release of political prisoners was just to give it credibility—or so we thought. So we can now wash out the Russians——'

'But can we?' I butted in. 'They need hard currency. Couldn't they be working it this way? Get the money, then short change us on the handover?'

'How the hell could they do that?' he demanded impatiently. 'They know bloody well that we wouldn't hand over that sort of dough without safeguards.'

'I mean that they might give us Palinovsky back—but in such a mental state that he wouldn't be much use to us. It has been known.'

'Could be,' he said. 'But it's highly unlikely. We believe that the Russians genuinely are bidding against the Americans for him.'

'All right then—that only leaves the Chinese.'

'Rees—the only thing I'd bet my pay and prospects of a pension on—and I rate the latter higher than my mamma's good name—is the correctness and completeness of our F.E.32 List. That's a compliment. You helped to compile the last one. Nobody's working for them on this one.'

And that was as near unarguable as any premise in the Business. The F.E.32 List was a roster, amended almost daily and kept rigorously up to date, of all Europeans known to be working for the Chinese. Chinese, for obvious ethnic reasons, can't do their own spying in the West, any more than we can in China.

'So who?' I asked.

'Wild joker. Like I said before. Some organization playing their own hand—just for the dough.'

'By God, they'd have to be big,' I said.

'If my guess is correct they *are* big. Bigger than anything we've ever been up against before—and different. We're like top league footballers suddenly being called upon to play top league ice hockey.'

'Organized crime in other words?'

'Exactly.'

'Mafia?'

'It's not them.'

'How do you know?'

'On the surface the police forces of the world may not

seem to be doing too well against the Mafia, but in actual fact they've got them pretty thoroughly penetrated—Interpol this side, and F.B.I. coping with Cosa Nostra in America. Anything as big as this, they'd know.'

'But there *is* a political slant to it all,' I insisted.

'I don't think so,' he said positively. 'Yes, yes, yes—I know. They asked for the release of political prisoners in the first instance, but in my considered opinion that was a bloody big fat red herring. Don't you see—? By giving it a political slant in the first instance they've got every Intelligence agency in the world—on both sides—buzzing—working against each other, treading on each other's toes and, more importantly, hampering the ordinary police. A shambles going on for weeks, with the papers, TV and radio screaming their heads off, during which time these people have got their prisoner safely tucked away, and their tracks covered. Then the real business starts—the cash end of it.'

'That's where they'll come unstuck. That sort of money couldn't be kept underground.'

'That's where you're wrong,' he said. 'The bigger, the safer. Swiss banks never reveal sources of payment. Skyjack dough almost invariably goes to one clearing house in Lausanne. Within a week of receipt it's been changed half a dozen times—dollars into pounds, pounds into Italian lire, pesetas, Belgian francs. The original dollars don't come back into circulation for a year or more—and then in small packets in Cape Town, Buenos Aires, the Persian Gulf. Try tracing it back then.'

'I see,' I said slowly. 'But all this is still assumption. I mean the money hasn't been paid over yet.'

'Not the Palinovsky money—but this isn't their first dabble. If my theory is right these people started in business a couple of years ago. At first it was straight skyjacking—Cuba, Jordan, Greece. A gun in the pilot's ribs and he flew where he was told. Then the airlines tightened security. The skyjackers beat them. The airlines tightened up further—tightened to a point where it was impossible to be jumped in the air again—so this crowd went into something else—straight old-fashioned kidnapping. They snatched a French industrialist first, then the small son of an immensely rich German banker. They collected a hundred thousand dollars for the first—chickenfeed to their previous takes—but they missed out on the hundred and fifty thousand they were asking for the boy, and damned nearly got caught. Can you guess why?'

I shook my head.

'Because the police of different countries work in with each other—directly and through Interpol. We in the Business don't. Like I said, once the political angle comes into it we're all loners. A top Scotland Yard dick can sit round a table with the Sûreté Nationale, F.B.I., German Kriminal polizei and the Carabinieri and they all lay their cards down face up. Can you imagine us buggers doing that? It'd be against the laws of nature. The British sometimes have a loose working partnership with the C.I.A., like in this one, but we never completely trust each other. Knowing this, I think they've hit on the idea of giving things a phony political face to keep the police out of it. And, of course, dealing with Government money they can raise the stakes way up out of sight. What individual would fetch twenty million dollars from private sources?'

'How much of this is theory, how much fact?' I asked.

'Ninety-five per cent and five per cent respectively,' he answered promptly.

'Give me the five per cent.'

'They snatched two foreign diplomats in South America a year ago. They were fronting as Maoists then. They demanded the release of certain political prisoners, who had to be flown to Algeria. One government agreed—the other stuck its heels in, so they shot that one.'

'I remember those two cases,' I said. 'There was no money involved in either.'

'There was,' he said positively. 'A million bucks each. That detail was kept dark. No government likes to appear a bunch of tightwads bargaining for a man's life with dirty dollars. Kept to political prisoners it's principles. The crowd that actually *was* flown to Algeria is still there, begging round the souks. Nobody wants them.'

'So that's fact, is it? Where did you get it?'

'That's fact. Where I got it from doesn't matter, but if you think it does, it came from certain high-up officials in the Uruguayan, Brazilian and German police respectively—all of them furious that we cloak-and-daggerers wouldn't let them combine and get on with the job. Yes—it's fact all right.'

'Is it too late to get the police in with us now?'

'The Americans are sensible,' he said. 'They always work with their own police—C.I.A. through F.B.I. down to State level. Our police don't come into it because this crowd hasn't worked in England—which doesn't mean that they won't some time in the future if it suits them. Out here I did get the Indian police in on it—after a hell of a fight—but you know what happened to Nadkarni. They pulled out quick after that. Pakistan? Not a chance. They're too preoccupied with their semi-hot war with India. That leaves the Russians. I hardly need tell you that there's not a chance there either.'

'So it's us—on our own?'

'Us, on our own, cocker, just like you said—and all we've got to go on at the moment is a possible link between the original ambush and these people who may, or may not, be sitting high in Sitlo. Pardon the pun.'

'Two of us against the whole field.'

'Two and a half. I'm staying out here until this is wrapped up, or we've drawn a complete blank.'

'Who's the half?'

'You've thrown a slug of scotch into my kisser, but don't be *too* cheeky. We keep Wainwright in as the bumboy—*faute de mieux*.'

I said flatly, 'Nothing doing—for two reasons. If Wainwright is kept on you've got to stop riding him into the ground. Given a chance he's all right.'

'Just my little joke,' he said. 'What's the second reason?'

'I'm not taking you up to Sitlo. You'd never make it.'

'You're goddam tooting you're not taking me up to Sitlo. Think I'm nuts? No—I'm establishing temporary H.Q. right here.'

'Will Yev stand for that?'

'You leave Yev, and all other Children of the Widow, to me,' he said, and it was the first I knew of his being in the Club too, but it did not make me feel any more fraternally towards him.

'How much of all this have you told Wainwright?' I asked.

'General outline—nothing in detail. You can tell him as much as he needs to know, according to the situation. He knows already that you're in complete charge, so you won't have any trouble on that score.'

'All right,' I said. 'Suppose we get down to briefing?''

'Whenever you like—sooner the better.'

'I want maps—and I also want Wainwright in on it,' I said. I expected argument, but he just nodded and went out. I poured myself another drink. Things seemed to be going fairly smoothly, but I was still shaking inwardly. He, the Gaffer, with a glassful of whisky in the chops. Yes, I'd *have* to watch it when this was over. Well, at least it had made up my mind for me finally. This would be my last job for him—and I couldn't see myself working for anybody else. Not this sort of work, anyhow.

He came back after a while with a roll of Ordnance Survey of India maps under his arm, followed by a completely expressionless Wainwright.

'Okay,' he said. 'Let's get down to it. Yev says he can have you put down in the area by chopper tonight.'

Chapter Fifteen

THESE MAPS WERE BETTER than the one Wainwright had given me, and in them Sitlo stood out in all its starkness. It was just a dot in the middle of nowhere—literally—because the upper slopes above the dot were marked 'Unsurveyed'. It was exactly two hundred miles ENE of Lahore, and not a road or a railway ran nearer than a hundred and fifty miles of it, though a trail back into India proper was indicated—and marked 'Impassable between November and May.' It was now October.

'Don't let that worry you,' the Gaffer said. 'We can pick you up when you're ready to come out.'

'How will you know when we're ready?' I asked.

'You'll be taking a VHF set in with you. Yev's radio man will be listening in on a fixed frequency every night between ten and twelve.'

'How heavy is the damned thing?' I asked sourly. I hate radio at any time, particularly if I have to hump it.

'Does it matter?' he snapped. 'You'll cache it near wherever he sets you down, and you'll come back to it.'

'Fine,' I said. 'Just so as we don't finish up fifty miles across the hills from where he sets us down—and the batteries don't go flat in the meantime.'

'Tell him all about it, Wainwright,' said the Gaffer tiredly.

'Inert sealed pack,' Wainwright said. 'You activate it with a flask of acid when you're ready.'

'Sort of thing they teach you on the Course,' said the Gaffer. 'Pity you never went on one.' That had always been a sore point with him. He was proud of the spy school, which he himself had set up in an old rambling country house in the Wirral, and he was inclined to regard my refusal to go there as a personal affront.

I said, 'I know Yev maintains his own communications centre here, but how the hell is he able to whistle up a helicopter, just like that? I thought private flying had been clamped down on tight in these parts.'

'Not Yev's private flying. He's sub-contracting on the Indus Dam scheme—flies the engineers around and does their aerial survey work for 'em.'

'Yes, but even so,' I said doubtfully, 'isn't somebody likely to start asking questions? The Indus Dam is away to the north-west. Our route is almost due east—smack across the military zone—terra interdite.'

'Forget it,' he snapped. 'Sit back and enjoy the ride. Yev isn't risking an expensive chopper just because he likes us. He knows what he's doing. Anyhow, the gink *you* saw made it all right, didn't he?'

That was true, certainly, and I drew a little reassurance from it. I put my finger on the small dotted rectangle that marked the abandoned airstrip. 'That's all we know,' I said. 'He was making for here. That being the case, I'll want to be set down at least ten miles from it. Does our pilot know that part of the hills?'

'According to Yev, no. He's a new boy—not long out.'

'I want to see him—now,' I told him.

'You can't. He's out on a job with the engineers, and won't be back until nightfall.'

'Then we put it off,' I said flatly.

'You can't do that either,' he answered. 'Sorry, Rees—nobody's being awkward, but that's just the way it is. He's due back on the Indus tomorrow and he will have to stay there just as long as they want him—and God knows how long that will be. Tonight is the only time we can have him—and even then it's going to be as tight as a badger's arse.'

'Do you realize what we're asking him to do?' I raged. 'A blind flight in the dark, with not a known landmark—just the occasional bunch of oil lamps in the villages we pass over—villages that aren't even marked on this map. He's got to locate Sitlo somehow or other, then judge where the airstrip would be, then try to work out a spot some ten miles from it—then finally come down in the dark—without signal fires. It's impossible.'

'The difficult we do immediately—the impossible takes just a little longer,' he quoted. 'Okay—so you're going to walk it, are you? Sooner you than me—but please yourself.'

It was a hell of an alternative. I looked at Wainwright, but got no help there. He was looking blankly non-committal.

'How good is this pilot?' I asked the Gaffer.

'Search me. He's Yev's man—and that cookie demands the best for any money he pays out. Let's ask him.' He went out, and came back some minutes later with Yev, who pursed his lips and fingered his chin.

'A good man, Idwal,' he said. 'I don't employ others. He flies that machine well, and services it himself. Yes—a good man——'

"But——?' I said, watching him closely.

He spread his hands. 'He came to me from London, well recommended by the company who supplied the machine——'

'But—?' I said again. 'Come on, Yev—you're stalling. That's not like you.'

'I am not stalling,' he said sharply. 'What I am trying to say is this—without giving rise in you to doubts—I have not employed him in any work of a confidential nature. All has been open. He has flown only with the sanction of the government. Your work *is* confidential. It is also dangerous. I have therefore to warn him of this beforehand—to give him the option of declining it if he so wishes. He is a young man—adventurous—so I do not think he will decline it, especially since Mr Gaffney is willing to pay danger money at a high rate. But his discretion—whether he will keep silent afterwards——' He spread his hands again.

'He's a talker, in other words?'

'How do I know, Idwal Rees? That which he has done for me *could* be talked about without harm. What I am trying to say is that I cannot give guarantees. I can warn him——'

'And by Christ, so can I,' said the Gaffer. 'He gets a damn nice bonus for this—but it carries a three monkey pledge with it. See nothing, hear nothing, and above all, say nothing afterwards—not if he wants to stay healthy.'

'An empty threat,' said Yev quietly.

'You think so, do you?' the Gaffer chuckled dryly.

'I *know* it, my friend,' Yev told him. 'That young man is in my employ. Even when he is flying for you he is still in my employ. I would not willingly see one of my people dealt with as roughly as you imply because he indulged in a little youthful boasting.'

He turned to me. '*You*, I think, understand what I am trying to say?'

'I do, Yev,' I said. 'For all you know, the chap's all right—but you've never had occasion to test his discretion, so you can't vouch for him.'

'Exactly.'

'Very good,' I went on, my mind now made up. 'We take precautions. One, he mustn't know that Wainwright and I are Europeans. Two, he mustn't be given the slightest inkling that this is in any way Intelligence business. Can you think of a plausible reason why three

Punjabi Mussulmans would be wanting to be dropped out in the wilderness like this?'

'Sheep,' said Yev promptly.

'Sheep?'

'The flocks are coming down from the hills now. Soon will be the time of buying and selling in the fairs at Jullundur and Amritsar. I could be sending my agents up to make their bargains in advance.'

'Bloody good,' said the Gaffer approvingly.

Yev smiled. 'It *is* bloody good, as you remark, Mr Gaffney. It's something I've never thought of in the past—but most certainly shall in the future. Forward buying.'

'All right then,' I said. 'Third point—the less he sees of the three of us the better. I gather that we'll be taking off after dark?'

'You will—from my own airfield the other side of the Ravi. It is ostensibly a night flight to test instruments. It has been done before—genuinely.'

'Fine—then that being the case, somebody else had better brief him, and we'll keep our mouths shut and our faces muffled. What languages does he speak?'

'Only English.'

'Couldn't be better,' I said. 'Now, about the briefing?' I turned to the Gaffer. 'Could you do that?'

'Are you nuts?' he asked. 'Of course I couldn't do that.'

'You never went on one of your Courses, I take it?' I said innocently. I put a mark down on the map arbitrarily, ten miles to the east of the airstrip. 'Quite simple really. You've just got to tell him that he's to find that place on the ground——'

'Funny feller,' he sneered. 'You know damn well what I mean. I *wouldn't* do it.'

'I shall do it,' Yev said. 'Just give me the co-ordinates of that spot, Idwal.'

I measured them exactly with the protractor, giving the

full six figures of both eastings and northings and interpolating the height between the contour lines. In theory the pilot could do it quite easily by dead reckoning—two hundred miles on the correct compass course, checking on a bearing to the lights of Sitlo—always providing that there *were* lights at Sitlo, and that his compass was absolutely accurate, and that he was able to estimate distance flown from his instruments—and that cross winds did not blow him off course, or head winds cause him to overestimate—or tail winds to underestimate. Any one of those factors could, I knew, throw him out by as much as twenty miles. A combination of more than one of the factors—I shivered and stopped thinking about it.

'It's the pick-up that will be chancy,' I told Yev. 'It doesn't matter quite so much if he's a bit out the first time—but he's got to come right to the same spot when we whistle him up. We can help him a bit there, of course. If it's at all possible we'll have four fires going in a hundred yard square—and I'd like a couple of powerful electric torches. We'll flash a series of dots upwards as soon as we hear him overhead.'

Yev noted it all down and nodded. 'He is a good man,' he said. 'Technically a *very* good man—and, as far as I can judge, in the matter of integrity also. I have no fears myself—but I had to warn you, Idwal.'

'I know,' I told him. 'And I'd back your judgment as unquestioningly as my own. Thank you, Yev.'

'Thank me when you return,' he said. 'Now let me find Solomon, so he can arrange for all your needs. Come back safely, Idwal Rees.' He went on.

'That's another cookie I'd like to get on the books permanent,' the Gaffer said, sucking his teeth. 'How about talking him into it, Rees? There'd be a bonus in it for you.'

'I'd sooner sell my grandmother to a brothel,' I told

him. 'And now push off, will you. Wainwright and I have to work our lists out.'

He went off looking sour. If he had an administrative weakness, it was that. He could not bear to be kept out of anything, however trivial. On the yearly confidential report form that went in on each of us was a question: 'Does he show balanced judgment in the delegation of duties to his subordinates?' If I, God forbid, had been his boss I'd have blackballed him on that one.

Solomon drove us out to the small airfield as soon as it was dark. We were sweating like June brides under our heavy mountain clothing but I knew that we would be grateful for it up there in the hills. He had once again fitted us out with a kit that was a miracle of compactness while still covering most foreseeable contingencies, packed into three manageable loads, with the radio disguised in a fourth bundle.

'The old man and meself briefed the pilot,' he told me. 'He looked a bit old-fashioned about it, but he'll do it all right if anybody can. Good lad—name of Grant. Used to fly choppers in the navy before he signed up with the company.'

'Can he keep his mouth closed?' I asked.

'Why shouldn't he? He's got a good job with us—with a nice little bit of extra lolly for this caper,' he said. 'Anyhow, what's he got to talk about? Three wogs being dropped in the hills on a bit of private business for me father. Nothing to electrify the boys at the club in that.'

The big helicopter was idling on the pad in front of its hangar when we arrived, and the whole place was lit up like a ballroom, so we kept in the shadows until our stuff was loaded and it was pushed out into the centre of the field, then we slipped across and climbed in the back in the darkness. Solomon gave a thumbs-up sign and muttered 'Okay, Idwal—we'll be listening in every night as from tomorrow. Best o' luck.' Then the door was slammed and the engine opened up, and we lurched into the air in the disconcerting camel-like manner of all choppers.

Lahore below us was a huge island of lights in a surrounding sea of darkness. The cloud base was low that night and I could see our flashing light reflecting back off it, but after a while it went out, and only the dim glow of the shaded cockpit lights up forward relieved the pitch darkness. We sat hunched on the floor of the freight compartment, and Safaraz, who disliked flying even in a relatively stable fixed-wing aircraft, after rumbling gloomily for half an hour, was finally sick. He went to sleep after that.

I was conscious of Wainwright's silence. We had hardly exchanged a direct word since our return, and yet I did not feel that he was sulking. He was just crushed. It was in an effort to get him back on to an even keel that I had insisted on the Gaffer's including him in on the final briefing, but even there the old devil had been vicious. He kept implying that Wainwright was only in it at all because he was a skilled radio operator, and I wasn't, breaking off in mid-sentence and saying, 'But I've briefed you on that, Wainwright, so we needn't go into it again,' or 'Full "need to know" procedure will be observed throughout this operation, Wainwright—I don't have to impress that on you, do I?' etc. etc. I expected Wainwright to blow his top at any minute, and I, for once, wouldn't have blamed him. I have said that I would have faulted the Gaffer in his inability to keep his nose out of detail work. On looking back I could add another to that. He couldn't keep his personal spleen under control either. He certainly had it in for Wainwright. And, I reflected wryly, he had it in for me now also.

I said, 'How are you feeling?' just for something to say.

'All right,' he said flatly. 'You needn't worry.'
'I'm not. You'll have to watch that arm though.'
'Yev's doctor has seen to it. It's practically healed.'
'I'd better tell you what I intend doing when we get up there.'
'Do I need to know?'
'I wouldn't tell you if you didn't. Anyhow, I'm open to any bright ideas *you* may have. I think we ought to concentrate on the airstrip first. See if it shows signs of recent use. If we're lucky enough to get a lead there, we'll follow it up. If we're not, we'll have to start getting in among the local residents—bending our ears around the chaikhanas for gossip—that sort of thing.'
'You're assuming that they are still in that area?' he said doubtfully.
'We've got to assume *something*,' I said. 'Where else could we try at this stage? That fellow on the stretcher looked too sick to be moved far. I think they must have some sort of at least semi-permanent hole-out up here.'
'They've moved him once by helicopter. Couldn't they have done so again?'
'That's what I'm basing my premise on. They have a helicopter at their disposal. If they were moving out of the area altogether wouldn't they have gone to a more accessible spot than this? I mean, why bring him up here to the edge of nowhere first?'
'To transfer him to a fixed-wing aircraft—something bigger—perhaps.'
I said, 'I think you have a point there—although I hope you haven't. There are lots of abandoned airstrips along the Indian frontier, far more accessible than this one we're going to.'
'Yes—but would they be as unobserved?'
'Some of them. Anyhow, if it comes to that, proximity to an airstrip isn't so important. They could put down in any

quiet spot back in India and then transport the guy by car.'

'Transport him where?'

'How do I know? Your guess is as good as mine. As I see it, they've got to have a place where he can stay until he's fit to travel—up on his feet again—because a man on a stretcher is conspicuous. The hospital suited them ideally, but Claire scared them out of there by telling the German that she thought she was due for a going over by the police. No, I still think it's a logical conclusion to assume that they're going into winter quarters in Sitlo. Here's hoping, anyway.'

He was silent for a time, then he said, 'All right then, supposing they are there—what then?'

'That will all depend on how many of them there are,' I said. 'If it's only the doctor and the patient we have to deal with, there'll be no problem. We arrest them and bring them back to Lahore in this thing.'

'Arrest them on what authority?'

'Gun law. I'd say that we were Indian plainclothesmen and that we had reason to believe that they were prohibited immigrants—aliens in a forbidden zone—and that we were taking them back to New Delhi for questioning. Once we got to Lahore we'd whip them along to Yev's place after dark and put them through it.'

'Just suppose they are in fact what they represent themselves as,' he said. 'Television people—no connection with the ambush crowd?'

'They're still on the wrong side of the law. They asked Claire not to report them to the authorities, remember. We could always hold that over them. No, I can't see any squawks going in about unlawful arrest, even if they're as pure as the driven snow. They'd get a stern warning from either the Gaffer or myself, fronting as Indian police officials, and they'd be turned loose with an injunction to keep their noses clean and their mouths shut. Can you see any holes in that?'

'I don't think so. Whatever they are, I don't suppose they'd worry Claire again—and that's the only thing I'm really interested in now.' He was silent again for a long time, then he said, 'What happens if it's a true bill? If, for instance, the doctor is the chap who was holding me?'

'No problem there, either,' I said. 'They'd have to answer three questions. Who are they? Who's employing them? Where's Palinovsky?'

'You think they'd talk?'

'I'm bloody certain they'll talk. The Gaffer has got sky-jacking, kidnapping, extortion and murder stacked up against them—and the death penalty still applies in both India and Nepal. Oh, yes—they'll talk all right.'

'You think he'd play it legal?'

'*He* wouldn't play it any way at all. He'd just see that the evidence went along to the Indian police, and then fade out. That's if the clients were lucky.'

'If they weren't lucky——?'

'He'd play it highly *il*legally. Do his own interrogation. I wouldn't like to be on the receiving end of that myself. He learnt the business in China.'

'Ugh, the filthy old bastard.'

'As you remark—Ugh, the filthy old bastard. Anyhow—I've told you everything now,' I finished.

'He won't thank you for that.'

' "Need to know". You heard him say that. I think you do need to know.'

He said, 'Thanks,' quietly, and then I think he went to sleep. I know I did.

It was the changed note of the engine that woke me. I looked at the luminous dial of my watch. We had been up something over two hours, which meant that we were somewhere in the vicinity. I crawled across the floor of the freight compartment and wiped a small window clear of mist. There was a three-quarter moon and I could see snow-covered mountains rising all round us in a solid, frightening phalanx. The air was turbulent and the chopper was dancing and lurching. Safaraz had awakened also, and was being sick again. Faintly in the dim glow of the cockpit light I could see the pilot's back. He appeared to be quite unperturbed, and I felt that nice reassured feeling that all scared passengers draw from the sight of a professional doing his job without flapping. Then I felt Wainwright tapping me on the shoulder.

'Look down,' he said, and pointed to the larger window on his side.

I peered through it and saw two pinpoints of light below us, then, as the chopper swung, I saw a third—then a fourth—and they were in the form of a square.

And if that wasn't enough, a light started to blink right in the dead centre of it.

'It looks as if we're expected,' said Wainwright dryly.

Chapter Sixteen

I WENT THROUGH TO THE COCKPIT in a headlong rush, pulling out my gun. I jammed it hard behind the pilot's right ear and yelled, 'Go up—*up*—do you hear?' He turned and looked up at me, and I saw his face for the first time. It was the man who had picked up the German and the patient.

He stared at me, startled, then said, 'Unless you want to be smeared all over these hills, you'll get out of here and leave me to handle her.'

'The moment she touches down I pull this trigger,' I told him. 'Do you understand?'

He hesitated, and I jammed the gun in again, painfully. He winced and then nodded, and made adjustments to the control column and throttle, and she checked, juddered and started to rise. Through the Perspex bubble I saw the lights below slide past us and recede.

Behind me, Wainwright said, 'Get his headphones. I think they're talking to him.' I pulled them off. A crackling voice was saying, '—Angels One. What the hell's the matter with you? Over.'

Without a moment's hesitation, Wainwright pushed the button of the chest mike and said, 'Angels One. My cyclic pitch has jammed. I'll have to go up to try and shake it loose. Call you later. Out.' I really admired him for that. That was quick thinking.

I said to the pilot, 'Right, Grant, we know all about you. Just put us down in a nice quiet spot about ten miles north-west of here.'

'Get stuffed,' he spat at me. 'What do you think this crate is? Ali Baba's magic carpet? I'm not putting her down anywhere where there isn't a properly marked landing ground.'

'Okay,' said Wainwright over my shoulder. 'Get your arse out of that seat, and I will.'

Grant turned and looked at him for a moment, then he grinned ironically and unbuckled his straps. 'All yours,' he said, but when Wainwright started to squeeze past us, he changed his mind. 'No, if it's all the same to you, I'd rather not risk it.' He pushed the control column and we went into a tilted turn. 'You may be a hot pilot, but I'd sooner you were checked out under less hairy conditions than this. Ten miles north-west, you say? Do you know what the terrain is like?'

'Sure—nice and flat,' I told him.

'Like hell it is,' he said. 'Look at the chart. There's a bloody great mountain roughly five miles ahead of us on this course.'

'Go round it,' I directed. 'Put us down in one piece and you've got a chance. Get clever and I'll blow your head off—and my friend takes over.'

'I doubt it,' he said, 'but I'm in no position to argue.' He peered forward through the Perspex. 'See what I mean about the mountain?'

I did. High above us the snow-covered crestline was showing white against the dark sky. Wainwright craned forward and looked at the compass.

'Course three-one-five,' he said. 'Put her on reciprocal —one-three-five.'

Grant nodded and brought her round. Wainwright was straining his eyes out into the darkness, and I realized that he was checking to see whether or not the signal fires were still in sight. They weren't. 'All right—back on course,' he said, but right at that moment we ran into cloud—thick and impenetrable, piling like cottonwool against the Perspex, and the chopper was being shuttlecocked up and down in wild turbulence.

'You crazy bastards,' Grant screamed. 'I told you——'

I prodded him with the gun and said, 'Do as you're told, or get out of that seat.'

He pulled her round again, and I could almost hear his teeth chattering. We came out of the cloud and the mountain ahead of us swung back into sight—a tilted white plain with black patches of rock thrusting through the snow. Grant yelled, 'We'll be into it in a minute. Let me deflect round the shoulder!'

I looked questioningly at Wainwright. He had switched on the light over the chart-flap in front of Grant. 'Port twenty degrees,' he said, and Grant sighed gustily with relief. The crestline dipped into a saddle before us on the new course, but it was still above us. Wainwright jerked at my sleeve and drew me back.

'We're over a pass here,' he muttered. 'It looks as if it's full of snow. It would cushion things a bit if he put her down here.'

'You're the expert,' I answered. 'You'd better handle her yourself. He's gone chicken.'

'Don't be stupid,' he said. 'I've never been in one of these bloody things in my life before.'

I stared at him, the pit of my stomach doing somersaults. I took a deep breath, swallowed hard, and got my voice under control before moving back to Grant.

'Put her down,' I said.

'You goddam fool,' he howled. 'It's all snow!'

'Sure,' I said. 'It'll cushion her.'

'But there may be rocks, pits, crevasses underneath the damned stuff.' He grabbed my arm. 'Look—whoever you are—call it off. I've got enough fuel to get back to Lahore, but only just.'

And for a moment I was tempted to take him up on that, but then Wainwright butted in. 'Put her down, you windy bastard or I'll do it for you,' he said, and clipped Grant over the ear, painfully.

I hate to think back over it. The wind was funnelling down the pass and it was making us dance like a drunken dragonfly. I could see the sweat beading Grant's face as he eased her down—lower—lower—until we were in the spindrift being whipped up off the surface. Then there was a soft thud underneath us, and I breathed freely again, but not for long, because she rocketed up then, hovered, stood still, then plummeted down again, lurched to one side and finally came to rest at a steep angle.

Grant was slumped in his seat, making whickering noises, Wainwright and I were in a tangle on the floor, and Safaraz, whom I had forgotten, was looking wretchedly through the door from the freight compartment, calling aircraft and all kindred inventions of the devil some very dirty names.

The radio had come to life, and I could hear a crackling in the earphones.

I picked them up.

'Angels One—calling—calling—calling. Do you read? —Over,' I heard, then, 'I say again, Angels One. Do you read? Over.'

I switched it off and drew Wainwright to one side.

'How far do you think we are from those fires?' I asked him.

'Fifteen minutes flying,' he said. 'Knock off five for the turn-about we did—say anything between ten to fifteen miles north-west of them.'

'Do you think they might have seen us land?'

'What, in this ice cream sundae? Not a chance. *Look out!*' He lunged past me and dived on Grant, who was just picking up the earphones and chest-mike. He hit him really hard this time, then turned to the set and pulled out various plugs and leads.

'You're making it hard for yourself, Grant,' I said.

'I was only picking the bloody things up in case somebody trod on them,' he snuffled.

I told Safaraz to search him, then stand over him, and I tried to open the cockpit door, but realized that I was pushing against solid snow. Wainwright found a shovel and an axe strapped to the bulkhead then, so we levered the door open a few inches and scraped a hole behind it, and eventually we were able to tunnel our way out.

Picture a large family-sized dining-table covered with a white cloth and tipped to an angle of forty-five degrees, then put a spot right in the middle of it. The spot was us. We had gone right in, so that only the tip of the rotor pylon and a small segment of the tailspinner were above the surface, and as soft feathery snow was falling it looked as if it would only be a matter of time before these, also, were covered.

It was about as neat and thorough a camouflage job as I've ever seen.

'What now?' asked Wainwright.

'Nothing until daylight,' I said. 'Let's get back in out of the cold. I've got a question or two to put to sonny boy in the meantime. Incidentally he's the pilot who picked up those two from the hospital.'

'Then how the hell does he come to be working for Yev?' Wainwright asked in tones of deepest wonder.

'I haven't the faintest idea,' I said, 'but I'm going to find out—and quick—even if it has to be done the rough and nasty way.'

'I hope he'll be sensible,' Wainwright said. He didn't like the seamy side of intensive interrogation.

'I don't think he'll be difficult to crack,' I said. 'He certainly wasn't too eager to call your bluff in the air.

Congratulations on that. You scared the pants off me. Come on.' I dived back into the burrow.

Grant was sitting on the floor with his back against the sloping bulkhead, nervously eyeing Safaraz, who was absently playing with his Khyber knife.

Now that the engine was dead the heaters weren't working, and the cold was intense, although the battery-powered lights were still on. I snapped all of them off except the one over the chart-flap, which was on a universal swivel. I turned this one full into Grant's face, while we sat behind it in darkness.

He blinked nervously at us. He was somewhere in the upper twenties or low thirties—goodlooking in a smooth-faced, toothpaste-ad sort of way—gingerish, with a trendy shoulder-length hair do. He was in every way a type which reacted on me like poison ivy.

I said, 'I haven't much time, Grant, so you can either answer my questions without finagling, or I'll have this Pathan take you outside and cut your throat.'

He blinked and shivered and his tongue flickered round his dry lips.

'There's no need for that,' he bleated. 'What is it you want to know?'

'Who were those people you were handing us over to?'

'I don't know.'

I told Safaraz to give him a Peshawar shave. He chuckled and bent forward and got a handful of Grant's hair and jerked his head back so that the skin of his throat was stretched tight, then he stroked him gently on the carotid with the razor edge of his knife.

Grant screamed.

'Who are they?' I asked again.

'I tell you I don't know—I don't—I don't—I met a man in the club who offered me a job——' he chattered.

'Go on,' I said.

'Let me go—*please*—tell him to let me go——' He was in a lather.

I grunted to Safaraz, who released him.

'He knew I was flying this thing for Mr Shalom, and he asked me if I'd do a little job for him on the side. I'd be helping somebody who was in trouble, he said.'

'And Big-Hearted Grant, Everybody's Friend, said yes, of course. What was the job?'

'A sick man to be picked up from near a hospital in the hills——'

'And taken where?'

'Brought up here—just where I was going to drop you. He told me that I'd be given every help from the ground —both that end and this—but even so I didn't like it. You don't seem to realize how dangerous it is flying a chopper in these hills, especially at night——'

'But you still did it,' I said. 'Actually on the night of the seventeenth. Yes, we know that. Cut out the bullshit, Grant, and get on with it.'

'I dropped him here. He was on a stretcher, and there was a doctor with him——'

'A German by the name of Reutlingen—yes, we know that too. You see, we know a lot—so don't risk whipping in a crafty little fib from time to time, or that knife will do more than tickle you. You dropped them up here. Who did you actually hand them over to?'

'Just a bunch of wogs. There was a white man in charge of them, but he didn't speak to me directly until I asked him a question about the route back—then he was bloody rude.'

'In what way?'

'He told me to start up and sod off, and if I ever opened my yap about this, I'd be rubbed out.'

'All right—now the man down in Lahore—the one who retained you? Who is he?'

'His name is Robson—he's got a small import-export agency—offices on the Mall near Nedou's Hotel.'

'What was his interest in the matter?'

'He said that there was a girl up there running this hospital. She wanted to help these people—he wanted to help *her*.'

'I see—like we said—just pure goodness of heart all round.' I stretched my foot out and kicked him hard on the shin. He yelped, and tears came to his lovely big sad eyes. 'Goodness of heart and what else, you little fart?'

'Five hundred pounds sterling,' he whimpered.

'Right—go on. We come to this job now. Who engaged you for it?'

'Mr Shalom himself, and his son Solomon—so I thought it was quite legit. I thought you were two Indians going up to buy sheep. Then when I saw where it was you wanted to be set down I got worried. I knew the terrain now, and the thought of landing without markers terrified me—so I phoned Robson. I asked him if it would be possible for him to make the same arrangements with these people—to set out lights, I mean. I said I was willing to pay.'

'What did he say to that?'

'He questioned me about the job, then told me that he'd call me later—and that I was to keep my mouth shut in the meantime. He came to my hotel about an hour later. He said I was to carry out this job, and that there would be marker lights set out for me, like before, and he gave me a radio frequency to use when I got within twenty miles of the estimated position. That was all. I didn't know that I was doing you or anybody else any harm. Just the reverse. It would now be a safe set-down.'

'But you never thought of mentioning any of this to Mr Shalom?'

'How could I? That would have meant telling him that

I'd previously used his helicopter—without permission when I was supposed to be out night-testing instruments.'

'I see. Now think hard. Is there anything you've missed? Anything at all, however unimportant it may seem to you?'

His face wrinkled, then he shook his head. 'That's the lot,' he said.

I stretched out my foot and kicked him again, harder. He screamed.

'The money you took the girl at the hospital?' I said. 'Hadn't you forgotten *that*?'

'I didn't know it was money,' he wailed. 'Robson just gave me an envelope to give her. I'd forgotten it.'

'Well don't forget anything again,' I warned him. 'I told you we knew a lot already. All right—what did the German and the patient tell you during the flight?'

'Nothing—not a damn word. They never spoke. I don't think the German spoke English, and the other fellow was too sick to talk. Anyhow, I don't make conversations during a nightflight—it's too tricky handling the bloody thing at the best of times.' And I was in wholehearted agreement with him there.

I thought for some time, then I said, 'All right, Grant. I think you're in one hell of a position.'

'You don't have to rub it in,' he sniffed dolefully. 'I did a bit of moonlighting that meant no harm to anybody—I even paid for the fuel for the trip out of my own pocket, *and* tested the instruments at the same time. Now I've landed myself in all this.'

'You're telling me?' I said, and started counting on my fingertips. 'Taking and using an aircraft without the owner's permission. Flying in a prohibited area. Aiding and abetting a gang of international heroin smugglers. Kee-rist! Under Indian Law you've chalked up about fourteen years already.' He moaned softly. 'That's if I decided to hand it over to the policc. If I *didn't* hand it over, you could find yourself in even worse grief.'

'I've still got the five hundred,' he said hopefully.

'You're going to need it.'

'If you need it more than I do——'

'Ah, trying to buy my silence, are you? To bribe me?'

'Yes,' he said simply.

'Good. I'll collect it off you when we get back.' I looked out of the window behind me. The rising sun was playing multi-coloured tricks on the edge of the snow surrounding the pit. 'All right, now get outside and tell me whether this thing will ever fly again.'

He climbed out ahead of us and inspected the rotor blades critically. 'One of them will need a torque wrench on it,' he said, then went and looked at the tail. 'Possibly all right, but I won't be able to tell until I start her up—then she's going to take a hell of a lot of digging out.'

'Keep on looking,' I told him, then Wainwright and I retired some distance up the slope out of earshot, while Safaraz brewed tea and warmed chapattis over canned heat.

'What do you think?' I asked.

'Write me down among the naïve,' Wainwright said, 'but it rings true to me. A yellow little jerk twisting on his employer. I didn't think he was making any of it up. He was too darned scared.'

'I'm inclined to agree with you. The thing is, what the hell are we going to do with him?'

'Leave him here—fixing the radio so that he can't talk to anybody,' Wainwright suggested.

'There's always the chance that he might get her flying again, and go off and warn somebody,' I said.

'Take him with us—hands tied, gobful of cotton-waste kept in position with insulating tape? That's what the bastards did to me.'

'Bloody nuisance. He may be one of those magnificent young men in their flying machines, but he still looks a city sparrow to me. He'd slow us up.'

'What then?'

'There *is* only one thing for it,' I said, and he looked as if he wanted to be sick. 'No—I don't mean to knock him off. Let's dig him out and send him back. Calculated risk. We promise to hold off from the police, and also not to put the mockers on him with Yev, just so as he returns direct to Lahore. That way I can send a long code message to the Gaffer, and he can start doing something about our friend Mr Robson.'

'Um—I see what you mean,' he said dubiously. 'There's always the risk that he'll fly off to Them, though.'

'I doubt it. Of course I *could* send Safaraz with him to make sure——'

'But you'd rather not. I don't blame you.' He looked away into the distance. 'I take it you want me to go with him?'

And I couldn't do it. It would have been the sensible thing—but I just couldn't. 'Christ, no,' I said. 'I need you with me.'

He didn't say 'Thanks'—that would have been too embarrassing for both of us, but I could feel his relief.

I went on, 'We'll hold him here until just after eight, then get him off. We'll get through to the Gaffer on our set at ten, just before Grant arrives in, and he'll pick him up and keep him out of mischief.'

'I think you've got it,' Wainwright said.

Fortunately the snow had stopped by now and we were able to clear right round the chopper, so that her rotors had a full circumference. It kept us warm up until mid-afternoon, then Grant got in and started her up without much difficulty—but he had a tricky task in readjusting the pitch of one of the rotors. He lifted off then, with

Wainwright beside him in case he got any ideas, and then set her down again and said he was reasonably satisfied.

I sat in the snow working out a message to the Gaffer in our standard random code, and when I'd finished it I sent for Grant again.

'We're giving you a break,' I said, and he looked as suspiciously at me as a Persian being sold a carpet by an Armenian. 'It's not that I think you deserve it,' I went on, 'but we can use you. Go straight back to Lahore and deliver a message to somebody there, and thereafter keep your mouth shut, and we'll say nothing either to the police or to Mr Shalom. As far as you're concerned you put us down here, and had a slight mishap, but everything is now okay again. That way you keep your job—and don't eat curry and rice in an Indian jail for the next decade or so.'

'How do I know you'll stick to that?' he asked.

'You don't know—but maybe you'd like to hear the alternative?'

'Go ahead.'

'We wreck the chopper and leave you here with it.' I saw the fear that leapt to his eyes. 'Your chances of walking out without supplies or a knowledge of the hills would be negligible. I reckon you'd survive maybe three or four days.'

'I'll take you up on your offer,' he breathed.

'Wise man,' I said. 'And I'll be wanting that five hundred you were talking about, when I see you again.'

'Sure, sure,' he agreed. Graft he understood perfectly.

'Well, that's fine,' I said. 'Just one thing to clinch matters.' I slapped the VHF set which Safaraz had unwrapped from its bundle. 'We'll be in touch with them down there. You'll be timed, and a friend of ours will be waiting for you. Don't get any ideas about calling in anywhere else en route. Pull a fast one on us, Grant, and

I promise you that you'll be picked up as soon as you show your nose out of these hills—anywhere and everywhere. No place to hide. Get me?'

He nodded and moistened his lips again.

'Right,' I said. 'Well get those engines warmed up. You take off at eight.'

Chapter Seventeen

HE LIFTED OFF just before eight o'clock, without too much difficulty, although the wind had risen again and was buffeting down the pass. In the faint moonlight that came intermittently through the scudding clouds we watched him hover and circle, then set off due west. We had taken every precaution we could think of against a doublecross, even to wrecking his radio and landing lights, so that his only chance of making a safe descent would be on a properly lighted, plainly marked landing ground, but I was still worried and I found myself indulging in a welter of argument, counter-argument and self-justification. We should all have gone back with him. We had a lead there now in this man Robson. No—that way we would have lost valuable time. Our abortive landing would have scared them and they might even now be taking off for somewhere else, and the trail would be broken. I should have sent Safaraz back with him. No—I needed Safaraz up here with me. I should have wrecked the chopper and left Grant to die here. No—I had no right to rob Yev of a highly expensive piece of equipment which he needed in his business and had lent us purely as a favour.

Always it came back to the one indisputable fact—that I should have sent Wainwright with him. Against that I could put up no argument at all. I had taken a totally unjustifiable risk here, because I hadn't the moral guts to put paid to Wainwright's last chance to redeem himself.

I wouldn't willingly go through those two hours again.

We sat in the snow hollow while he activated the batteries and tested his circuits. He had done it all in a practice run-through before leaving Lahore, but here the light of the shaded torch was inadequate and his fingers were frozen, and he was muffing things badly. He was also worried about the fixed frequency. It was very close to that which Grant had been using in the aircraft, which meant that anybody listening in up here might easily cut in on us. For that reason I had decided not to risk anything *en clair*. I would give my number in Urdu, followed by the words, 'Pilau kharab', which to us meant 'Bad security'—then I had a message already prepared in the five-figure blocks of our random code—'Helicopter due back with you now Stop Pilot insecure Stop Carrying message Stop Acknowledge when all clear Ends.' I could imagine the Gaffer wondering why the hell a message had been entrusted to an insecure pilot.

Wainwright started calling at exactly ten o'clock. He was still calling at midnight. We gave it up then.

He said in a flat voice, 'I'm sorry, Rees. I've got the power, my circuits are correct and the frequency is fixed, as you know. Theoretically we should be in contact—but we're not.'

'Are we blanketed by the hills?' I asked him, and he shrugged hopelessly and pointed to the map.

'Not according to this,' he said. 'Here's our position. High ground to the north and east, but sloping away to the west. No, you can put it down to an unexplainable atmospheric phenomenon, or a typical Wainwright cock-up—whichever occurs to you as the more feasible.'

'Don't start feeling sorry for yourself,' I told him. 'What I know about radio, plus a nickel, wouldn't buy the ghost of Gandhi a haircut. Let's get going in the general direction of the airstrip. We'll take the set with us and try again tomorrow night.'

Safaraz and I shared the contents of Wainwright's pack between us and I let the latter carry the set. It was heavier than the pack and he felt better sweating under this self-imposed penance.

I had been up the snow slope during the day and taken compass bearings on the northern and eastern peaks. The route back to the airstrip appeared to be fairly straightforward. It was about twelve miles away in a direct line, and the valley below us appeared, on the map at least, to lead directly to it. We ploughed down the slope through the powdery top snow until we reached the inevitable water-course in the valley bottom, then turned south along it. The going was heavy at first because, although the snow was kept clear down here by the funnelling wind, there was a carpet of ice over the goat track that skirted the stream, and we kept slithering and falling in the dark. But we were at least going downhill, and therefore getting below the freezing temperature of the upper slopes.

We came out of the water-course at dawn, and the whole valley was spread below us. It was a huge bite out of the surrounding ramparts of the Himalayas themselves, a dozen miles or so wide at the mouth and running back into the hills perhaps twice that distance. To the west was the hot Indian plain shrouded in morning mist—to the east, the snows.

Through the centre of this valley ran a river, which I identified from the map as the Ravi—the one on which Lahore was built, two hundred miles to the west. It was still below snow level down there, and the slanting rays of the sun were showing up the terrain in bas-relief. The floor of the valley was as broken and tumbled as a brown blanketful of child's buildings blocks. Stunted trees grew along the line of the river, but other than that there was no vegetation to be seen except patches of thorn scrub. Here and there in the far distance I could make out small fields, but only from their symmetry because it was too late in the year for standing crops.

I combed the ground with my binoculars, counting only half a dozen tumble-down mud huts in the whole area until, in the far eastern apex of the valley I made out a sizable village. I took a compass bearing on it and confirmed from the map that it was Sitlo. But of an airstrip, abandoned or otherwise, there wasn't a sign.

'Sitlo it will have to be in the first instance,' I said to Wainwright. 'And a bastard of a trek it's going to develop into. Look at that ground.'

'No sign of a trail in or out of it,' he said, peering through the glasses.

'It will probably be running along the river bank,' I told him. 'Hidden by the trees. The question is do we make for the nearest point of it and put a possible five miles on to the trip over easier going—or strike out obliquely over the rough stuff?'

'Up to you,' he said.

But it wasn't. Safaraz was much better at this sort of fine judgment, so I put it to him.

'There *is* a trail beside the river, sahib,' he confirmed. 'Look hard and you will see it through gaps in the trees. It is the only way into the valley—and if we use it other people will be using it too. I say the rough way.'

He was right, of course, so we brewed coffee and ate again, and then rested for a couple of hours before starting the climb down.

And a hell of a climb it was too. The stream we had been following came out through a gap in the cliff wall behind us and fell in a white pencil a sheer thousand feet before hitting a ledge and bouncing out in a smother of foam to fall another thousand feet to the valley bottom. Trees and clumps of shrubbery growing in the niches helped a little, but at times we found ourselves on patches of naked cliff face, desperately searching for toe and fingerholds. I told Safaraz, surefooted as a goat, to take the radio and thought he had done so, but Wainwright, still sweating out his penance, wouldn't hand it over—and half-way down the inevitable happened. It got caught up in some scrub and he had to slide his arms out of the carrying-straps to free himself, then he slipped, and the set fell like a plummet the whole way. It was the last straw for Wainwright, and I thought for a moment that he was going to jump after it. He clung to the cliff, white and shivering with rage and shame, and Safaraz and I had to climb up each side of him while I talked some sense back into him.

'What the hell does it matter, anyhow?' I said. 'The bloody thing wouldn't work.'

'God damn it!' he yelled. 'I'd have *made* it work—*tonight*. It was our only link. We won't know now whether or not that bastard made it back or flew off and warned these people. We can't call the bloody chopper when we're ready to go out. It's my fault—my bloody fault again—why the hell didn't you send me back with Grant?'

'Because I needed you up here, you stupid bastard,' I told him. 'Now go on—down you go, before I take a swing at you.'

He was right of course. I'd been pinning my hopes on that damned set. I had intended to halt when we got to the bottom to give him the opportunity of overhauling it properly in daylight. And now the set had gone and I was stuck with a crumbling man. It had been his *raison d'etre*. With it he had felt he had a place and a purpose with us, and that now he was just a passenger. And there again he was right.

I tried once more to reassure him when we got to the bottom, but it was no use. He snarled, 'Stop playing the comforting nursemaid, Rees, for Christ's sake,' and thereafter we marched in silence, if you could call it marching.

The terrain was worse in actuality than it had appeared from up above. It was just one seemingly endless plain covered with rocks that were too far apart to allow jumping, and too higgledly-piggledy to form reasonably straight paths between them, so it was one continuous climb up and slide down, with the ever present liability of losing direction. We made, I think, about two miles in the four hours we had left before sunset.

But at least we were able to camp comfortably that night, well down in a crevasse with a warm fire going under an overhanging rock, and we cooked a solid and satisfying meal. We all felt the better for it when we woke at dawn next morning, even Wainwright, who I gave the job of checking the map and working out our position by dead reckoning, because down here we could see nothing but the tumbled rocks around us, and the surrounding hills where all landmarks looked alike. I worked out our position also, and when we compared results we agreed to within a few hundred yards of each other. The river lay away to our right, about some three miles, and according to this the airstrip should have been ahead of us another five, but I'd lost faith in it. There undoubtedly had been an airstrip somewhere, but it had merged back into the terrain since the war, and had just been marked in arbitrarily on the map by someone since. What Grant had landed on last time, and almost this time, was probably just a natural clearing in these rocks, or perhaps even a patch of cultivation.

I debated on the advisability of swinging away to our right and making for the river, because water was going to be a problem before long, but decided to play it safe at least for the next few hours and continue on the line we were on. Wainwright came up with a good suggestion which saved us a lot of time in line-checking. I would take a bearing from the map, then climb on to a high rock and send Safaraz out on the bearing on the ground, four or five hundred yards in advance of me. Then Wainwright would go out and pass him, continuing in the same line for as far as I could see him, and would halt on another high rock. All one had to do thereafter was to keep the distant man in sight, leap-frogging each other and checking only occasionally on a back-bearing.

It was while we were doing this in the early afternoon that we came to the airstrip. One minute we were doing the mountain goat act over the rocks and the next Safaraz was yelling to us from out in front.

There it was—a strip about a quarter-mile long where the rocks had been pushed back into a rough perimeter on three sides. The fourth side was the river, running swift and deep at the bottom of a sheer drop of some fifty feet or more. The alternately frost-riven and sunbaked earth was cracked and crevassed and thorn bush was growing in patches, but there was nothing wrong with it that fifty or so coolies with mattocks couldn't do to make it serviceable. There were even the remains of a rough stone-built control tower at one end, and dispersal bays had at some time been cleared irregularly to one side. We spread out and started to walk the length of it, and almost immediately Safaraz shouted. He had spotted the fresh ashes of a fire—and then Wainwright found another, and then it was an easy matter to find the other two, which completed the square.

I climbed up into the crumbling control tower and ran my glasses round in a full circle. The place was completely deserted, but I knew we would have to be careful from now on. I stayed under cover then and kept Wainwright with me while Safaraz bird-dogged around. He came back with the complete picture.

'A path, sahib,' he said. 'It starts from those trees over there, where once a hut has been built, and runs north east. Ponies have been over the path recently, because there are fresh droppings there. There is a durga there also —a devil-frightener like these damned idolators put up to scare people away—two durgas—a lady showing her this and a gentleman showing his that. Very vulgar.'

We checked with the map again. I had done the cartographer an injustice. The airstrip was just where it should have been. I realized now why I had missed it when viewing the ground from up on the cliffs. Subconsciously I had been expecting to see a concrete runway, symmetrical and easily recognizable. This was just part of the landscape. It had been well constructed nonetheless, and apart from the superficial signs of wear had stood the test of time well. It would originally, of course, have been just for emergencies—the odd Dakota struggling over the Hump on its way back from the long wartime haul to Chiang Kai-shek's China. They'd have had a primitive radio beacon here, and a fuel dump, and the strip would have been outlined with oil 'gooseneck' lamps when required, with an R.A.F. corporal and half a dozen poor devils of erks running it. A place of ghosts.

I went over with Safaraz to the ruins of the hut. Inside it was a pile of freshly cut brushwood and a battered oil drum that had held kerosene, and each side of the doorway stood a crude clay figure as frankly obscene as a lavatory wall graffiti—the animist equivalent of 'Beware of the Dog' which would be quite sufficient to make the average superstitious Hillman keep a respectful distance. We inspected the path. It was obviously an old jeep track, although no wheeled traffic had been over it for many a year as the rough wall each side had collapsed and fallen across it in places, but ponies had used it recently.

The village was out of sight from here, but I judged it to be some two miles away and that the track went straight to it.

I said to Wainwright, 'Well, we're in the same parish anyhow. They're here—somewhere. Let's get away from the strip just in case somebody happens along.'

We went back among the rocks and sat huddled in a council while Safaraz brewed coffee and warmed chapattis over canned heat.

'Europeans,' I mused. 'Semi-permanent camp. They certainly wouldn't be living in the village. Too many people pass through the chaikhanas and caravanserais. It would be something on the outskirts—possibly a farm-house.'

'It shouldn't be hard to check,' Wainwright said. 'The place isn't all that big.'

'The village itself isn't,' I agreed, 'but there are possibly dozens of farms tucked away up the side valleys. Unless we get a lucky break it's going to take time.'

'How much time have we got? Before the trail is closed, I mean?'

'Not quite a month, according to the map footnote—but I'm hoping the Gaffer will have acted before then.'

'How can he act if we don't get in touch with him?'

'He knows the position now from the report I sent with Grant. When he doesn't hear from us tonight or tomorrow he'll assume that something has happened to us and he'll probably come up with Grant himself for a looksee.'

'Always assuming that he *has* got your report,' Wain-wright said gloomily. 'That's been bugging me all day. The possibility of Grant's having doublecrossed us after all.'

'Forget it,' I told him. 'He knows he's got a chance if he plays along with us—and *more* than a chance of finishing up in an Indian jail if he doesn't. The Grants of this world play it safe.'

'He might have thought better of it once he got in the air.'

'Like hell. He couldn't get in touch with anybody by radio. He is far too careful of his own neck to risk setting down up here without lights—therefore there's only one place he could go. Lahore. He knew we would be in radio contact with them, so they'd be expecting him. He also thought I had a vested interest in keeping him out of trouble with either the police or Yev.'

'What was that?'

'The five hundred pounds. To him I'm a bent cop on the make. That would be something he would understand and appreciate. No—Grant will be firmly on the side of the angels now.'

'I hope you're right,' he said, still gloomily.

'I think I am. So do you, really—but if we're both wrong, we've still got a saver.' I was sweating in my efforts to get him out of the slough of guilt he was wallowing in.

'What?'

'If the Gaffer doesn't show up here by the day after tomorrow we'll assume that either Grant has doublecrossed us or that he's crashed on the way back. That being the case, you and I will continue our efforts to find these people's hide-out and I'll send Safaraz back on foot with a message.'

'That will take a hell of a time, won't it?'

'According to the map it's seventy miles to the nearest railhead—a place called Pathankot at the foot of the hills. It would take him a day and a night—the way *he* travels. Then it's only four or five hours into Lahore by train.'

He brightened visibly, so I went on, injecting far more optimism into it than I was really feeling: 'All right, Course One—Grant has arrived back and the Gaffer has my report, which was, in brief, that we now know that there's somebody up here and that we're going to look for them. He will accordingly be expecting us to call him tonight. The call doesn't come. He'll wait a further twenty-four hours. Still no call. Knowing him I would bet on his coming up himself then—probably bringing three or four Indian Special Branch men. With me so far?'

He nodded.

'Grant will make for this spot. If he comes by day we'll go out on the strip and identify ourselves. If it's by night we'll morse upwards with a torch, "Pilau safe", as soon as we hear them overhead. Got that?'

'Yes.'

'Meanwhile two of us will go on a recce to see what we can pick up—but one will have to remain here constantly.

'That will be me, of course,' he said, and for a moment I thought he was back in the doldrums, but he went on, 'You two are better with the language, and Safaraz couldn't send morse.' It looked as if he was climbing back and seeing sense once more.

'Good,' I said. 'Well, Course Two—if there's no sign of the Gaffer by the day after tomorrow, Safaraz starts back, and you and I keep digging. Tonight I'll go out on my own for a preliminary nose round.'

We watched the sun go down, then I set out. Wainwright was quite cheerful, but Safaraz was miffish about being left behind. It was like driving a pair of bullocks in a Punjab cart. You can never get both the bastards pulling together at the same time.

Chapter Eighteen

I LEARNT VERY LITTLE on that stroll. The track from the airstrip joined the main one that ran beside the river after half a mile, and then continued into the village, which consisted of two parallel streets and a small central square. The houses were mud-and-stone built, single-storied for the most part, and such shops as there were fronted on to the square. A few of them were still open. A tailor, cross-legged and hunched against the cold, crouched over his handcranked sewing-machine in the guttering light of a hurricane lamp—a couple of silver-smiths, guarded by the inevitable watchman with a muzzle-loading shotgun, tapped on miniature anvils—a grainshop was still functioning, and there were no less than three chai-khanas, open-fronted and noisy, with huge tea kettles swinging over charcoal braziers.

This cheered me. Chai-khanas are where one picks up gossip—chai-khanas and doctors' surgeries. There was one of the latter next door to the tailor's shop, plastered with notices in Urdu, Nagri and, impressively, English, proclaiming the practitioner to be one Doctor Bhansi Lal, 'Specialist in Aryuvedic, Tibetan & Western Medicine, Obstetrics & Pocks Cured or Money Back'. I made a mental note of this one. If all else failed, a visit tomorrow with some excruciating symptoms plus a little judicious pumping, might yield results.

I thought of spending an hour or so in a chai-khana, but decided against it. A man on his own is conspicuous, and excites speculation. Two or more, talking naturally to each other, attract no undue attention. This would be a job for Safaraz and myself tomorrow. The morning food market would be another covert worth drawing too. Shopping for the ordinary Indian household is normally done by the women, who buy their grain, ghee and vegetables by the pennyworth daily. Europeans, even up here in the wilderness, would inevitably employ a cook, who would buy in bigger quantities. The main thing was that I had at least got the layout, size and feel of the town.

I found my way back to the airstrip without incident, until Safaraz suddenly loomed up in front of me with the point of his knife stopping a bare millimetre short of my Adam's apple. I jumped and cursed him. He loved doing that. We settled down in our hollow and I looked at my watch. Just after midnight. I could picture the Gaffer fuming and swearing in Yev's radio centre. I wondered if he had already gathered in the man Robson, and what he had twisted out of him. He might even now know more about things up here than we on the ground did——

And then I heard, high above us but unmistakable, the faint clacking buzz of a helicopter. Safaraz heard it too, but we had to wake Wainwright. We stood up, straining our ears. It seemed to pass overhead, and the sound died away to the south.

'A wild one,' I said. 'Probably military.' But then we heard it again, more distinctly, as if it had swung round and was coming back, lower. And then, almost overhead, we saw a single flash of light.

'Not military,' I said. 'In this sector he would have his blinker light going.'

'Perhaps these people have another chopper on tap,' Wainwright suggested.

'They can't be expecting one or they'd have the fires going,' I said.

'Then who?'

'How the hell do *I* know?' I snapped.

'Grant? He *has* doublecrossed us——'

But I rejected that one. 'Grant would only have gone to one place,' I said. 'Lahore, like a homing pigeon—and once there he wouldn't dare to pull a fast one, for the simple reason he believed us to be in radio contact with the Gaffer. No, he's handed the letter over, the Gaffer has leaned heavily on Robson and has got enough out of him to come up here pronto.'

'Would he risk it at night—without signal fires?' Wainwright said doubtfully.

'It would be a bigger risk by daylight,' I said. 'Two military zones to fly over—Indian and Pakistani. He could possibly clear it with one, but not both—so there'd always be a chance of the other crowd sending up a fighter if they saw him.'

There was another flash then, directly overhead.

'Bloody good instrument flying if it *is* him,' Wainwright muttered.

'Don't forget he's been here before, and he's probably taking a cross-bearing on the lights of Sitlo,' I said, more to convince myself than him.

'Grant was terrified of a blind landing,' he answered.

'He'd be a damned sight more terrified of the Gaffer breathing down his neck,' I told him. Then I made up my mind. 'I'm going to risk it.'

'What? The fires?'

'No time,' I said, rummaging feverishly in my pack. 'No—our codeword, "Pilau".' I grabbed the torch and climbed over the rocks towards the strip. 'You and Safaraz cover me from different points, just in case.'

I went out into the centre of the strip and pointed the torch upwards and flashed 'p-i-l-a-u', and almost immediately a shaky 'a-c-k' came back. That would be the Gaffer, I decided. His morse was even worse than mine.

Lower and lower he came. He was too far to one side, so I flashed a series of dots rapidly, and he corrected. Then he was right above me and I could feel the down-draft of the rotor, and the noise was deafening. His landing lights snapped on and I was in the centre of a blinding circle. I waved jubilantly and then stepped out of it, and something hard jabbed into my back.

'Get your hands up and keep them up,' a man's voice roared in my ear over the noise of the engine, and jabbed again, harder, to emphasize it.

Another man ran into the circle of light and waved both his arms and then skipped back to safety, and the engine, after a final burst, cut out, and the chopper settled, and the silence was broken only by the dying clack of the rotor. The other man went back into the light then, and I saw that it was the German doctor.

The man behind me said, 'Thanks for the assistance, fella. We didn't need it really. We've been talking the bum down for the last hour.' I turned my head and the gun went into my back harder. 'Watch it.' he warned, then he yelled into the surrounding darkness. 'You other two out there—come in with your hands up or this guy gets it—right in the back.'

Grant had jumped down now. Just Grant—nobody else. He came towards us, daintily pulling off his gloves. 'Hairy, ducks,' he beamed. 'Just plain bloody hairy—but I did it.' Then he recognized me and spat in my face—not full-throated Eastern fashion, which I could have borne—but delicately, like a deb clearing the tip of her tongue of a shred of cigarette tobacco. The man behind me must have sensed the tensing of my muscles, because he jabbed me again, and said, 'Hold it!' Then he said to Grant, 'Get the hell out of it, you goddam fag, or I'll turn him loose on you.' He raised his voice again and called. 'You'd better come on in. The strip's surrounded and you haven't a chance. I'm going to count ten, then I'm pulling the trigger on your pal if you're not in here. One—two—three——'

I bellowed in Urdu, so they could both understand, 'Khara ho jao—dono!' (Stay where you are, both of you.) The gun went in really hard this time. 'One more break like that, fella, and it will be your last,' he said, and then added, 'You can belt him now, pansy, but you better be standing well to one side when I reach ten. Four—five—six—seven——'

And then Wainwright, the bloody fool, came in with his hands up, just as Grant took a swing at me. He dropped his hands and let Grant have it under the angle of the jaw—a beautiful curving left hook.

And the man behind me removed the gun from my back just long enough to shoot Wainwright straight through the head.

I'd gone down on my knees under the impact of Grant's punch, which hadn't been flowerlike, and the man spun round with the gun pointing straight at me. And he actually got the shot off, but it was wide, because half his head had disintegrated under the heavy bullet from Safaraz's rifle. I dropped flat, tugging my gun from under my left arm, and scuttled lizardlike out of the light. The German doctor had gone back to the helicopter and had taken out a package. He turned gaping at the sound of the shots. He must have been a quick-thinker, because the package had a red cross prominently marked on it and he held it up in front of his chest, yelling in terror, 'Nix shoot! Nix shoot! Doktor!' But Safaraz must have thought he was holding it up as an aiming mark, because the bullet smacked straight through it—and the doctor.

I got unsteadily to my feet and looked round for Wainwright, but he wasn't there. Safaraz came running forward out of the darkness.

'The river, sahib!' he was shouting. 'Wainwright sahib is in the river!'

I remember yelling to him to cover me, but that is all, because then I was in the river myself, screaming, 'Wainwright—Wainwright—you stupid, *stupid* bastard——' and I was being swept away through the rapids like a cork until I felt myself grabbed and pulled sideways on to a rocky bank and Safaraz was trying to hold me and I was bashing him in the face.

He said gently, 'It's useless, sahib, he's gone. Would he thank us if we, too, died?'

And then the fight went out of me, and I was crying like a kid. Safaraz went on,

'He said, "I must go forward, Safaraz, or that man will shoot Rees-sahib." I couldn't help you because you were in my line of fire until the man moved round to shoot Wainwright sahib. So he didn't die in vain—and it is wrong to grieve for the death of a brave man.'

We climbed back up the cliff to the strip. Grant was chewing at his balled fist and making whickering noises. He screamed like a woman when we came into the light. When a man is as frightened as that one needn't fear lies.

I said wearily, 'All right. What happened?'

He gibbered, 'I didn't dare go back—I landed at Jullundur—and phoned Robson. He came out by car—brought another radio—got in touch with them here. They told me to come back. What could I do? Robson would have shot me if I'd refused—your people would have dealt with me if I'd gone on to Lahore. Give me a chance—give me a chance, for God's sake——'

'How many of them are there up here?' I asked.

'I only know of these two—the American and the German doctor I brought up—and the sick man on the stretcher——' he broke off and vomited.

'Where do they stay?'

'I don't know—I swear—please—I've never seen this place except in the dark. Robson said something about a house near the river—not far from the strip——' This was the truth all right, but I had to test it further. I said to Safaraz, 'A Peshawar shave again—a little closer than last time.'

He dropped to his knees behind Grant and jerked his head back and pushed the point of the knife in slowly. Blood started to trickle down his neck and over the front of his jacket. Grant shrieked, 'That's all I know—I can't tell you any more! No—no, NO!' Then he passed out.

I told Safaraz to tie him and drop him out of sight among the rocks, then I searched the two bodies. The American was wearing a pouch belt next to his skin. There was a lot of money in it, in dollars, Swiss francs and rupees, and three passports. The photos were all of the same man, but the names were different—Edwin James Foster, Harley Winston Greenslade and John Renshaw Booth. Home addresses were Portland, Oregon; Dayton, Ohio and Washington D.C. respectively, while occupations were given variously as engineer, salesman and art dealer. The German yielded nothing but a gold cigarette case with some small paper folders of white powder in it—and a hypodermic syringe in a leather case. I touched the tip of my tongue to one of the powders and then spat quickly. So that was the doctor's little load of bother, was it? A junkie. He hadn't looked that type to me, but lots of them don't show it providing they're getting their supplies regularly.

I called Safaraz and said, 'The pilot told me that these people may have had a house near the river, not far from here.'

'There is one,' he answered promptly. 'About a mile to the south of here. I walked around while the sahib was away last night. I saw and heard nobody there, but I smelt smoke and there was a dog that barked loudly, so I didn't go close. Other than that there is no house nearer than the village.'

'Let us go then,' I said. 'But with care, because I do not know how many will be there, and it is getting light.'

He led off through the rocks and we came to the edge of a small gorge through which the river ran in a series of cascades. Directly below us was a house, dilapidated but with a recently repaired roof in sharp contrast to the crumbling walls. Patches of overgrown and neglected cultivation ran along both banks of the river. There was no sign of life about the place other than a thin plume of smoke from the single chimney, and a yellow pi-dog sleeping in the pale sunshine.

I left Safaraz to cover me with the rifle from the top and climbed down carefully. The dog got my scent and started to bark. I froze for some minutes, but nobody appeared, so I went on. There were eight windows in total, two up and two down, front and back. All were shuttered except the two lower ones on the side that faced the river. I crept round and peered over the sill of the nearest one. It opened into the big single ground floor room. It was furnished with rough locally made stuff—a table with a few frame-and-hide chairs—and logs were smouldering in the big open fireplace. On a yakdan against one wall I could see a large radio receiver-transmitter. A man was lying back in a chair by the fire, with his leg stretched stiffly in front of him on a stool. He sat up as I watched, and yelled towards an open window at the dog, 'Shut up—damn and blast you—Shut up! Shut up! Shut up!' The barking really seemed to be bothering him.

I went back round the house and signalled to Safaraz to come down, and when he arrived I went through the door, gun in hand. The man gaped at me. I crossed to him and frisked him quickly. He was unarmed. Safaraz darted for the stairs and went up them. He reappeared and said, 'One room, sahib, like this. Three beds and some luggage, but nobody else.'

I told him to keep watch from the upstairs windows, then turned back to the man. He stared at me and said in halting Urdu, 'Tum kaun ho?' (Who are you?)

I said, 'All right, you can speak English. Who are *you*?'

He ignored the question and said, 'Where's Doctor Reutlingen?'

'Being taken care of,' I said. 'Now come on—I said who are you?'

'Mind your own bloody business,' he spat at me. 'Where's the doctor?'

'Have it your own way,' I told him. 'It can wait until I get you back down below.' And his manner changed immediately. His face twitched and for an awful moment I thought he was going to burst into tears.

'I'm sick,' he whined. 'You don't know how sick. I've had a busted leg and a cracked skull, and I've got to have constant attention—and I've been left here—*alone*—since last night. Those bastards have got no consideration.' He ended on a wail.

'My heart bleeds,' I said. 'Never mind. You'll get all the attention in the world when we get back.'

'Please,' he begged. 'I've got to see the doctor—*now*.' I could see beads of sweat on his forehead and upper lip, and he had begun to shake and twitch—and then it came to me in a flash. I felt for the cigarette case and the hypodermic and held them up.

'Is this what's worrying you?' I asked.

I thought he was going to pass out. He tried to get up from the chair, but he fell back into it, and his fingers were clawing at the air. 'Give it to me! Give it to me! I'll answer any questions you like then,' he gasped.

'Questions first,' I said. 'Or you can wait until we get

down—tomorrow, or the next day—or the next.' I shoved the case and needle back into my pocket and turned away towards the stairs.

'What the bloody hell do you want to know?' he shrieked.

'Name first,' I said.

'Roderick Temple-Hall——'

That could be taken as true. Nobody ever thought of one like that on the spur of the moment.

'Where do you come from?'

'Sevenoaks, Kent—look, I've got to have a fix, I tell you——'

'What are you doing here?'

'We had a crash—*Please*——'

'Who's "we"?'

'The doctor and Mike and——'

'Who's Mike?'

'I don't know—not his real name I mean—Greenslade, Booth—what the hell does it matter? He had a dozen.'

'What did you have a crash in?'

'A light aircraft—a Cherokee. I'm not talking any more without a fix——'

'Where were you going? Where had you been?'

'Picking up that Russian bastard from a strip in Nepal and bringing him back here——'

'Where's the Russian now?'

But he was past talking. He was blubbering and gasping and his nose was running.

I said, 'Can you fix your own dose?'

'Hot water—a glass——' he whispered.

I dragged an iron pot from the hearth. He picked up a glass from a table beside him, but he was shaking too badly to hold it, so I went through the horrible ritual of it guided by his pointed directions. A spoonful of water. The contents of one of the packets. Stir until dissolved. Fill the barrel. Fit the needle. He fumbled a bandanna handkerchief from his pocket and signed to me to knot it round his left arm, then he twisted it like a tourniquet with a piece of wood from the hearth, until the big vein in the crook of his elbow came up prominently. I turned away as he shoved the needle in, too sick to watch any more.

He lay back in the chair with his eyes closed, and gradually the twitching stopped, and his breathing became more even.

I let him rest for some minutes, then I started again.

'All right,' I said. 'You can go on talking while you feel up to it, or I'll leave you alone until you've really got the rats again. But next time there'll be no fix. What's it to be?'

'Rot in hell, you bastard,' he said, without opening his eyes.

'Up to you,' I shrugged. 'Just so as there'll be no misunderstanding about it, this lot goes on the fire first.' I stepped across to the hearth and held the paper packets over the smouldering ashes. He sat up quickly and grabbed at my jacket.

'No—no—for God's sake,' he implored. 'All right—get on with it.'

'You crashed——'

'Yes—and I got smashed up. Mike sent Reutlingen and me to a hospital over the hills, and he came on here on foot, with the Russian——'

'Where's the Russian now?'

'Down below, poor bastard.'

'I see. Now, who did the actual skyjacking? When you snatched Palinovsky, I mean.'

'Me. Who else? I did all the flying. Mike is the big executive, the bloody swine. He drums up the business and does the dickering afterwards. He's made a balls of this one though. He complicated it too much. The Russians retained him to snatch Palinovsky in the first place—then he heard that the Americans were in the market for him too, so he played one against the other.'

'How did the whole thing start?'

'He retained me to knock off a Boeing to Cuba a couple of years ago. Great success—so we teamed up after that—A couple to Jordan—one out of Montreal—two to Egypt. Then skyjacking on the classical pattern became impossible—so we branched out.'

'How did Reutlingen come into it?'

'The original idea was to keep Palinovsky under drugs the whole time. That can be tricky if you don't know what you're about. We needed a doctor. This fellow used to practise in Beirut, but he got into trouble over heroin running and had to scoot. The bloody fool had talked too much to his second-in-command, a wretched Arab——'

'Ib'n Shakoor?' I asked.

'That's right. He was blackmailing Reutlingen. Mike decided that he was too dangerous to have around loose, so he arranged to have him knocked off—but he went into the one place where he was safe—jail. Mike, clever bastard, got him out of there though and had him fixed in Nepal. Smart—but too complicated. Where is he now? Mike, I mean? Have you got him too?'

'Being looked after,' I said. 'So you killed Palinovsky too? Why?'

'Search me. I didn't even know he was dead. Look, I've got enough on my plate without having things stuck on me——'

'You said he was down below. I took it to mean——'

'Down below *here*, for Christ's sake——' he pointed to the floor. I saw a trapdoor in the rough planking for the first time. I went to the foot of the stairs and called to Safaraz. He came down, and I covered him while he lifted the trap and shone a torch down. The light fell on a figure lying on a charpoy. I went down.

He was bearded, unkempt and filthy, and he appeared to be in a coma. I left him there for the moment and came back up.

'All right,' I said. 'I've got a few more questions before we leave.'

'Leave for where?'

'That needn't concern you for the moment,' I told him.

'You bet it concerns me,' he said. 'I'm not talking any more without a deal.'

'You'll talk all right,' I assured him. 'Either now, or as soon as that shot wears off. Still, purely as a matter of interest, what sort of a deal had you in mind?'

'Give me that cigarette case and the needle. I'll talk then, I promise you. You don't know the half of it yet.'

'We will,' I said. 'No case. You'll get a fix when you absolutely need it—from now until I hand you over to the proper authorities. That's if you're sensible. If you're not sensible, then you're on cold turkey as of now.'

'That's what I'm afraid of,' he said. 'The *only* thing I'm afraid of. Cold turkey. Look, whoever you are, I'll tell you the lot—what we've done, what we were going to do, a list of Mike's agents, where the loot is stashed—everything. And then——'

'And then?' I prompted.

'Let me go out my own way—a quadruple shot will do it. That's what I've been wanting to do ever since the crash. That's why that bastard Reutlingen was holding my supplies.'

'Not bloody likely,' I told him. 'You'll tell us the lot anyhow, laddie. Then you'll face trial. I hope it will be out here—where hanging is still on the books.'

'All right then,' he said. 'Have it your own way.' He brought a gun up from under the cushion of the chair. 'Give me that case.'

But he never got it, because Safaraz shot him from the

top of the stairs. All in all, I suppose that was really the best solution.

We got Palinovsky up from the cellar, then we pulled dry brushwood in from outside and I found a tin of kerosene, then I threw a lighted brand into the middle of it.

Grant took some shaking before we got him into a fit state to get the chopper off the ground at sunset, then he lost himself in cloud and we had a rough ride until we finally got down on Yev's airfield, with about a pint of gas left.

Solomon drove us back under cover of darkness. 'We was worried about you, Idwal,' he said. '*And* the chopper. There's fifty-five thousand quid's worth there. What happened to your bloody radio?'

'Dropped it, I'm afraid,' I told him.

'Another hundred quid's worth,' he said sorrowfully.

Chapter Nineteen

THE GAFFER stood at the foot of my bed and sucked his teeth. 'All buttoned up,' he said. 'The Yanks flew Palinovsky out of Calcutta this morning—dressed as a Marine corporal. I hope they'll be able to get something out of him. The poor son-of-a-bitch didn't know whether it was eight o'clock or Nevsky Prospekt. Christ knows what sort of dope that Kraut doctor was keeping him on.'

'Robson?' I asked.

'He didn't know much. Only a little man. Radio link, that's all. I'm getting a persona non grata chit stuck on him, so the authorities will be asking him to get the hell out of it. Grant was a bit unlucky though—or will be.'

'What happened to *him*?'

'Well, first of all Yev fired him for moonlighting. Then the spooks got at his baggage.' He looked at his watch. 'They'll just be pulling him off the London plane in Beirut about now—with a kilo of heroin on him. *That'll* stop him breaking wind in church for the next five years. I can't stand poofs—particularly airborne poofs.'

He walked to the door and then paused and turned and said awkwardly, 'Look, I don't expect you to believe me —but I'm sorry about Wainwright. Really sorry.'

I said, 'Let it drop.'

'Funny, you know,' he went on musingly. 'He was so damn good at some things, and yet——'

'*Let it drop*,' I repeated.

He looked at me, then nodded and said, 'All right. But you let this balls about quitting drop too. No hard feelings on my side. A drop of scotch in the kisser never hurt anybody.'

But I told him to stuff it, and left that afternoon and went up to see Claire—and tried to tell her about things.

She didn't want to listen, so I came down again, and there was a message for me at Yev's to ring the Gaffer in London about something or other. I'm waiting for the call to come through now.

She was right of course. 'You'll only quit the way James did, Idwal,' she told me as she looked out over the hills. 'Or you'll develop into something like the Gaffer. Either way, I'd rather not be involved.'